BOUND TO OBEY

Francis leant closer to Caroline and stroked her breasts gently before Caroline felt the pain of the nipple clamps he was using on her.

'Poor little slave,' he said, again stroking her now tortured nipples. 'What a lot you have to endure – but it's worth it. One day you will submit to my sexual pleasures willingly. You will bring me the ropes to tie you with and the whips to beat you with, but not yet. First you have to learn.'

By the same author:

BOUND TO SERVE
BOUND TO SUBMIT

BOUND TO OBEY

Amanda Ware

This book is a work of fiction.
In real life, make sure you practise safe sex.

First published in 1995 by
Nexus
Thames Wharf Studios
Rainville Road
London W6 9HT

Reprinted 1998

Typeset by TW Typesetting, Plymouth, Devon

Printed and bound by
Caledonian International Books

ISBN 0 352 33058 9

To John,
my Master and my love

Chapter One

It was a lovely sunny morning as Caroline drove through the countryside to her appointment. She felt both nervous and excited. Who would have thought that, after the disastrous day when she had lost both her job and her home, she would be looking forward with such pleasurable anticipation to the forthcoming interview?

It had been an appropriately dismal day, grey and wet, when her employers had informed her that her services would no longer be required. Of course, it had nothing to do with her accusation of sexual harassment against a director of the company for which she was working, had it? With one agitated hand, Caroline impatiently pushed her long blonde hair over her shoulders as she remembered the interview with the directors that had followed her accusation. They had intimated that it was all the fault of the way she dressed and walked – in fact her whole attitude. They had also impugned her work record with the firm, saying that they had been considering her dismissal for some time. She had protested vehemently. Her work was good and it seemed very convenient that, if dissatisfied, their decision to sack her had coincided with her complaints about one of the directors. To cap it all, the flat she was renting went with the job. She was still considering an approach to an industrial tribunal to pursue a claim for unfair dismissal, but new employment and a new home were her top priorities and anything else would have to wait.

She reflected on the stroke of good luck that had led her to try a new employment agency at just the right time. The smiling recruitment consultant, after a long chat, had informed her that, just that morning, a new vacancy had been registered with them. A wealthy and highly intelligent married couple had just returned to England from America and were looking for a live-in secretary/personal assistant. A new job and new home in one! Apparently, this couple were successful lecturers and authors with no children and a full domestic staff. They were embarking on an interesting new project, full details of which would be revealed to her at the interview.

Caroline found the entrance to the long driveway to Beech House; the way was fringed with luxurious trees on either side, whose thickly leaved branches interlaced overhead, almost obscuring the daylight. She emerged into a circular, gravelled area in front of a rambling, beautiful house, where she was able to park. Colonial porticoes and its woodland setting made Caroline think of the American South at the time of their civil war. She took a deep breath, smoothed her navy-blue dress and got out of the car. Caroline ascended the wide stone steps and rang the bell. The door was answered almost immediately by a pretty, petite girl in a maid's uniform.

'You must be Miss West,' the girl said. 'Mr and Mrs Stevens are waiting for you. Please follow me.'

The house had all the ingredients usually found in a Gothic novel, Caroline reflected as she followed the maid up the wide staircase. Her hands were cold with nervousness but she knew that she looked her best. Her long blonde hair was brushed and shining. The dress she wore fitted her slim figure, following the curves of her body and showing off her shapely legs. The high-heeled, black shoes she wore further enhanced the image, as did the dark red polish on her long nails.

The maid paused before an imposing, polished wooden door and knocked. Permission was given for them to enter and, when they did so, Caroline drew in a breath as she looked at her prospective employers. They were, possibly, the best-looking two people she had ever seen. Mr Stevens was well over six feet in height, his wife perhaps a little less. They were both dark-haired with regular features and exuded – what? Caroline felt a warmth coming from them but also a definite sense of control; of themselves and everything and everyone around them.

'Ah, thank you, Annette,' said Mr Stevens. 'Would you take Miss West's keys and give them to Evans.'

Caroline looked queryingly at her prospective employer and the explanation was quickly given.

'Evans will park your car in the main garage which is behind the house and will, of course, drive it round for you . . . when you leave.'

Not wishing to look awkward or hesitant, Caroline looked in her bag for the car keys and handed them to the maid. With a work of thanks, Annette disappeared, closing the door behind her.

'Now, Miss West, please be seated,' Mr Stevens continued, indicating a chair in front of the desk. 'My name is Francis and this is my wife Lynne. We don't use surnames here. Is it all right if I call you Caroline?'

By this time she was so fascinated by the setting and by her interlocutor that Caroline felt she would have agreed to anything. She nodded her compliance and seated herself in the proffered chair. Lynne

3

smiled warmly at her and then walked towards the door. Caroline turned around quickly on hearing a key turn in the lock.

'We don't want to be disturbed, do we?' Francis asked her rhetorically, when she turned startled eyes to him. 'Our servants are all very loyal and have strict instructions not to enter, without knocking, into a room that they believe we are occupying. However, there have been mistakes made in the past – resulting in appropriate punishment, of course.'

Caroline settled herself into her chair, trying to ignore the slight dampness between her legs. Was it caused by the strangeness of her surroundings making her slightly nervous or was it the use of the word 'punishment' awakening the, as yet, unacknowledged submissive side to Caroline's nature? She became aware that Lynne was standing very close to her and she felt a hand brush her hair – or did she imagine it? She told herself to calm down. She needed this job. She smiled tremulously at Francis as his wife joined him again. Francis sat in a chair behind the desk and sifted through some papers.

'I've been told all about your employment and housing problems,' he said, and then raised his hand at her worried expression. 'Please don't be concerned, I'm on your side. From what Miss Summers at the agency has told me, you were the victim of a rather unscrupulous set of people. You haven't got any close relations or emotional attachments, I understand?'

Caroline was so relieved at his earlier words that she nodded agreement.

'I have some relatives somewhere in Wales, I think, but we haven't communicated for some time. As for boyfriends . . . just a few casual relationships, but nothing that's really meant anything.'

Francis and Lynne both smiled at her.

4

'So you can devote yourself to this job? We really do need someone who is able to give us all her time and attention without distractions.'

'I like to get very involved in my work,' Caroline enthused, 'and this is such a beautiful setting, I think I could be happy here.'

'I'm sure of it,' Francis enthused. 'Well, Caroline . . .' He managed to make the use of her name sound like a caress, while his eyes frankly appraised her. 'Your qualifications are excellent and you are quite . . . stunning. However, you will need to know about the special requirements that will be expected from our very personal assistant. We would like you to stay overnight as our guest so that we can tell you all you need to know in a relaxed atmosphere. There are also some . . . tests we would like you to undertake before we all agree to formally sign the contract.'

'Tests? What sort of tests?'

Caroline felt a real concern. The agency had not mentioned that she might have to undergo tests.

'Please don't be concerned. Perhaps I used the wrong word.' Francis smiled and, having risen, walked over to a broad bay window and looked out. He turned back into the room quite suddenly, as if he'd made a decision.

'Caroline, we need to assess you, your personality, likes, dislikes and so forth. After all, we are going to be living together under the same roof and we need to be sure that there won't be any, ah, problems. We need to be as certain as we can be that you will fit in here. Do you have any difficulty with that?'

The question almost startled Caroline. She was finding Francis a very attractive person and realised that her nipples were becoming hard as she watched him moving about the room. She thought that she might agree to anything he cared to suggest. Realising that she was blushing, Caroline bent to retrieve her handbag which had slipped on to the floor and, in so doing, recovered a little from her confusion and managed to find her voice.

'I think I'd like to accept your very kind offer and stay the night. I have no plans for this evening and an overnight stay in this beautiful house would be a pleasure. Thank you.'

Lynne and Francis both smiled at her.

'It will be a pleasure for all of us, Caroline,' Francis said. 'Believe me, my dear, a real pleasure.'

Caroline lay on the massive four-poster bed and dreamily wondered if this beautiful room would be hers if she got the job. It was light and airy with a double bay window looking out on to the well-kept grounds. The furnishings suggested that they had been selected for their warmth and comfort. With a deep sigh of contentment Caroline nestled into the velvet softness of the bed's counterpane. She could not help thinking about Francis and, as she did so, felt her nipples hardening in response. Her fingers strayed to her nipples as she lost herself in one of her favourite fantasies. In her imagination, she saw again the black-leather-clad male figure. It was this figure who was stroking her breasts, closing his mouth firmly about each nipple in turn, as his fingers gradually found their way to the wetness of her clitoris. She gasped as he bit one of her nipples, the pain increasing her sexual arousal, making her struggle against the ropes that bound her wrists and ankles, ropes that ensured her submissiveness, her compliance to this man's needs and desires – her needs and desires. The man looked up at her and smiled cruelly. 'You are very wet, you little slut! I think you are enjoying yourself!'

'Please, Master. Please let me feel you inside me.'

The man, who had turned into Francis, smiled again. 'Where would you like to feel my cock, little slave? Beg for it!'

Caroline writhed against her bonds, feeling the pleasurable restraints that took away her choices, made her feel deliciously helpless.

'Please, Master. Please let me have your cock in my anus.'

'I am always happy to make my slave feel she is getting just what she wants, what she deserves.'

Caroline felt her sexual tension increasing, felt herself building to an inexorable climax as her fingers pushed aside her knickers and found the pleasure bud that never failed her, particularly when accompanied by her fantasy images. She imagined her 'Francis' tying a gag in her mouth 'to ensure your silence, little slave'.

The knock at the door stopped her. Caroline took a few seconds to realise where she was and at whose behest, before she managed to shout that she would only be a moment. She slid off the bed and desperately straightened her rumpled clothing, letting go, reluctantly, of the fantasy images and forcing herself back to reality.

Taking a deep breath, Caroline opened the door to find Lynne standing there.

'I hope I didn't wake you,' she said. She took in Caroline's flustered state with a somewhat knowing smile, as if she knew what Caroline had been thinking about, what she had been doing.

'No, I was just thinking.' Caroline's voice sounded ineffectual even to herself.

'Pleasant thoughts I hope,' Lynne said as she held out a box. 'I realised that you didn't have anything with you to change into and so I've brought you some of my things. I hope you don't mind.'

7

Caroline took the box.

'That's very kind. I was going to suggest that I drove home to get some things.'

'Well, now there's no need. I think you'll find the sizes are OK. These things are all too small for me. Francis bought them for me some time ago and, well, you know men. They haven't got much of a clue about what fits and what doesn't!'

This somehow did not quite ring true. Caroline could not imagine Francis getting anything like that wrong, but she was grateful for the clothes and simply smiled her gratitude.

'Please keep them,' Lynne said, carelessly. 'If you join us here, you will find that these are the sort of clothes you will need – a sort of uniform really. Dinner will be in an hour if that's OK.'

'That will be fine, thank you.'

Lynne smiled and turned to go but, almost as an afterthought, turned back and put her hand on Caroline's shoulder.

'I do hope you decide to join us here, Caroline. I feel we could be real friends.'

Lynne's hand just brushed Caroline's left breast as she turned and closed the door behind her.

Caroline sat on the bed and wondered if the touching of her breast had been accidental. Her thoughts were in a turmoil. This was a strange household. There was an undeniable sexuality about both Francis and Lynne and they both seemed to find her attractive.

Wondering if she really knew what she might be getting herself into, Caroline turned her attention to the box and opened it.

What sort of a 'uniform' was this, Caroline wondered, as she unpacked several items of clothing in red and black PVC, leather and rubber. With undeniable sexual excitement, Caroline examined a black leather harness, consisting of an assortment of straps which formed the shape of a bra, except that this bra had no covering for the breasts, just the outline. She took out a couple of rubber skirts which could only be described as micro when defining the length, a red PVC studded dress and a black rubber dress with straps and a front zip holding the skin-tight contraption together. There were also a selection of long gloves in rubber and PVC, together with some sensuously thin black rubber stockings.

Caroline discovered that her crotch was, yet again, very damp. These clothes were a fetishist's dream. Caroline had only ever fantasised about wearing such clothes and now, if Lynne were to be believed, she was to wear them as part of her new job. If she got it, she reminded herself. Breathing in the alluring aroma of leather and rubber, Caroline knew that she just had to get this job, no matter what it entailed.

Francis and Lynne were waiting for her in the dining-room, where the maid who had conducted her to the earlier interview now showed her. Caroline was very self-conscious, but aware of the fact that she looked good – very good – as she walked into the room. She had chosen the black rubber dress, enabling her to try on the rubber stockings, which she was longing to do. She felt very sexy, a feeling which was evidently shared by her hosts as they eyed her appreciatively.

Francis walked over to her, his eyes openly expressing his admiration as they travelled over her. She could almost feel the heat from his gaze. Without apology or explanation, he ran his hands down her body, feeling the sensuous heat of her through the tight rubber.

'You are delightful, my dear, truly delightful, isn't she, Lynne?'

9

Lynne joined them, only a slight narrowing of her sometimes predatory gaze belying the warmth of her reply.

'She is, indeed, Francis. That dress might have been made for her.'

Caroline felt herself relaxing under their complimentary looks and felt only excitement as Lynne walked around behind her. 'I have a present for you, my dear, something that will go with your outfit. Lift your hair up.'

Caroline did as she was told and felt something being strapped around her neck. She felt Lynne arranging her hair for her and turned to look at herself in a big wall mirror. She felt a momentary confusion as she looked at her reflection in the mirror. She saw a blonde girl with a shapely figure encased in shiny rubber and, fitting snugly around her neck as though it belonged there, a wide, black leather collar. The collar had a silver-coloured metal ring inset in the front for – what? The possibilities of the use to which that ring could be put excited Caroline. She knew what the collar was. She couldn't be wrong about that, could she? She suddenly realised that she was desperately hoping she wasn't wrong. She turned to face her would-be employers and smiled, a little uncertainly.

'It's a slave collar, isn't it?'

Francis came up behind her and turned her back to face the mirror. Now she could see the black rubber-clad girl again, but this time there was someone else, too. A man whose arms effectively imprisoned her, as he caressed her rubber-clad breasts. She could feel his cock straining against her. Both he and Lynne were dressed in black leather catsuits. But they didn't seem frightening. It all suddenly seemed so right. She felt that she had come home and was suddenly aware of how very much she wanted this to be her home.

Lynne joined them and, smilingly, clipped a steel chain to the ring in her collar.

'Yes, my dear,' Lynne said, her voice full of barely suppressed excitement. 'The position for which we are interviewing you is that of our slave. You will be required to serve and obey us in all things, no matter how sexually perverted some of those things might be.'

Caroline stared at Francis and Lynne, her mind a mass of conflicting emotions. Was this what she wanted? In spite of all her former difficulties, she'd always been independent, made her own decisions – been free. Free to do what? Free to be lonely, insecure, dependent on other people's largesse to keep herself fed and clothed. Yet, what was she being offered now? To be a slave, to lose her identity, be at the whim of someone else's perverse desires. Did she really want that?

Caroline's thoughts became frantic. She had to say something. Lynne and Francis were looking at her expectantly. Then, surprisingly, Francis' voice came to her rescue.

'We know this is all very sudden. We intended to talk to you, try to assess what you might or might not accept, but when I saw you – looking so very sexy and, yes, so very willing . . .'

Francis trailed off and looked at her with his usual warm smile, but making no attempt to conceal the desire he felt for her.

'You don't have to decide anything now. Let's have dinner, as we planned, and we'll tell you more about what we would like from you. If, at the end of dinner, you decide not to stay with us, you are completely free to go. You can remain here overnight and leave in the morning.'

Caroline could only nod her acquiescence. Her

11

body was definitely urging her to accept, but she knew that she needed time to think this through. Such a drastic, unplanned, alteration to her life-style could not be decided just by her body's overpowering sexual needs. All this – the rubber dress, the leather collar and the lead – was causing her to feel that she would like nothing better than for Francis – and Lynne – to take her and do what they wanted with her.

Over dinner which, delicious though it was, did not merit much of Caroline's attention, Francis told Caroline of how he and Lynne had decided to look for a willing girl to be their sex slave.

'You see, Caroline, both Lynne and I are very dominant people. We have a very good relationship with each other but, sexually, you will realise that we need more than the other can give. We have certain needs that only a submissive can offer. Miss Summers at the agency you went to is ... how shall I say ... a special friend of Lynne's and she therefore knew exactly what we wanted. She's been on the lookout for someone like yourself for some time. She told us that you more than fitted the bill. You are on your own, in need of a job and a home, no close relationships. You are also very beautiful, my dear; something that Lynne and I both appreciate. You wear those clothes as though they were made for you and with, unless I'm mistaken, obvious enjoyment. Miss Summers also felt that you exhibited certain submissive qualitives, but we obviously couldn't be sure until we'd talked to you. Wearing the clothes we'd bought for you was the first test.' Francis smiled at her surprised expression. 'Yes, we did buy them for you after we'd taken your measurements from the agency application form.'

A lot of things now began to make sense to Caroline. She'd wondered why the agency had needed to know her sizes and so much about her private life.

'You said the first test.' Caroline looked directly at Francis. 'I assume there are others?'

Lynne smiled and, reaching across the dining table, patted her hand.

'Nothing for you to worry about, Caroline. I have the feeling you will pass any tests with ease.'

Francis reached across the table and held one of Caroline's hands, unable to completely conceal the triumphant smile that was caused by the sight of her traitorous nipples immediately hardening and pushing against the tight rubber of her dress.

'Tell, me, Caroline. Do you think you'd enjoy being put in restraints?'

The embarrassment caused by this discussion of what Caroline knew to be her own innermost secret thoughts, at least, secret until now, made her try to pull her hand away, but Francis exerted a firm but gentle pressure to keep her hand in his.

'I've never . . .' Caroline couldn't finish. She wasn't even sure what she was going to say.

'Never, what, Caroline?' Francis asked, his eyes intense. 'Never been tied up? Never thought about it? Is that true, Caroline? You've never thought about being tied up by a sexual partner?'

'No, I mean, yes, I've thought about it, but I've never . . .'

Caroline was furious with herself. Normally so erudite, she was stumbling with her words like a child.

Francis released her hand and moved around the table until he was standing in front of Caroline. With an undeniable thrill, she realised that Francis was holding a length of white cord in his hands. Surprisingly, he knelt in front of her.

'Don't be afraid, my darling. I won't do anything

13

you don't want me to. You only have to say stop and I will. I just want to show you how good being tied up can make you feel. Will you let me?'

Suppressing the fear that the reality might not be as good as the fantasies she'd so often enjoyed, Caroline looked at Francis and nodded, unable to hide the sexual excitement she was experiencing.

Francis gently put both Caroline's wrists together in front of her and tied them. Caroline's clitoris was pulsing with its desire to be touched, touched by Francis. Caroline experimentally struggled a little, feeling the excitement build as she realised that she was unable to free herself – no fear, just an added thrill as she told herself that she was totally at the mercy of Francis and Lynne. Supposing Francis didn't keep his word and, anyway, did she care? No, it only added to her sexual enjoyment, this delicious feeling of helplessness.

Francis seemed to know exactly what she was feeling and moved behind her, cupping her rubber-clad breasts in his hands and squeezing the large nipples. Lynne was watching intently, her own excitement growing. She wanted to join them, but didn't want to frighten Caroline – it might be too soon.

Without saying anything, Francis moved his hands to Caroline's tied wrists. Untying them, he gently pulled her hands behind her and secured them again, this time quite tightly. To ease any sensations of fear this might have caused, Francis' hands returned to Caroline's small, but perfectly shaped breasts, massaging the nipples sensually, feeding Caroline's growing arousal.

'Does it feel good, my darling?' Francis asked, not really expecting a reply. Caroline's body was sending unmistakable signals to him. He nodded at Lynne who had been eagerly awaiting just such an invitation.

'Lynne wants to join us and, as I know you're not sure about that, I'm going to make this easier for you. After all, if you become our slave, you won't be allowed to make any decisions when it comes to sexual pleasures, yours or ours.'

As Lynne approached Caroline, Francis wadded up a handkerchief and thrust it between Caroline's lips, silencing any protest she might have been about to make. Dreamily, Caroline knew she wouldn't have protested. Her clitoris demanded urgent attention and, at this moment, it didn't matter who supplied it.

Francis felt his cock straining against the leather of his trousers as he knotted a length of cord behind Caroline's head, securing the handkerchief in place. Lynne knelt before Caroline, slipping her hands between Caroline's warm, rubber-clad thighs, noticing with delight that Caroline, of her own volition, had decided not to wear any panties. Lynne breathed in the exciting scent of warm rubber mixed with the smell of Caroline's female juices, as her sex demanded attention. Lynne's fingers located the slippery clitoris, engorged with desire. Caroline's head was thrown back against Francis. She was pulling desperately at her bonds and making mewing noises through her gag, not because she was trying to escape, but because she was enjoying the tight restrictions which showed her that she had no choice. The choices had already been made for her. As Lynne's mouth closed over the pulsating clitoris, Caroline screamed into her gag as her orgasm, much stronger than any she'd ever experienced, took possession of her, made her twist and struggle against Francis, who held her tightly. The sight of this gorgeous rubber-clad creature, helplessly bound and gagged who, he now knew, was undoubtedly his sex slave, in the throes of her orgasm, was enough to make him briefly regret not freeing his penis from its leather confines as his own powerful orgasm made him spunk profusely inside the leather trousers of his catsuit.

Caroline was still feeling weak from her orgasm as she signed the piece of paper in front of her. What did it matter? She knew this was what she wanted, even though some sections of the contract bothered her a little. What would the punishments be like and how could she avoid incurring them?

'Right, Caroline,' Francis said, drawing the signed contract towards him and briefly checking that all was in order.

'Lynne and I have never owned a slave, so this is in the nature of an experiment for us too. We want to train you to participate in all manner of sexual delights – some you will like and some you may not. We want to show you how experiencing some measure of pain can lead to undreamed-of ecstasy. We are now your Master and Mistress, to be addressed as such at all times. You will not be expected to participate in domestic tasks – we don't want that sort of a slave. You will be well looked after and, in return for your sexual services, will want for nothing.'

'You mean I'll be a sort of prostitute?'

At Francis' frown, Caroline added falteringly, 'Master.'

'You will certainly not be regarded as such. You will be expected, occasionally, to entertain our guests, but that is part of your duties. Initially, as part of your training, you will be expected to obey all the members of our staff. They will be briefed on what they are and are not entitled to do with you.'

'Will I be told as well, Master?' Caroline found that it was easier than she had expected to use that form of address, especially as it was to Francis and she wanted to please Francis in all things.

'No, you will discover these things in due course. You will know that, whatever our staff say or do to you, they have our permission.'

Francis got up from his seat across the table and stood behind Caroline. He ran his hands down her body appreciatively.

'You really are delightful, Caroline.'

She felt his hands moving to her breasts and then the straps of her dress as, with practised hands, he unbuckled the straps and, slowly and sensually, eased the zip downwards.

'Step out of the dress, Caroline,' he instructed her as he came round to face her.

Totally unselfconscious now, Caroline released the bottom of the zip and peeled the dress from her body. Francis stood and admired her for several seconds before ordering her, gently, to stand with her hands behind her. When Caroline complied, Francis walked behind her again and she felt an undeniable sexual response from her clitoris as she felt the cords again being tied around her wrists. As he tied her, Francis dropped kisses on her neck.

'You were made for this, Caroline. You were meant to be a slave. You look so good in ropes.'

Caroline could hear the growing excitement in his voice, could not but be aware of her own wetness, her nipples hardening. Francis was tying her elbows together and, looping the cord across her arms and breasts, left a long piece of cord dangling in front of her while he walked around her admiring his handiwork. Then, quite suddenly, he pulled the piece of cord between her legs, securing it tightly to her bound wrists. Caroline gasped as she realised that, whenever she moved, the cord rubbed against her clitoris, further exciting her.

17

'Frustrating, isn't it, my dear?' Francis asked, smiling as his hand caressed her pulsating bud. 'You are in a state of constant arousal, but can do nothing about it because your hands are tied behind you. You are dependent on the whim of others.'

Francis stood behind her again, squeezing the nipples of her bound breasts – the bondage already making them extremely sensitive.

'No, please, Master . . .'

Caroline gasped with pain as Francis cruelly tweaked her nipples. She felt one of his hands close over her mouth as he pulled at the rope between her legs, causing her further, yet delicious, pain.

'No? No is a word for which you have no further use, Caroline. We do not permit the use of that word here and, until you learn total obedience, we must enforce that rule by other means.'

Francis removed his hand and forced her to her knees in front of him.

'I think we will have to keep you gagged for most of the time, in various ways. This for instance!'

Francis pulled down the zip on his catsuit and allowed his erect penis to spring outwards, the purplish tip already wet with a mixture of his earlier spunk and the new evidence of his highly excited state. Francis caught a handful of Caroline's hair and wound it roughly around his hand, forcing her inexorably closer to his penis and then thrusting its swollen length between her lips.

Caroline could not struggle very much. She was too tightly bound and could not move without causing further aggravation to her swollen clitoris. She moved her lips up and down the shaft of Francis' penis, sometimes instinctively licking around the tip, until Francis rammed his cock almost down her throat with the violence of his orgasm. Caroline swallowed

the warm saltiness and felt Francis gently withdraw-
ing from her and kneeling in front of her. He raised
her chin and smeared the spunk dribbling from the
corners of her mouth across her lips.

'Thank you, slave.'

'*My* turn now, I think!'

Lynne stood there. She looked angry. Neither Caroline nor Francis knew how long it had been since she
had come silently into the room and Lynne herself
could not tell why it was she was so angry. She was
flexing a riding crop in her hands and looking straight
at Caroline.

'Time for your first taste of pain, slave!'

Caroline could only stare at her, frightened yet
strangely fascinated. Lynne exuded sexual excitement.
She knelt beside Caroline, suddenly gentle, but sinister in that very gentleness. She bound a wide leather
strap across Caroline's eyes.

'You will find your sense of touch magnified because of the blindfold.'

Lynne's soft voice was dangerously insistent, the
very sound of it causing waves of pleasurable anticipation to flood Caroline, removing the slight sense of
fear or, maybe, delightfully enhancing it.

Caroline tasted rubber as something soft was forced between her lips and strapped tightly behind her
head. Lynne started inflating the rubber gag until it
filled Caroline's mouth.

'Not quite as yielding as your Master's cock, perhaps, but equally efficient at keeping you quiet.'

Lynne's voice was now filled with unmistakable
menace. Caroline's thoughts raced. Was she jealous
of what she must have seen? Where was Francis?
Surely he wouldn't let Lynne really hurt her?

Caroline felt a delicious shiver of anticipation as

she felt the riding crop being stroked down her back. Yes, she was afraid. She didn't like pain and she didn't know how severe the beating would be. She knew there would be a beating, but couldn't deny the fact that the cord between her legs was now sodden with her love juices. Maybe Francis was right. Perhaps this was what she was meant for, to be bound, gagged, blindfold and totally at the mercy of others for their sexual desires, however perverse. She could not deny that this thought was making her grateful for the gag in her mouth, however uncomfortable. Without it she would be screaming for someone to fuck her – give her the much needed release that she craved, that she must have!

'Can I have your assistance, please, Francis?' the seductive voice of her captor filled Caroline with exquisite dread. What were they planning? She could see nothing beneath the tightly tied blindfold, could only hear Francis approach and kneel beside her. Suddenly she found herself being pulled over his knees, the cord pressing painfully on her clitoris, but with that pain a certain sense of pleasure. She felt Francis' hand in the small of her back, pressing her firmly on to his knees, inexorably holding her still to wait her punishment.

'Mmmf!'

The first hard stroke of the riding crop caught Caroline unawares, even though she'd thought she was ready for it. She made her protest uselessly into the inflatable gag, which allowed very little sound to escape.

She became aware of fingers probing her swollen clitoris, soothing and exciting it. She could feel how slippery she was, but how wonderful it felt to be totally restrained, at the mercy of people who could inflict pleasure or pain in equal measure. She could feel her orgasm building, then another stroke of the riding crop making her gasp into her gag while she feebly struggled against the unaccustomed pain. Yet with that pain, she felt pleasure, pleasure because she had no choice, she could not free herself, could not stop what was happening to her, couldn't even cry out for help, although Croline knew that that was the last thing she wanted. She could not deny she was enjoying her situation and continued to think this even when the succession of blows from the riding crop, interspersed with the massaging of her clitoris, kept coming. Her orgasm could not be denied and Lynne smiled as she felt the increased moisture on her fingers.

Caroline heard movement, but did not understand what was happening as, although the gag was removed from her mouth, the blindfold was left on. It was not until she was made to lie on her back, grateful for the fact that the pain from the beating had subsided to a dull ache, and smelled the unmistakable smell of a highly excited female, that she realised what she was expected to do. Her tongue willingly probed Lynne's slit, tasting her juices, until she found the bud of pleasure and sucked gently on it, drawing Lynne quickly to orgasm.

It was some little while after this that Caroline felt the cord being untied from between her legs and gentle fingers massaging her painful clitoris.

Her wrists and elbows remained tied, but the cords were released from her swollen breasts. Caroline was helped to her feet and guided out of the room, down a hallway and into another room. She was helped to lie on what felt like a bed, a bed which was covered with, as Caroline could tell from the feel and smell, a rubber sheet. She was about to ask whether her blindfold was going to be removed when a wide strip of adhesive tape was applied to her mouth, silencing any such questions. She felt rope being tied around her knees and ankles and a strap binding her to the bed.

'You look so pretty like that, my dear,' Francis' voice told her, 'and so damn desirable too, but, unfortunately, there are other things that require my attention.'

Caroline felt his lips brush her forehead and then her breasts. She then felt a rubber sheet being drawn up to her chin. There was the sound of retreating footsteps and of a door closing.

Caroline lay there, experimentally testing her bonds and finding, to her delight, that there was no escape. So this was what it meant to be a slave. There would, undoubtedly, be times in the future when she would regret her situation, but overall she was glad she had signed that contract. It was strange to think that, bound, gagged and blindfold as she was, she was here of her own volition. Caroline struggled against her bonds and felt the pleasurable restrictions that held her in place and the sexual stimulation she derived from that imprisonment. For the first time in many years, she felt that she belonged somewhere at last. She was needed – Francis and Lynne needed her. She remembered how she had been able to bring pleasure to them – in a way that, strangely, gave *her* power over Francis and Lynne.

Yes, she was content in the knowledge of her true submissiveness which Francis and Lynne had revealed to her.

Caroline was aware of the discomfort in her bound arms and tried to settle herself a little more comfortably, as far as the strap would allow her to move at all. Her clitoris pulsed a reminder that too much wriggling would make her inability to satisfy herself keep her awake all night. Francis had expertly tied her so that, although there was no chance of escape, her circulation would not be cut off if kept in bondage over a long period of time, which was obviously what he intended. Under the rubber sheet Caroline's nipples were hard and sensitive. She realised the subtle torment of the rubber, as the sensuous material confined her straining nipples. The increasing wetness of her sexual discharges demonstrated the usefulness of the second rubber sheet.

'Just another test, darling. Just another test.'

The words were spoken close to her ear and so softly that she wasn't sure if she was asleep and dreaming. She felt hands peeling away the rubber sheeting, removing the tape, untying the blindfold and releasing her from her bonds. She knew it was Francis, even though the room was very dark, and felt an undeniable thrill as she wondered what test he wanted her to undertake for him. She didn't mind. She was ready to prove herself in any way that he might choose. She wanted to please him, to ensure his happiness with his new slave.

She was helped to stand and suddenly the room was flooded with light. Caroline blinked and was grateful for Francis' steadying arm while she accustomed herself to the brightness.

She became aware of a second visitor in the room as a darkly handsome man appeared in her line of vision. A powerful hand glinting with gold jewellery reached out and stroked her breasts sensuously, bringing the nipples to immediate arousal. The stranger was of continental appearance, well-dressed in obviously expensive clothes.

'You were right, Francis. She is beautiful. She will make a delightful slave.'

The voice was richly cultured. Caroline could not

23

help swaying towards him. Remembering herself, she looked at Francis who smiled encouragement.

'This is – well, we'll call him Michael. There's no need for you to know his name. Michael is a very, very good friend of mine who has just returned to this country from abroad. We have many things in common, particularly our shared appreciation of beauty.'

The accent on the word 'shared' was unmistakable. Caroline looked at Michael. If this was a test, she was more than willing to participate.

Michael's appreciative hands were sliding down her body, one hand insinuating itself between her legs.

'Why, Francis, your little slave is wet – very wet.'

Francis checked for himself, bringing his fingers to his nose and sniffing Caroline's juices.

'I do believe you are right, my friend. I think the slave is in need of some attention – as are we of course.'

Caroline felt as if her nipples and clitoris were almost crying out their sensual demands. She wanted – needed – some attention and she was more than happy to give as well as to receive.

'Are your slaves normally allowed this much freedom, my friend?'

Michael's voice held only a mildly questioning note as if he and Francis had already rehearsed this conversation.

'You are of course right. Slaves should always be treated as such, so that they are constantly reminded of their position. As my guest, you may choose the restraints. You will find quite a selection in that cabinet.'

Francis indicated a pine-fronted cabinet in one wall, which Caroline had not noticed before. Michael went to the cabinet and opened the door.

'A very good selection, my dear Francis. Ah, this will be very suitable.'

There was a clinking of metal as Michael reached into the cabinet and picked up a long length of chain. Francis, meanwhile, was behind Caroline stroking her clitoris and sometimes using her own juices as lubrication to facilitate his finger's easy entrance into her anus. Caroline gasped with pleasure, her arousal already fuelled by the sound of the chains and all that they implied.

As Michael approached, Francis regretfully removed his fingers from Caroline's sex and stood in front of her while Michael draped the chains around her. Caroline had once fantasised about being tied up in chains and her bodily excitement, as she saw the realisation of this fantasy, was very apparent. Francis used his fingers to manipulate her arousal, making her moan with pleasure.

The chains were light-weight and Michael proved himself to be an expert as he tied them around Caroline's breasts and arms, threading a long piece down between her legs, settling it snugly into her crease, before taking it back up and chaining her wrists tightly together behind her back. As he snapped a padlock into place, Michael declared himself satisfied while Francis' admiring gaze confirmed his approval.

Caroline watched as Francis walked around behind her and then felt his gentle but insistent fingers on her shoulders indicating by their pressure that she should kneel down in front of Michael. When she was suitably positioned sitting on her haunches, Michael removed his clothes, slowly and sensuously, occasionally squeezing her nipples, which were so excitingly framed by the lengths of chain. His cock was already erect, springing free from the restraints of clothing, long and hard, glistening with secretions. Francis softly whispered to her to kneel up and, as she did so, Michael's cock was able to push past her eager lips. She tasted the saltiness of him, using her lips to gently massage the stem as her tongue flicked along the plum. Francis was watching with growing excitement as his friend rested one hand on Caroline's head; his eyes closed as he gave himself up to pleasure.

Francis knelt on the floor behind Caroline and inserted two fingers into her slit, lubricating his fingers prior to gently inserting them into her anus. Caroline momentarily lost her grip on Michael's cock as her mouth opened in a surprised gasp of pleasure, before returning happily to her task as she sucked enthusiastically on the rigid member. At the same time, she automatically bore down on the intruding fingers inside her rectum, increasing the flow of sexual feelings for herself and Francis.

Judging that the time was right, Francis unzipped the trousers of his catsuit and released his own tumescent organ. Caroline's clitoris throbbed with excitement as she became aware that Francis was again using her own juices as a lubricant on his cock. Francis frequently rubbed against her clitoris as he slid gently in and out of her slit, making his cock gleam with the slickness of Caroline's juices. Caroline felt her orgasm building as she became conscious of the fact that Michael's fluid was seeping in greater quantities into her mouth as his own climax approached. She sucked determinedly at the friendly invader in her mouth as she felt Francis' cock nudging at her anus, before sliding gently in. She knew she could not hold out any longer as Francis's fingers squeezed her nipples, which were standing erect within their chained confines. Michael chose that moment to spunk into her mouth, copious amounts of semen which it seemed only natural that she should swallow. Michael's cock slid out of her mouth as her orgasm shook her, making her struggle against the restricting chains with the force of it.

Francis pulled her back hard against him as he spunked into her rectum. She felt his hot breath on her neck as he groaned with pleasure.

Weak from her own orgasm, Caroline felt a sense of pride as she looked at the two men who had sought and received their satisfaction through her, felt the thrill of power as she realised that she had done this. Somehow it seemed only natural that Lynne should walk through the door at the moment of her triumph.

Although Lynne had changed out of the catsuit, she was still dressed with all the dominant force that she knew well how to exercise. She wore a black leather knee-length dress in a severe style, its very severity making it extremely sexy. The soft leather clung to her curves and went right up to the neck. With it she wore black leather high-heeled boots, the tops of which disappeared beneath the skirt of the dress. In her hands, she carried a riding crop, the top of which was shaped like a penis.

'Having fun, children?' she asked as she walked commandingly into the room.

Francis smiled languidly at her.

'Come in, my dear. You are very welcome. You know Michael, of course.'

Lynne flicked the tip of the crop playfully against Michael's cock, which sprang to an immediate erection.

'Nice to see you again, Michael. You have, I trust, found our hospitality to be no less than it should be.'

'As always, Lynne. As always.'

Lynne walked over to Caroline, who felt her clitoris stirring as she eyed the crop.

'Well, slave. I trust you are enjoying your servitude?'

27

Caroline smiled almost dreamily.

'Oh yes, thank you, Mistress.'

Lynne pushed Caroline until she was leaning with her back against the bed and squatted down beside her.

'Very nice,' she commented, as her approving glance swept over Caroline and noted the way in which she was chained. She watched with a smile as Caroline gasped with the feeling of pleasurable pressure that the chain between her legs gave her as Lynne deliberately moved it into a more sensitive position, so that it rested tantalisingly over her clitoris.

She used the crop in stroking motions over Caroline's body while the men watched, their erections straining. She brushed the penis-shaped head over Caroline's mouth, forcing it between her lips and suggestively sliding it in and out.

'Suck it!' she ordered and Caroline quickly complied, tasting Lynne's own juices as she did so.

'Gentlemen, I think the slave should be unchained. I need to be pleasured.'

The men hastened to obey, unpadlocking and unwinding the chains. Michael smiled as Caroline groaned with pleasure when he moved the chain between her legs. After all the chains had been removed, Caroline was lifted back on to the bed, the contact with the rubber sheets again sending waves of pleasure thrilling through her.

The men stood aside to wait patiently for Lynne's next move. Keeping her eyes on Caroline, she started to pull down the zip at the front of her dress, then changed her mind.

'Stand up!' she ordered.

Caroline immediately obeyed, scrambling quickly – if a little regretfully – off the bed to stand in front of Lynne.

'Undo my zip!'

As Caroline moved her hands to the zip fastening, Francis almost telepathically formulated his wife's real intent. Grabbing Caroline's wrists he drew them behind her and tied them tightly together. Lynne smiled with quiet satisfaction as Francis tied the knots. Caroline looked at her in bewilderment but then suddenly understood and, leaning forward, took the tip of the fastening into her mouth and pulled it all the way down, until she was kneeling on the floor and the dress fell at Lynne's feet revealing her nakedness.

Michael and Francis both picked Caroline up and, as Francis untied her hands, Michael gently pushed her back onto the bed. She felt her arms being pulled upwards and ropes again tying her wrists together. Michael pulled her bound wrists further upwards until he was able to tie the ends of the rope through a pine ring that protruded from the wall. While he was doing this, Francis had parted her legs and tied her ankles to each side of the bed. She was now very open and vulnerable to all three of the people who stood beside the bed, looking at her with faces flushed with sexual excitement.

Caroline experimentally wriggled, testing her bonds. They held firmly, as she had known they would. She had only wanted the feeling of the restrictions to complete her sense of helplessness which, in turn, fuelled her feelings of arousal.

Lynne got on to the bed, her knees on either side of Caroline's head. Caroline could feel and smell the sexual heat of her as, eyes glittering, she grabbed a handful of Caroline's hair and forced her mouth close to Lynne's bush.

'Suck me.'

Caroline felt her own growing wetness as she

probed her tongue into Lynne's pubic hair, feeling for the slit which she was eager to invade, at the same time trying to arch her body off the bed in indication of her own sexual needs. As Caroline's tongue found its target, she heard Francis's voice.

'I'd say the slave was trying to tell us something, wouldn't you, Michael?'

'I certainly would. Have you got something to blindfold her with?'

The answer to this was apparent when Caroline felt some material being tied over her eyes, plunging her into a world of darkness which only increased her fevered desires. She found the bud of pleasure she was seeking and closed her mouth on it, sucking gently at the engorged clitoris. She became dimly aware that someone else had climbed onto the bed, her nipples were being stroked and squeezed, her sexual bud teased. There was the unmistakable feeling of a tongue swirling around her clitoris, sending her further into paroxysms of desire. She felt the tip of a penis probing at her vagina, demanding entrance. But whose? Francis or Michael? She couldn't see, only feel. Someone's fingers pinched both her nipples, the exquisite pain bringing her close to a climax. She felt her Mistress' juices increase on her tongue and the hand in her hair pulling harder and knew that she had achieved her objective. Now, however, the unknown penis was in her and she was being shafted with some ferocity. She could hear loud and laboured breathing and moved her head frantically from side to side, but could in no way dislodge the blindfold. Her Mistress climbed off her and she opened her mouth to ask who was inside her, who was giving her such extremes of pleasure, but her questions remained as only ideas in her mind as she felt an erect cock pushing between her lips. Almost gratefully, she accepted its length

30

into her mouth. Now she didn't have to ask questions – she again had a task to perform. She felt the exhilaration in the freedom this gave her. Whoever was shafting her reached his climax and shuddered with the strength of it. The cock in her mouth was leaking its pre-come fluid and she tasted the saltiness just as someone's hand – Francis, Michael, the Mistress? – flicked across her clitoris, knowing that that was all she needed to bring her to orgasm. Hot spunk was jettisoned into her mouth which she swallowed as she gasped out her pleasure.

Caroline awoke with a start. It was dark again in her room and she was alone. The rubber sheets were sticking to her as a result of her perspiration. Even when she moved as much as she was able to, she could not dislodge any part of the sheets that were now very firmly anchored to her body, almost like a second skin. As her whirling thoughts settled, Caroline realised that someone, after releasing her from her spread position on the bed, had retied her as she had been before the night visit, even re-applying the tape over her mouth. She stretched as much as she could within the confines of her bonds and the strap. She could remember the events of the night in vibrant detail, feel the stirrings in her clitoris again as she remembered being fucked, remembered the pleasure she had given and received.

Caroline wondered how they had managed to get her back in bed, retie her and leave without her being aware of it. She could not remember anything after swallowing the anonymous spunk. That thought made her freeze. No, she couldn't remember anything at all after that until she woke up back in bed. Had she dreamed it all? Of course she thought it was dark – she was blindfolded just as Francis had left her earlier. No, she reasoned, she couldn't have had such a dream that she could remember in such minutiae, could she?

Caroline remembered the frustration of not being able to touch herself after Francis had left her tied up for the night. Perhaps her longings and frustrations had combined with an exhausted sleep to produce such vivid dreams.

Caroline decided she was too tired to try to figure it out any further and thought that, whether she had dreamed it all or not, it had been a very enjoyable experience.

Wriggling herself into as comfortable a position as she could, Caroline thought with pleasurable anticipation of her new position as a slave. Whether she had been dreaming or not and, on reflection, she thought she must have been, she hoped that when sleep, which was not far off, claimed her, she would be able to return to that wonderful land where her complete and total submission to kinky sexual desires was expected and to which she knew she would gladly acquiesce.

Chapter Two

'Before I remove your gag, there are a few rules of which you should be aware, disobedience of any of which will result in severe punishment. No allowance is made for new slaves. You must learn immediately.'

This was a new and business-like Francis who had woken Caroline from her fitful sleep, unstrapped her from the bed and, after helping her to sit up, removed her blindfold.

After allowing Caroline a few minutes to adjust to the brightness of the sunlit room, Francis pulled a chair up in front of her.

'When you are not gagged, you will not speak unless spoken to and, even when you are, must ask permission to speak. You will address me as Master and Lynne as Mistress. You will keep your eyes down at all times unless spoken to. You will not be allowed any clothing that is not of our choosing. As you know, we both have a love of fetish clothes,' Francis' eyes became bright with remembered desire, 'and you of course wear rubber so well. You can therefore expect to be made to wear quite a lot of rubber and leather and other materials of our choosing. You will wear a chastity belt when you are alone. You will not be trusted not to give yourself pleasure without asking and receiving permission. The chastity belt will ensure your obedience. You will learn to give pleasure to both of us. Learn those lessons well, my dear, because failure will not be tolerated. Occasionally, you will be given to someone who has particularly pleased us, as a reward. That person will keep a video record of your behaviour during their custody of you, which we will watch, and woe betide you if any misdemeanours come to our attention. You will be whipped on a daily basis as part of your training. Extra punishments will not take account of these daily beatings but will be additions. When you are beaten, you will count each stroke of the implement that is used. Failure to do so, or errors during the counting, will result in extreme punishment. You will normally be restrained during your punishments, but occasionally you will not be. It is very much in your best interests when this occurs to remain perfectly still in the position you have been ordered to adopt, whatever the severity of the punishment. Failure will result in your being tightly restrained and soundly beaten for an extended period of time, to be decided by myself or your Mistress. After each beating, you will thank myself or your Mistress for the beating. Do you understand?'

Caroline, filled with confusion at Francis' colder attitude, could do nothing else but nod her acquiescence, knowing that all resistance was pointless. She had voluntarily signed the contract, thereby making herself a slave. Francis now seemed to be treating the whole thing as a scientific experiment.

Seeing her confusion, Francis relented slightly and, leaning forward, took one of Caroline's nipples into his mouth and sucked gently. Then he reached out and tore the tape from Caroline's mouth, quickly, to minimise the discomfort. He turned his attention to her clitoris, stroking it into immediate awareness.

'Caroline, you can stop this now by asking to be released. I hope you won't, but it is your choice. The contract can be torn up. I think we have begun a very interesting relationship. I am going to treat you as a sex slave. I want to see your reactions. I want to find out what you enjoy, what you can tolerate. I want to test the boundaries. Everything I told you last night still applies. You will be well cared for but, as a sex slave, you have to accept that you cannot be allowed to say yes or no and pick and choose what happens to you. I am offering you your freedom right now, but after that, if you choose to stay, you must stay no matter what. I can't operate a Master/slave scenario if I am forever wondering whether you are going to stay or accept what is going on. You must make your choice now but, if you stay, I repeat the warning, you will not be offered such a choice again until the contract expires. It runs for a period of one year. At the end of that time, you will of course be free to renew it or leave, as you choose.

'I'll leave you now for half an hour while you think about it and will expect your decision when I return.'

So saying, Francis bent and pushed his tongue into her slit, already wet from his earlier attentions to her breasts. He found the clitoris and sucked gently on it, unfairly dulling her ability to think clearly. With a smile, he left her.

When the door had closed behind Francis, Caroline tried to sort out her feelings in the light of what she had just heard. She was strongly attracted to Francis, there was no doubt about that. She could still feel his warm mouth closing around her clitoris, treating it as if it were a special prize he yearned for. She shuddered as she remembered how she had felt last night and the strength of her orgasm. She liked being tied up, liked the feeling of giving up choices, of letting someone else do the choosing for her. No matter what? Yes, no matter what. She liked having all the decisions made for her and *she* was the one that was making the choice for that to happen. She could feel the strong sexual attraction she had for Francis and knew that that was playing a major part in her decision. She wanted to belong to him, wanted to be a slave to him, wherever that might lead. As for Lynne, Caroline remembered the sexual excitement of the previous evening. She had enjoyed the pleasure she had derived from bringing Lynne to orgasm and the similar treatment she herself had received. Pleasuring her Mistress would not be an onerous task. As for the punishment, she knew she could learn to enjoy even that as part of her submissiveness.

When Francis returned, he found Caroline with her eyes demurely cast downwards.

'Well, Caroline, have you reached a decision?'

'May I speak, Master?'

'You may.' Francis' voice held a note of eagerness.

'I would like to stay and serve you as my Master. I would like to be your slave.'

'Very good,' Francis said, taking a moment to survey his beautiful slave, tied up and awaiting his sexual desires, no matter how perverse.

Francis moved over to Caroline and smoothed the bent blonde head, resisting the strong impulse to fuck her, tied and helpless as she was. He would savour that delight for later, he promised himself.

'Now, I think the servants have prepared your room for you.'

So saying, Francis untied her. Caroline was so relieved to be free of the tight ropes that for a moment she could only stretch her aching limbs and massage them. Francis, however, was again busy at her ankles, strapping on a pair of leather cuffs which were connected by a short chain.

When the cuffs were in place, she was assisted to stand up, whereupon her wrists were drawn behind her and another pair of cuffs put on. These were joined together by a metal clip.

At that moment, Lynne walked into the room. Seeing Francis' activities, she smiled coldly.

'I see I must welcome our new slave.' Lynne's voice was full of the suggestions that the sight of Caroline evinced in her. Lynne was a natural dominatrix. She enjoyed power and control. She knew she would enjoy beating Caroline hard and often.

After admiring Francis' handiwork, Lynne attached a length of chain from Caroline's cuffed wrists down to her ankles and padlocked the chain in place. She then approached Caroline with another length of chain, this one fashioned into a leash, which she attached to Caroline's collar.

'You've been very good,' Lynne said. 'I won't gag you just now, but I think a blindfold will totally dispel any thoughts of escape that you may have.'

Caroline wanted to say that she had no intention of trying to escape, that she was here of her own volition, but she remembered she would have to ask permission to speak and, besides, she felt it was all part of the game, a serious game, where everyone played their part without question.

'Being a slave can be quite pleasant,' Lynne continued, 'but it depends on you and how fast you learn. You'll find it quite painful at first, but that's the best way to learn. I can't wait to introduce you to my friends.'

For the first time, Caroline realised that Lynne was now holding a black leather riding crop in her hands. Startled, she raised questioning eyes to her Mistress and immediately felt a burning pain on her backside, which took her by such surprise that she almost fell, and would have done so but for Francis' restraining arm. The pain was indescribable and seemed to reverberate through her for several seconds before beginning to subside. The beating of the previous evening now seemed almost playful. Caroline began to plead. 'Please, don't . . .' which earned her another stinging blow.

Francis exchanged glances with Lynne; strangely satisfied looks.

'I think the time has come for our slave to learn her first real lesson,' he said.

Then he grabbed Caroline and pushed her face down over the desk. As he tied her tightly to the table and pushed a wadded cloth gag into her mouth, he enumerated her crimes.

'Firstly, you looked up at your Mistress. Secondly, you spoke without asking permission to do so and thirdly, you didn't count. All strokes during punishment must be counted.'

'Which implement, Master?' Lynne asked.

'The cane I think. Six strokes.'

Francis bent close to Caroline.

'I realise you cannot speak, but you will be expected to remember the number of strokes, and to thank me for the punishment as soon as you are able. Failure to do so will result in the punishment being repeated, only doubled and the severity increased.'

The cane made an ominous swishing noise as it fell on to Caroline's buttocks, making six startling red marks against her white skin. Caroline moaned with pain into her gag, her pleas for mercy effectively muffled. The pain was intense and, as she was untied and helped to get off the table, she was aware of the hot and stinging sensations in her bottom. She could feel, rather than see, the six expertly placed weals. Even so, she wondered at her erect nipples. Why was her clitoris pulsating with desire after the treatment she had just received?'

As soon as the gag was removed, she remembered to ask permission to speak and, when granted, she recounted the number of strokes.

'Thank you, Master, for my punishment,' she finished, staring at the floor, hoping that she might have earned a reward.

'That's all right, slave,' Francis said as Lynne tied a black silk scarf over Caroline's eyes, prior to leading her from the room. There was obviously not going to be a reward this time, she must learn to wait for her pleasure.

'You are learning,' said Lynne, 'but you have a lot of instruction and lessons ahead of you. I shall enjoy administering every painful one of them. I think, tomorrow, we shall begin your anal instruction, my dear. It is a slave's first duty to learn how to pleasure her Master and, if she fails, the pain of punishment is of course correspondingly the greater.'

Caroline lay inert. The pain in her bottom had almost completely subsided but the memory of her humiliation was still very prevalent, as indeed her disappointment when her sexual arousal remained unsatisfied.

Caroline sighed in frustration and moved her head to one side, impatient at the fruitlessness of her feelings of thwarted desire. The abrupt movement brought a fresh reminder of her status, as the pain in her neck reminded her of the short length of chain which was connected from her collar to the headboard of the bed. She was naked beneath the bedclothes but, apart from the chain on her collar, she was not otherwise tied. There was really no need for that, as the bedclothes were not of the usual material.

Caroline remembered how she had gasped with shock when she was taken into what she now thought of as her cell. Of course it was furnished like a bedroom, but it was pointed out to her the uses to which the room could be put for the restraining of a difficult slave. When her blindfold was removed, Caroline took a few moments to get used to the light.

'We think you'll be comfortable here,' Lynne said smilingly.

The cane with which Caroline had been beaten had now been replaced in Lynne's unrelenting grip by a leather tawse, which she swung threateningly.

As she said this, she bent down and ran the tip of her tongue around Caroline's left nipple, which sent a tingling shock through her system. Caroline found herself trying to move nearer to the source of this pleasure, but only succeeded in nearly overbalancing as the chain between her wrist and ankle cuffs became taut with her movement. Lynne gave an unpleasant laugh.

'As you get used to being in restraints, you will learn to accommodate your movements to them. I hope you do, for your own sake. We really don't like our slaves to be marked with unnecessary bruises.'

She stroked Caroline's hair.

'You really are adorable. I'm going to have such fun training you to pleasure me.'

'In good time, Lynne my dear,' Francis said. 'Let's first show our guest the delights of her new accommodation.'

Caroline looked at the imposing four-poster bed which looked very comfortable and harmless, until Francis took her closer and showed her the lengths of rope and chain dangling from each of the four posts.

'This will keep you in whatever position we decide to put you while we take our pleasures. These will include teasing and tormenting you, whipping you when necessary . . .'

Francis put his mouth close to her ear so his words were like a caress.

'I think the need will arise very frequently, don't you, my darling?'

Caroline felt his hands manipulating her nipples, felt herself straining towards Francis, her body begging for satisfaction. She heard him give a deep sigh of pleasure.

'I do love it when a slave is chained and available for my pleasure.'

Caroline felt her body responding to the stimulation which somehow seemed to be increased when she struggled against her bonds. Francis' hands moved to her cunt.

'My darling, you are very wet. I wonder why that is? Anyone would think you liked being a slave.'

Caroline kept her eyes lowered, trying to hide her body's yearnings. Francis continued his demonstration of the room's delights.

'You see this nice table? Well, it too has many uses.'

Displaying the four leather cuffs at the four corners of the long table and the wide black leather strap which hung from the middle, he turned to Caroline and said, smilingly, 'Can you imagine how snug you'll be, strapped to this when you need to be beaten? If you've really been misbehaving, we might even leave you strapped here all night. How do you think you'd like that?'

Caroline knew that she would find it far from intolerable, if only Francis, or Lynne, kept her company, caressing and stroking her clitoris, stimulating her nipples with sucking and licking motions, their skill in which they had already demonstrated.

41

'I think our slave looks tired. Shall we get her into bed?' Francis enquired of Lynne, whose eyes were alight with anticipatory pleasure, as she guided Caroline to the bed and then, amazingly, removed the cuffs and chains that bound her.

'We have decided to be lenient with you, as it's your first day,' she informed Caroline.

'You will permitted to use the bathroom before you get into bed,' she said, taking Caroline firmly by the arm and leading her through a door to a large bathroom.

'Mistress, may I speak?' Caroline asked, as Lynne showed no sign of leaving the bathroom.

'You may.'

Caroline swallowed, but she was determined to speak.

'I'd like to use the bathroom and ... and I'd be grateful if I could do so alone.'

Lynne laughed and turned to Francis who had followed them in.

'You are a slave,' she explained patiently, as if to a child. 'Slaves are not permitted privacy. How do we know what you might get up to if we left you alone and unrestrained? You may proceed, while we watch, or you may decide you don't need to use the bathroom after all.'

Caroline had a desperate need to go to the toilet and, her face suffused with the red of embarrassment, under the watchful and approving eyes of her captors, she emptied her bladder. When she was finished, she sretched her hand out for the toilet roll but felt a firm grip on her arm restraining her. She was ordered to stand up, and watched with fascination as Lynne licked the drops from her cunt.

'Mm, very nice. I can't wait until you do that for me.'

Caroline was then led back to the bedroom. She stared at the sheets of the bed, almost welcoming them as old friends, as Lynne pushed her on to them. The sheets were slippery to the touch and she could already feel the material adhering to her flushed skin. The sheets were made of black latex and, as they were pulled up to her chin and tucked in firmly by Lynne, Caroline realised why she was not going to be tied up for the night. She couldn't move at all, as the rubber seemed to mould itself to her body, and the tightly pulled sheets were impossible to dislodge. Lynne pulled a length of chain forward and attached it to Caroline's collar, padlocking it into place.

'Just in case,' she said, and brushed Caroline's mouth with her own. 'Get some sleep, my darling. You have a very busy day ahead of you and I think you might have a visitor.'

Left to herself, Caroline pondered Lynne's parting words. A visitor? Was this to be the first of the guests to which Lynne and Francis might lend her? She wasn't ready for that. Yet, even as she thought this, Caroline was very conscious of her body's unsatisfied yearnings, not helped by the sensual pleasure of being wrapped in latex. She knew that the fabric would have to be peeled from her in the morning. Her fetishistic body would be reluctant to leave its sexy prison. Feverish with frustration, Caroline struggled to free at least one hand to reach her demanding clitoris, to give herself some relief. Her attempts only made the rubber cling more firmly to her and she realised that this in itself was a punishment. The latex was proving itself to be a very efficient chastity belt. Francis and Lynne knew that she would not be able to satisfy herself in any way until they chose the time and the method. In increasing frustration Caroline moved her head on the pillow, which only resulted in making the chain pull on her collar, reminding her of what she now acknowledged as her excitingly enforced servitude to her new Master and Mistress.

Caroline had hardly slept. Because of the restricting sheets and the chain on her collar, she was unable to move and was forced to wake up every time she had a natural bodily urge to try to turn. The latex sheets were now well and truly stuck to her body by her perspiration. She was desperate for a drink and felt overwhelming relief when she heard the door open and saw the maid, Annette, come in with a tray.

'Annette,' Caroline cried with genuine pleasure. 'I'm so glad to see you.'

Annette approached the bed and smiled shyly at Caroline.

'I'm here to get you ready for the Master. I'll help you to sit up first, then you can have a drink.'

Annette set about untucking the sheets which, as Caroline had anticipated, had to be peeled away from her body.

'I'm sorry about this, miss,' Annette apologised as she fastened a pair of leather cuffs on to Caroline's wrists and linked them together. 'You're new here and I . . . well . . . I remember what my first few days here were like.'

Annette released the short chain from Caroline's collar using a key she took from a bunch attached to her waist and helped Caroline to sit up.

'Annette, do you mean that you were a slave?'

This was so unexpected that Caroline was a little shocked. She had assumed, from what Francis had said, that this was the first time that he and Lynne had embarked upon such an experiment. If that was not true, how much of what Francis had said could she trust?

'A slave, yes, miss. I still am and proud of it, as you will be one day.'

Caroline accepted the cup of cold water between her cuffed hands and drank gratefully.

As she spoke, her words obviously rekindled memories to Annette. She sat on the bed.

'When I was brought here, I was just like you. I didn't really know what was expected of me. I was continuously beaten, because I kept forgetting the rules, but I came to realise that the Master is right.'

'What about?' Caroline asked, intrigued in spite of the mistrustful thoughts she had been having and desirous to know more.

'About the pain,' Annette continued. 'How it can become pleasure and the more I endured, the more I got to like it. You see, Miss,' Annette faced Caroline with an eager smile, 'once the Master and Mistress realised I was enjoying what they were doing to me, they gave me more and more freedom. Now I can come and go as I want, because they know I'll always come back. I couldn't imagine life away from Beech House.'

'How long did it take before they stopped tying you and beating you?' Caroline wanted to know.

'Oh, I'm still tied up when I'm not on duty and regularly beaten . . . because I want to be,' she added quickly as she saw Caroline's expression. 'I found that I liked being tied up, liked the feeling of the ropes biting into my skin as I struggled.' She laughed. 'It's all a game now, you see. The Master and Mistress like tying me up and beating me and I like that treatment, but I still struggle when I'm tied because the Master likes that, and I enjoy it. When he plays my body . . .'

Caroline interrupted with a demand, realising that she felt a twinge of jealously. 'What do you mean, plays your body?'

Annette smiled with remembrance of her Master's caresses.

'He knows every inch of my body, how to get pleasure and pain from it, when to stop the delicious torment and let me orgasm, when to increase the severity of a beating and when to insert his fingers into me so that I can't hold back any longer.'

She smiled at Caroline.

'Oh, he's an expert all right and I would do anything he told me to do.'

Her voice had hardened as she looked at Caroline and added meaningfully: 'Anything at all.'

Caroline rightly took that to mean she would forcibly restrain the new slave from attempting to leave. Just as quickly, the hard expression disappeared from Annette's face and she stood up briskly.

'I can't stand here gossiping all day! I've got to get you showered and breakfasted before I take you to the Master. You're going to be his sole pupil for most of the day before your visitor arrives.'

'What visitor? Annette, please tell me.'

Annette smiled.

'A very good friend of the Master and Mistress, but I'm not allowed to tell you any more than that. Now let's have you in the bathroom and showered.'

She helped Caroline to stand and walked her through into the bathroom. In the shower cubicle, Caroline was made to stand with her arms above her. Annette then fastened her cuffed wrists to a metal ring set in the wall of the cubicle. Caroline had to admit that the warm water felt good as Annette soaped her and cleaned away the night's perspiration. Seeing that Caroline was about to ask her more questions, Annette left the shower cubicle and returned with a black rubber ball-gag.

'No please don't . . .'

Caroline's protests were effectively stifled as the ball was wedged hard into her mouth and strapped behind her head.

'Sorry, miss, but time's getting on and I have a lot to do to get you ready.'

The rest of the shower was carried on in enforced silence on Caroline's part. Annette caressed her breasts as she soaped them.

'Mm, small but very nice,' she remarked.

She pinched the nipples hard and smiled at Caroline's undeniable arousal.

'I am allowed to do pretty much what I like with you as I'm getting you ready. One of the privileges I've earned for being a good slave.'

She ran her hands down Caroline's bottom and tickled the tight little hole between the cheeks.

'Yes, the Master will approve. I hope I'm allowed to play with that sometimes.'

Annette turned the water off and then looked down at herself.

'Oh, goodness, look at me. I'd better get out of these wet things.'

She kept her eyes on Caroline as she took her clothes off. As her clothes dropped to the floor, she kicked them away and then took Caroline in her arms, pressing her nakedness against her prisoner's more than willing body. Annette's urgent fingers probed Caroline's cunt and played with the swollen clitoris which, after the night's frustration, was urgently demanding attention.

'Mm, I think you enjoy being tied up just like I do.'

Annette bent her head taking each of Caroline's nipples in turn into her mouth and biting down on each one.

'I like having you tied,' she told Caroline. 'I can do what I like with you. However, I think we should make you more comfortable.'

47

Annette reached upwards and released Caroline's cuffed wrists from the ring. Caroline was very aroused and started to put her arms around Annette. To her surprise, Annette pushed her out of the cubicle and forced her to lie on the floor. Annette was holding her down with a very powerful grip and, grabbing some cord off a table with her other hand, Annette soon had her wrists tied tightly behind her back. Caroline was now lying on her stomach and she felt Annette lying on her to keep her in that position while she tied her ankles tightly and then linked a piece of rope through her wrist bonds to her ankles, drawing them up and tying the knots tightly so that Caroline was in a bow shape. When this was done, she stood up and moved away, returning to tie a scarf she had obtained over Caroline's eyes.

'You must learn the rules, miss. I am allowed to give you pain or pleasure as I choose. *You* do not make the choices. I think you need a reminder of your place here!'

Annette pushed Caroline none too gently onto her back, then there was silence. In the darkness of her blindfold, Caroline was totally unprepared for the whip as it lashed across her defenceless breasts. She could only make muffled cries into her gag. The silence which followed was torture to Caroline. Where was Annette? What was she going to do next? The next stroke of the whip caught her painfully across both nipples. Caroline tried to roll on to her stomach to avoid subsequent blows, but Annette would not allow this. Rolling her back on to her side, Annette held her in place and applied the whip again to Caroline's sensitive nipples.

Caroline was moaning pitifully into her gag. She heard Annette kneel beside her.

'Such a fuss! Be quiet now or I might put some nipple clamps on you.'

Annette's voice took on a far-away quality as she remembered her own past torments.

'The Master has some beautiful little nipple clamps. They have hungry jaws. When he fastens them on your tits, they hurt like mad, then the pain eases to a merciful numbness. Then, when he takes them off! That's when you need to be gagged. Otherwise you would be screaming like a mad thing with the pain!'

Annette's voice became unexpectedly gentle.

'Don't worry. I'm not going to use them on you now. I think you need a different sort of attention.'

Caroline gasped as Annette's fingers stroked her sore nipples, but then relaxed as the soreness disappeared and pleasure took over. Caroline struggled in her bonds as her body strained towards the hoped-for release of its sexual tension. She could feel Annette's gentle tongue swirling around her nipples, feel a probing finger massage her clitoris, slip into her wetness.

'There now,' came the gentle voice. 'You will find pleasure as well as pain in this house if you are obedient and, you know, it is sometimes worth being disobedient.'

Caroline strained against the ropes imprisoning her as she felt Annette's lips sucking at her swollen bud, inexorably extracting the orgasm that Caroline had been denied during the night's enforced confinement.

Chapter Three

Caroline was left in the hog-tie for most of the morning. She was very uncomfortable, even though Annette had pushed her over on her side. She was also feeling the lack of sustenance and the ball gag made her mouth very dry. When she remembered the pleasure that Annette had given her, however, she forgave the maid her enthusiasm with the ropes. Caroline wondered if the almost perpetual state of arousal that seemed to be endemic to her when in bondage, was something she was going to have to learn to cope with, especially when her pleasures were denied her for any period of time.

Caroline heard the door opening and two sets of footsteps approaching. She felt someone testing her bonds and then heard Francis' voice.

'Well done, Annette. You did the right thing. As your reward, the Mistress and I will deal with you later.'

'Thank you, Master,' came Annette's voice. 'You know I am happy to serve you and the Mistress.'

There was the sound of retreating footsteps and the door opening and closing. Francis uttered a gentle tutting sound as he crouched by Caroline.

'You are being very difficult, my dear,' he said, and then, amazingly, he chuckled. 'I knew you would not disappoint me.'

There was a pause and then the sound of a chair being drawn up.

Caroline was aware of something stroking her body, sending pleasurable tingles through her. Francis smiled as he watched her. He was glad she could not see the vicious-looking whip he was using to stimulate her. Time enough for her to find out what it was when he brought it into its proper use on that delicious body. She looked particularly good in a hogtie, beautifully helpless and at his mercy. It pleased him immeasurably that she was finding the delicate touch of the whip so welcome. He could tell that by the quivers of her body and her little moans of pleasure audible through the gag. Francis was feeling particularly pleased with life. This wonderful girl had come willingly into his house and he was confident that she was indeed born to be a slave . . . his slave.

He frowned momentarily as he thought of Lynne. His wife had shown herself adept at the more sadistic side of slave training. He wanted to nurture this one. His wife would have to obey him as did everyone else. In any event, she was happy with Annette and the two of them could be useful in the early stages of this slave's training. She needed to be controlled and she needed to discover the joys of total and absolute submission. He stroked the whip against Caroline's hair then against her bottom. The marks of her caning were already fading. He would have to do something about that. He looked almost pityingly at Caroline before raising the whip and bringing it down with extreme force on her beautiful backside. If Caroline had not been gagged, her scream would have echoed through the house. The intensity of the pain was unbelievable to her and Caroline made mewing sounds of protest through her gag, trying to beg Francis not to repeat the process. The second stroke was laid across the first one and was immediately followed by a gentle admonition from Francis.

'You're a silly little girl. I'm sorry about the whipping, but you do appreciate that you have brought it on yourself. You were warned what would happen and I hope you now realise that we were not joking.'

He stroked the whip across Caroline's tear-streaked face and then removed the blindfold. He crouched in front of her, looking at those lovely tear-drenched eyes and tilted her chin upwards as he spoke to her in that deceptively gentle voice.

'In this house you are nothing but a slave. You will be treated as such and you can expect no mercy. You have forfeited the right to that. Caroline, Caroline, I want to be gentle with you. I want you to love your Master and long to serve him, and you will, my dear, you will.'

He held her face in both his hands and gently ran his thumb over her mouth, distorted with the cruel gag.

'I'm going to untie you now, my dear, I need to get you dressed for our guest.' He looked at her. 'I can make things very easy for you or very difficult but, believe me, my dear, I will have my own way.'

Francis moved behind her and untied her. Caroline's limbs were so cramped that she was hardly able to move. To her surprise Francis massaged her arms and legs until she was able to stand. He looked at her appraisingly.

'You look lovely with the marks of the ropes on you.'

Once the gag was removed, Caroline licked her dry lips. She almost protested as she felt her wrists drawn behind her again and the cuffs replaced and linked together. Francis smiled at her.

'I'm sorry, my dear, but the cuffs are gentler than the ropes. Now, stay very still.'

Caroline was in no fit state to resist in any event.

Leather cuffs were strapped around her ankles and a short length of chain was used to link them together.

'That's better,' Francis declared. 'I don't think you'll be running very far like that.'

In spite of the tenderness of her skin caused by the whippings she had received, Caroline knew that she did not want to run away from Francis. She wanted him to take her, here and now, wanted him to satisfy her abused body's constant arousal.

To her disappointment, however, he steered her back towards the bathroom and into the shower but, this time, it was Francis who removed his clothes and stood facing her as he turned the shower on, Francis who soaped her gently and fondled her breasts. She felt mounting pleasure as his fingers probed her clitoris and relaxed against him as he went behind her and held her. She stiffened with surprise as she felt a wet finger inserted into her virginal anus, but Francis whispered gently to her.

'Stay very still and bear down on my finger, as if you were using the toilet. I want to get you used to being fucked in this way. I want you to anticipate the feel of my cock in your arse, pumping back and forth until I fill you with my spunk.'

Caroline couldn't say anything, enwrapped in his arms as she was and enjoying the sensations Francis was awakening in her. She forgot that she was this man's slave, forgot that he could do anything he wanted with her, in the spill of such wonderful sensations and the sure knowledge that she didn't want him to stop. He could feel her enjoyment as her body responded to his touch, could feel her anus opening ever wider to accommodate his probing finger. He was careful with her. He knew how easy it would be to injure her by his actions and he didn't want that. He wanted her to want what he was doing, want more of it and give and receive that pleasure of which he knew her to be capable. He used the index finger of the hand that was caressing her anus to massage her clitoris and was rewarded with the undeniable knowledge that she was enjoying what was happening as much as he was. The thought increased his excitement and he felt his cock grow hard and fought the urge to thrust it into her anus. She wasn't ready for that yet. She was too virgin in that area. He would only hurt her and make her draw back in fear at the remembered pain whenever she saw him approaching her. He needed her to be open for him, to feel that she wanted more than one finger in her anus and then more than two, until she wanted his cock up her arse like the hot little bitch he knew that she was.

Francis had to admit that he was surprised at the power of his own feelings. What had started out as another game for him was fast becoming something more. He wanted to train this slave, yes, but he also wanted her to come to him willingly, to offer out her hands so that he could easily tie them, to ask to be gagged because she enjoyed the feeling of helplessness, to moan piteously as she saw him raise the whip and afterwards to offer him her sore and striped buttocks so that she could feel his eager cock thrusting into her. He felt that it was possible. He felt her desire, felt her need, thought he heard her whisper, 'Oh, yes, Master, harder' but couldn't be sure above the sound of the water, above the sound of his own pounding heart. He loved being in that shower with her, loved the fact that she was so helplessly restrained and yet so obviously enjoying his caresses. Francis knew he was very near an orgasm but deliberately held off. Unknown to Caroline, he was showing her the consideration of waiting for her own orgasm which he knew was very near. He held her closer as her climax neared and, intuitively, clamped his free hand over her mouth, further denoting her helplessness.

Francis whispered to her, 'Yes, my darling, come. Come now.'

Before he had finished these urgings, she strained back against him, biting the hand that covered her mouth, not in a bid for freedom, but in ecstasy, as her climax filled her and quieted those raging sensations she could not deny. Francis was able to let his own orgasm take him. He would have loved to have forced her on to her knees in front of him, thrusting his cock in her mouth as he had done before, making her drink his spunk, but that would have to wait. It was very early days in her training and he did not want to jeopardise that burgeoning sexuality of which he was more conscious than she. She would come to him one day, willingly, and take part in whatever acts he desired of her, because she desired them herself. Yes, this slave must be nurtured, and that meant he would have to exhibit a lot of cunning in dealing with Lynne, but he would not let Lynne spoil this one for him. Oh, yes, she could take part in the training, but, after that, this slave was all his.

Francis released his hand from Caroline's mouth, but did not relax his grip on her as the feelings engendered by his orgasm quieted. Caroline relaxed against him momentarily and then stiffened as she remembered Annette.

Forgetting her position as a slave, Caroline twisted around and stared accusingly at Francis.

'You lied to me!'

Now it was Francis' turn to stiffen. He grabbed both of Caroline's wrists in a cruel grip. 'What are you talking about?'

Caroline fought in his grasp. 'Annette. She told me she was your slave. Yet you said I was the first!'

Francis relaxed. His smile when it came was unpleasant. He looked at Caroline, raising a sardonic eyebrow.

'Jealous, my dear?'

'I'm not jealous!' shouted Caroline. 'How do I know I can trust you? You said I was free to choose –'

'And so you were,' Francis interrupted. 'Annette means nothing to me! She was the first in our experiment and, of her own free will, she has elected to stay with us. Our success with Annette made us want to try again, only this time we didn't want a maid. We wanted someone who is more on equal terms with us . . . if a slave can be such, of course. As for myself, I like you, Caroline, I like you a lot and I think you like me. At the end of your contract, you are free to leave, as I said. Until then' – Francis' voice became urgent, demanding in his desire – 'you are my slave and I will use you as I please!'

Francis was passionate in his arousal. He pushed Caroline out of the cubicle and into the bedroom. Grabbing some rope, he forced Caroline on to the bed so that she was lying on her stomach. Her wrists were tied behind her and she felt a handkerchief thrust between her lips and tied tightly behind her head.

'This is how I like to use my slaves!'

Francis' voice was loud in her ear: she could hear the passion and feel the heat of his arousal as his cock probed urgently at her anus. She could feel her own passion mounting again as his hands found her breasts, the pain in her nipples as he squeezed them turning into a pleasure-pain. She wanted him inside her, wanted to feel his cock in her arse. Her clitoris was rubbing against the rubber sheet with Francis' movements. She wanted to hold back her orgasm, wait for Francis, but she knew she couldn't. The waves of orgasm were unrelenting. She was bathed in pleasure, wrapped in it, didn't want it to end. As Francis' cock penetrated fully into her anus, she was still experiencing incredible pleasure and was only dimly aware of a slight pain as her anus surrendered its virginity. She was much more' aware of the warm liquid filling her as Francis spunked inside her. She only felt glad, glad and grateful.

They lay together, sated, for some moments. Caroline could not tell Francis how she felt because of the gag in her mouth. She felt an overwhelming sense of relief at his explanation about Annette. She wondered if she would be made to pay for her disobedience in addressing Francis as she had, then smiled sleepily as she remembered Annette telling her that sometimes it was almost worth being disobedient.

Caroline felt sleep encroaching on her and this was only prevented by Francis gently stroking her hair and murmuring to her that she had to be made ready for the visitor. Caroline was released from her bonds by a gentler Francis, one who exhibited great care as he washed and dried her tenderly, lingering lovingly over her anus with remembered pleasure.

Caroline asked no questions as Francis strapped her into a leather body harness, settling the vaginal strap snugly between already wet lips, chuckling at her indrawn breath as he tightened the strap.

'Comfortable, my darling?'

It was a rhetorical question and Francis smiled as he replaced the leather collar around Caroline's neck with a much wider one which forced her to hold her head up. Caroline felt an indescribable surge of excitement as the collar was not only strapped into place but also padlocked.

Seating her in a chair, Francis watched as she drew

on the seamed black hold-up stockings he had given her and then helped her to put on a pair of black high-heeled shoes. The heels must have been more than four inches in height and Caroline wondered how she was going to be able to cope with walking in them. The shoes had ankle straps and she watched, with hardening nipples, as Francis produced two small padlocks and attached them to the straps, locking them in place.

Caroline revelled in the feelings that this sort of attire produced in her. She could feel her clitoris emerging from its protective hood with her mood of growing excitement. She wondered about the identity of the visitor and what he or she might want with Caroline.

Her thoughts were interrupted as the door was thrown open and Lynne appeared in the doorway and stood with her hands on her hips. She was wearing a black leather corset which enhanced her shapely figure, thigh-high pvc boots with five-inch heels and her blonde hair was drawn back from her face in a severe bun, which somehow suited her. She had a riding crop thrust into the top of one of her boots, which Caroline eyed apprehensively.

'You took your time,' she accused Francis. 'I suppose you were taking your pleasures from our little guest!' She almost spat the words.

'I see you are in a lovely mood, Lynne,' Francis said pleasantly. 'Did Annette not pleasure you so well today?'

Lynne strode into the room and, reaching down, twisted one of Caroline's nipples, making her yelp.

'We should keep this slave gagged. She's too noisy.'

She walked over to a table and began sorting through some items in a drawer.

'Fun-time over, my dear,' Francis said apologetically. 'Our guest will be arriving shortly and, I must say, you look wonderful.'

Francis helped Caroline stand and walk a few steps in the unaccustomed heels.

Because of what had happened between them, Caroline felt able to break all the rules and plead directly with Francis. She spoke in a desperate whisper.

'Will you stay with me when I meet this visitor? Please, Master, I'm very nervous.'

Francis looked at her and merely smiled. He seemed different when Lynne was in the vicinity. He bent down and, taking one of Caroline's nipples between his teeth, bit down none too gently on it, eliciting a startled gasp.

Francis straightened as his wife came over to them, holding something black that looked very menacing to Caroline's eyes.

'I think you're right, my dear. The slave should be kept gagged. I will leave you to do the honours.'

With that, Francis turned on his heel and left the room. Lynne didn't hesitate but strode over to Caroline and stood in front of her, swinging the black leather mask by its straps.

'Don't even think about giving me any trouble. If you do, it will be the worse for you.'

So saying she pulled the mask over Caroline's face. The mask was made to exercise total control over an unsuspecting victim. There were no eye-holes and Caroline's ears were covered so that sound became muffled. There was an in-built penis gag in the mask which Lynne thrust into Caroline's mouth.

'Get used to that, you bitch,' she hissed at Caroline as she tightly laced the mask into place. 'Get used to sucking cock, because you'll be doing a lot of it.'

There were small holes in the nose piece so the

wearer could breathe but, other than that, Caroline was plunged into a world of darkness, with only the chilling sound of the voice of the woman Caroline now felt was her implacable enemy. Had she sensed the closeness between her and Francis, Caroline wondered and, if she had, what would it mean for the helpless slave? Possibly harsher beatings. Why did that thought so excite Caroline, who, before, had always sincerely professed her aversion to pain? Now she seemed to yearn for further experiences of pain as she acknowledged the exquisite sensations that could result from it.

Caroline was unable to see or even hear properly. Everything seemed to be increasing her sexual excitement as, even in the confines of the helmet, Caroline heard Lynne scream out.

'Annette, get in here!'

Caroline heard the door opening and footsteps approaching.

'All right,' the cold voice came again. 'Let's get the bitch trussed up really tight.'

Caroline's wrists were tied very tightly behind her and then her elbows received the same treatment, being tied in a way that almost drew them together. A chain was attached to her collar, which was jerked savagely until Caroline was forced to stand and follow her tormentors. She had no idea where they were going. She was only too aware of the tightness of the constricting cords. She tripped and almost fell at one point and was rewarded with a stinging slap across her bottom. When she stumbled again, she felt a whip biting into her breasts. She was saved from further punishment by Francis' voice.

'Steady, my dear. You are sometimes too cruel. I think we can discard this mask and loosen those ropes – they are a little tight.'

With bad grace, Lynne complied, tearing off the

mask so that she hurt Caroline in the process and loosening the ropes by a very small amount.

'Caroline,' Francis said pleasantly, 'come and meet our guest. Someone you already know I believe.'

Caroline blinked at the light streaming through the windows and saw a familiar figure coming towards her.

'Miss ... Miss Summers,' Caroline faltered. She did not know why she should be so surprised after what she had been told by Francis and Lynne. Perhaps it was the undoubted lasciviousness with which Miss Summers was looking at her.

'Caroline, how nice to see you again. You look . . .'

Miss Summers licked moisture from her lips. She didn't need to finish the sentence. Her whole attitude was one of frank and open admiration. Caroline could not help noticing the nipples pushing against Miss Summer's thin cotton blouse and felt a thrill as she realised that she had the power to so affect someone whom, in reality, she hardly knew.

Miss Summers approached her and stroked Caroline's erect nipples, framed by the leather straps of the harness.

'Very nice, my dear.'

She looked at Francis and Lynne with a questioning expression.

Francis moved to Caroline and stroked her clitoris, which was wet with desire.

'We are very pleased with our slave, Angela,' he addressed Miss Summers with warm familiarity. 'You have earned your commission and we have prepared her for you.'

Caroline was startled at this but, realising her duties as a sex slave, quickly recovered her composure and smiled at Miss Summers.

'I hope I please you, Mistress?'

Caroline felt the warmth of Francis' approval as he

slipped a finger into her wet and willing slit. What was she turning into? Right now, it didn't seem to matter. She only knew that she urgently needed some sexual release and, if Miss Summers could supply it, she was more than ready to play her part.

'You have been misbehaving, girl! Can you deny it?'

The words echoed around the schoolroom. Caroline was glad that the wide collar had been removed from her neck, enabling her to hang her head, admitting her guilt.

'Yes, Mistress, I have,' she mumbled, feeling the dampness in her school knickers. 'I'm very sorry. I won't do it again.'

'Not good enough, my girl! You have to be punished, you know that, don't you?'

Caroline's nipples immediately hardened at these words. She could feel them straining against the thin material of the white blouse that she wore as part of her school uniform.

The room they were in was at the back of the house. Caroline had been surprised to see that it was, in fact, a schoolroom, doubtless used to facilitate adult fantasies. Caroline had been told by a somewhat mollified Lynne that Miss Summers had long nurtured fantasies about being a strict headmistress and of being allowed to discipline her pupils. Angela's commission was to be the fulfilment of that fantasy. Caroline had been released from her bonds and given a complete school uniform to put on. Lynne's change of attitude was explained by her kissing and fondling Caroline outside the door of the schoolroom and her whispered assurance that she and Annette would join them later, an assurance that was far from unwelcome to a very aroused Caroline. Now she stood in respectful silence as Miss Summers enumerated her crimes.

'You were caught talking in class again and were late for your lessons on three occasions! Such behaviour will not be tolerated, my girl!'

Caroline said nothing, keeping her eyes lowered and wishing that Miss Summers would slip her fingers into Caroline's open moistness. Her body was crying out for satisfaction.

Angela, however, was placing a high stool in front of Caroline. She faced her, her outraged expression unable to totally conceal her excitement. Her fingers fumbled with Caroline's school tie, untying and removing it.

'You know that you are going to be beaten, don't you, girl?'

'Yes, Mistress.'

'You know that you have earned this punishment?'

'Yes, Mistress.'

Miss Summers licked some anticipatory spittle from her lips.

'Beg me for your punishment then!'

'Please cane me, Mistress. I know that I deserve it. Please cane me hard.'

With a grunt of satisfaction Miss Summers pushed Caroline over the stool, using some rope to tie her wrists and ankles to it. Pushing the wadded-up school tie into Caroline's mouth, she secured it with more rope which she then tied tightly behind her head.

'I don't want you disturbing the rest of the school with your screams, you bad girl!'

Caroline's knickers were pulled down. She felt the longed-for feelings of fingers stroking her clitoris and slipping into her wetness and knew she was on the verge of an orgasm.

'Why, you are soaking wet!'

Suddenly, the cane whistled through the air, making Caroline yelp into her gag. Time after time the cane cut across her helpless bottom, the stinging turning into fiery pain as she was repeatedly struck. Caroline desperately tried to free herself, but she had been too well tied, her struggles only serving to increase her arousal.

Just as suddenly as it had started, the caning mercifully stopped and Caroline felt eagerly probing fingers inside her vagina, more fingers pushing at her engorged bud. Her orgasm quickly overpowered her, making her sag weakly against her bonds.

No words were said as Caroline was quickly untied from the stool. Her wrists were then tightly re-tied behind her and, grabbing her by the hair, Miss Summers dragged Caroline to her knees in front of her, pulled down the ropes that kept the tie in place and jerked the tie-gag out of Caroline's mouth. With the other hand, she yanked up her own skirt. Miss Summers was not wearing any knickers and, grabbing a handful of Caroline's long hair, Miss Summers forced the girl's face on to her bush. Caroline's eager tongue probed willingly into the wetness offered to it, tasting the juices which the resultant excitement of punishing such an errant pupil had produced. Caroline swirled her tongue around the swollen clitoris, hardly aware of the pain caused by the tight grip on her hair, as she answered need with need. Miss Summers pushed her pubes into Caroline's face as her orgasm shook her.

Breathing harshly, Miss Summers controlled herself at last and then, releasing her grip on Caroline's hair, knelt in front of Caroline and kissed her gently.

'Thank you, darling girl, thank you.'

Caroline felt again the undeniable surge of power as she realised what she had done for this woman. Her triumph was interrupted by a knock on the door.

'I hope this is an opportune moment for us to join you,' Lynne said as she walked into the room, leading a tightly bound Annette. 'I thought we might both have some fun with our slaves!'

Lynne pushed Annette further into the room and, with a malicious smile, turned and locked the door.

'That should ensure our privacy!' she purred, tucking the key into her cleavage. 'Shall we change slaves, or do you want to keep that one?'

Lynne's expression made it perfectly plain what she wanted, as she looked possessively at Caroline.

Angela Summers was all too well aware that Lynne always got what she wanted . . . always.

'It's been a long time since Annette and I have tasted each other, so by all means let's swap.'

Wasting no time, Lynne marched over to Caroline and pulled her to her feet, using a tight grip on her hair. She looked behind Caroline and nodded approval of the tied wrists.

'You always do very good knots, Angela, I commend you!'

Angela Summers was re-introducing herself to the remembered delights of Annette's body.

'The new slave is a credit to you, Lynne. She sucks clitty very, very well.'

'As well as Annette, do you think?' Lynne asked with a look in her eyes that meant she was planning something.

Angela Summers looked at Lynne with some surprise but, catching her friend's eye, admitted she was unsure.

Caroline and Annette were made to stand side by side, both securely tied.

'Why don't we stage a contest?' asked Lynne, rhetorically, as she had already made up her mind that there would be a contest.

'Excellent!' enthused Angela, tweaking Annette's nipples and smiling approvingly at the resulting pain-filled expression on her slave's face.

Lynne walked around Caroline considering her next move. She noted the ropes that had formed part of the gag and decided to make further use of them.

'I think my slave has a little too much clothing on!'

So saying, Lynne put her fingers in the top of Caroline's blouse and ripped the material from neck to waist. Without any warning she pushed Caroline on to a chair, ripped her school knickers off and wadded them up. Forcing the knickers into Caroline's mouth, she pulled the ropes from around her neck back into place, securing the knickers and tying extra knots to make a very efficient gag. Caroline could taste her own juices on the thick material which was stuffed into her mouth.

With intense delight, Lynne observed her slave's growing fear as she swung the metal clips in front of her face and then, grabbing Caroline's left nipple, taking great pleasure in squeezing it cruelly, she closed the savage jaws of the clamp on the nipple. Caroline was still screaming into her gag as the second clamp was applied to her right nipple.

Lynne grabbed her by the hair and brought Caroline's face close to her own.

'Listen to me, you little bitch! I expect you to win this contest easily. If you don't, you will be beaten on the insides of your thighs. Do you know how painful that can be? And maybe the odd stroke of the crop between your legs. I think you might enjoy that. I know I will! In fact, I hope you lose the contest!'

Lynne stood back and admired her handiwork.

'Annette will go first. She will pleasure us both, Angela, and we will time her to see how long she takes. The other one can watch. She might learn something. Then it will be her turn.'

Lynne used long lengths of rope to secure Caroline to the chair, laughing cruelly as the tightness of the ropes were obviously causing Caroline a measure of discomfort.

'Now watch and learn, slave!'

Caroline *was* uncomfortable but she was also excited. She wanted to win the contest, not only to avoid what sounded like a very painful beating, but also because a sense of pride fuelled her combatant spirit. She could and would win!

Annette was glaring balefully at her, similar thoughts probably occurring to her. She hadn't much time to think, however, as Lynne dragged her to her knees in front of Angela, who was sprawled on the floor with her back resting against a desk.

'Pleasure your Mistress!' Lynne ordered and a very willing Annette embarked on her task with enthusiasm.

Angela was soon in the throes of ecstasy as Annette's knowledgeable tongue got to work. If she showed anything less than total enthusiasm, Lynne tugged viciously on the chain attached to her slave collar.

Caroline watched with what she had to admit was jealousy. She would do a better job when it was her turn. The chair to which she was tied was becoming very wet with her own juices, the gagging knickers reminding her of her earlier sexual arousal. She twisted in her seat, feeling the constricting ropes holding her in place, adding to her excitement.

Lynne watched her with a pleasurable anticipation of what she intended to do to this slave when she lost the contest, which she surely would. Annette was an expert at licking out her Mistress! In any event, Lynne intended to make sure her slave lost the contest, by hampering her movements . . . just a little!

These exciting thoughts fuelled Lynne's own desires, but she still remembered to click the stopwatch as Angela cried out in pleasure.

'Excellent, my dear!' Lynne purred as she reached down and stroked Annette's dark curls. 'My turn now, I think.'

Lynne knelt down and untied Annette's wrists.

'I would like you to pleasure my tits at the same time as you are licking my little bud, my dear.'

She looked triumphantly over at Caroline, who instantly knew that she would not be granted such favours when it was her turn. She tried to protest, but the thick material of the school knickers prevented more than a murmur escaping. The pain in her clamped nipples had now subsided and she thought of their eventual release and the inevitable resultant pain with a strange eagerness.

Smiling to herself, Lynne settled herself in position, exclaiming with pleasure as Annette's expert fingers teased her already erect nipples into vibrant life, sensations joining with those being extracted from her clitoris, which Annette was sucking gently, expertly. Annette knew how Lynne liked to be treated, had done this many times before. She could not repress the surge of excitement as she thought of witnessing Caroline's humiliation and subsequent punishment. Maybe the Mistress would even allow Annette to take part.

Annette moved one hand underneath her Mistress, until she found the tight little hole between her cheeks and stroked the anal channel into awareness as she gently inserted a finger into its tightness.

Lynne's orgasm washed forcefully over her, leaving her sighing exhaustedly with pleasure, watched by an increasingly frustrated Caroline.

Caroline could not believe what was happening. She had been untied from the chair and the knickers had been removed from her mouth. Her wrists were untied but, as she started to automatically reach to release the clamps on her nipples, Lynne caught her wrists and pulled them behind her again. This time, she strapped leather cuffs on to Caroline's wrists, cuffs which were joined by a short chain. A leather collar was strapped around Caroline's neck and buckled in front so that the ring was at the back. Through this ring, Lynne threaded a length of chain and fastened it to the chain connecting her wrist cuffs. This had the effect of pulling Caroline's head back and thereby restricting her movements quite drastically.

'Please, Mistress. This is not fair ...' Caroline began.

'I didn't give you permission to speak, slave. In fact I don't remember you asking for such permission. For that you will be severely punished. As for fair, I did not mention that you would or would not be restrained during this contest. It is up to you how you manage to achieve our satisfaction.'

Angela was sure her juices were already trickling down her legs as she took her place in front of this beautiful slave, chained and helpless, the leather collar already reddening the white skin of her neck.

Taking pity on her, Angela tried to seat herself to best advantage for Caroline, whose straining movements only aggravated the collar around her neck. Caroline was more determined than ever to succeed. Bringing her hands up as far as she could, thereby easing some of the strain on the collar, Caroline was able to slide her tongue quite forcefully into the opening in front of her, using her top lip to massage the willing clitoris.

Lynne's plans backfired, as Angela came very quickly and forcefully, doubly excited by the slave's chained limbs and struggles to lick Angela out to the best of her ability, even with the extra restrictions she had to endure.

As she felt the increase of juices on her tongue,

Caroline withdrew and could not resist a glance of triumph at Lynne and Annette.

Enraged at that look of triumph, Lynne quickly recovered herself enough to strap a pair of ankle cuffs on to Caroline, which were attached with a short length of chain. Using this, Lynne attached a further chain length from these cuffs to the chain joining her cuffed wrists, further restricting Caroline's movements. Smiling triumphantly, Lynne tied a short piece of rope around Caroline's mouth, forcing it between her teeth, effectively depressing her tongue to a certain extent, and tying it tightly behind her head.

Seeing Angela's concern at this unfairness, Lynne quickly explained. 'She is not gagged. She can still speak. It's true her tongue is a little restricted, but I like my slaves to show initiative.'

Lynne looked at Caroline challengingly.

'I'm waiting, slave!'

Caroline was at a loss for a moment then, with her chains jangling, pushed herself to where Lynne was waiting for her and, with difficulty, manoeuvred herself into a position where she could just about reach Lynne's slit, which was already oozing with her juices as she contemplated her slave's struggles. That, in fact, was her downfall.

Lynne was so excited by seeing Caroline struggle to achieve her objective that, when she felt the rope in Caroline's mouth, as Caroline used her tongue to press it against Lynne's pulsating clitoris, she could not hold back the waves of orgasm, which shook her body with a force such as she had never before experienced. Unknown to her, while she was enjoying this great pleasure, her slave was straining against her bonds, using the feelings that these restrictions evoked to achieve her own, long-desired orgasm, which was further fuelled by the triumph she could not conceal.

Chapter Four

Caroline awoke from a deep sleep. There was no one in the bed beside her and, although she was again chained by her collar, the length of this chain allowed her quite a lot of movement. She had awoken with thoughts of Francis in her mind and she smiled, cat-like, as she stretched and remembered her victory in the contest. She winced a little as her arm brushed her sore nipples. She remembered the agony as the clips were removed by Francis and how Francis had held her until the re-awakening pain in her nipples had subsided.

It was in fact the day after the contest. Angela Summers had gone, having partaken of her commission, and Lynne and Annette were so aroused by the earlier events, they had embarked on a session of their own.

Caroline smiled as she recalled how she and Francis had celebrated her victory in the contest. Francis had insisted that she demonstrate the amazing versatility of her tongue on his penis. He had used the same collar to once again chain her as she had been before, tying a rope in her mouth and laughingly challenging her to bring him off, hampered as she was by her restrictions. It wasn't long before the laughter stopped as both Caroline and Francis became aroused and Francis removed all the restrictions to enable Caroline to take the full length of him into her mouth, at the same time as she gently squeezed and fondled the metal rings which adorned Francis' nipples.

Caroline remembered the taste of Francis, the thought triggering an immediate response in her clitoris. She loved swallowing his spunk, loved the taste of her own juices as he inserted a finger into her slit and then smeared her own juices on her lips.

Caroline's thoughts were interrupted by the sound of the door of her bedroom opening. A maid stood there, one she hadn't seen before, who smiled uncertainly at her and came forward holding the loaded tray. Delicious smells reached Caroline and she suddenly realised how hungry she was. As the maid put the tray down on the bedside table, she curtsied to Caroline before returning to the door. It was then that Caroline realised that the maid wore two ankle cuffs joined by a length of chain. She was about to question her when Francis walked in. She tried to repress the surge of feelings his appearance generated.

'Good morning, my dear. How do you feel this morning?' he asked.

She realised that it seemed to be an unspoken agreement between them that, when they were alone, they conversed on more equal terms.

'I'm feeling OK, thank you,' Caroline said, and moved a little as Francis settled himself on the bed.

'You haven't eaten your breakfast. Come on, let me feed you,' he said and picked up a piece of fruit for her to bite into. She enjoyed the food very much, more so, it had to be said, because Francis fed her every bite.

'You have a new maid to attend to you. I won't subject you to Annette again. She has become extremely jealous and I'm afraid she might try to harm you in some way.'

72

Francis smiled and caressed her nipples.

'You are to go out today, as a slave of course.'

Francis slipped three fingers into her, being rewarded with Caroline's increased moistness. She could refuse him nothing and that pleased him immeasurably.

'It will excite me to take you out and only you and I will know that you are restrained. Tonight I want to abuse that beautiful body of yours.'

His words excited Caroline so that she strained against the chain in her collar, trying to push herself towards Francis.

Although her movement and the reason for it gave Francis great pleasure, he merely arose from the bed, bent down and kissed her.

'I'll see you soon,' he smiled at her and was gone.

Francis returned to his own room and went to the window. The sight of the green lawns with their flower beds and topiary always soothed him and made him realise his own good fortune that had brought him to this very beautiful part of England. He needed to think. Always in the past his plans had been neat and orderly and carried out without snags that caused any real concern or that couldn't be easily dealt with ... but this time? He hadn't expected or wanted the complication that his feelings for Caroline were engendering in him. He had wanted, as in the past, to train a new slave who would then either join his household or one of the others of his many like-minded friends. Caroline had seemed perfect. No job and no home, eager to please and prepared to dedicate herself to working for him. He knew immediately that she had submissive tendencies. He was an expert in assessing them. He also knew that she had excited Lynne as much as himself and so the auguries were very good.

He reflected on the shower incident when he had felt Caroline's genuine responses to him, felt her need and, for the first time, felt an unselfish desire to give her pleasure before his own. Did that alter his plans for her? He leant his forehead against the window pane and watched a small wren picking desultorily amongst the lushness of the green lawns. No, his plans were not altered except maybe insofar as Lynne was concerned. He sighed and moved to seat himself in a luxuriously padded leather easy chair. He remembered his exhilaration when he and Lynne had first met. Here was a dominatrix who was a match for him in every way. She excelled in her cruelty and had given him many hours of pleasure as he watched her training slaves. After a few sessions with Lynne, they turned to him with relief and gratitude and accepted his commands with alacrity and, yes, pleasure. He felt that Caroline had to be continuously exposed to Lynne's cruelties for the same purpose. Caroline was already more well disposed to him than she had been, but he wanted her to learn the way of complete subjugation and accept it as the right way for her. He remembered her response when he had held his hand over her mouth and precipitated her climax. She had accepted the pleasure to be gained by being completely helpless and he wanted to work on that. He would enjoy taking her out today, knowing that she was his, knowing that, although she was his voluntarily, she would not be able to run away even if she wanted to.

His thoughts were interrupted by a knock on the door. On his shouted 'Come in' Lynne made her appearance. As always, she had the ability to make him draw in his breath with appreciation. She was wearing a softly tailored black leather dress, which came to her knees. The softness of the leather moulded itself to her voluptuous body and excited him as she moved. In spite of her cruelty, or perhaps because of it, he felt the usual stirring of excitement as he appraised her.

'You look very lovely, my dear,' he said appreciatively.

She smiled at him, acknowledging the sexual tension that always existed between them and moved towards him.

'Have you forgiven me?' she asked as she walked behind his chair and leaned over the back to caress his shoulders.

'There is nothing to forgive, my dear. Your bending of the rules in the contest sounds most exciting and I only wish I had videoed the whole thing.'

Francis paused, searching for the right way to say what he wanted . . . needed . . . to say.

'From now on I want to supervise personally all of Caroline's training. You are not to administer any part of it unless I am present.'

'You want to stop the experiment! You've let the little slut get under your skin, haven't you?' Lynne accused him as she straightened and walked around the chair to stand in front of him with her hands on her hips.

'My dear, I don't ever let anyone get under my skin, you should know that, but too much of your particular brand of cruelty can be counter-productive. I think Caroline has all the makings of a very good slave and I want to allow her time to develop. I'm sure you understand.'

'I understand that you have more feelings for this one than any of your other conquests. I've seen the way you look at her. I know that you allow her to talk to you as an equal when you're alone together.'

'My, my. Your spy network never ceases to amaze me. Annette again? Speaking of Annette, I want you to keep her away from Caroline, at least for the time being.'

Lynne's rage, which had been contained, now broke through. 'Why are you protecting that little bitch? What is she to you? We had an agreement!'

'Which you are very close to breaking. We knew what we wanted from each other when we got married. That was mutual respect, appreciation of each other's talents but I don't recall any mention of love coming into it. You're beginning to sound like a jealous harridan and I will not put up with that!'

Francis' controlled temper was very effective, more effective than Lynne's rage, and she knew it.

'We have an agreement that works. We both wanted to try this experiment of having a sex slave and we've been very successful so far. I think you're a stunning woman, Lynne, and we have a relationship that is profitable to both of us. Your desires run much more to the female than the male and that's OK with me. I don't interfere with your life and I would appreciate the same consideration from you.'

He rose and went up to Lynne.

'Let's not quarrel, my dear. We have a slave to train today and you can employ your own special talents when dealing with her, within very narrow restraints if you'll pardon the pun. I need you, Lynne, never forget that.'

She appeared slightly mollified and kissed him affectionately. 'You're right, of course. It's just that I've never seen you behave this way with any woman and I'm not sure how to deal with it.'

Francis laughed and put his arm around her.

'Don't worry about me. Now scoot, I have to get ready too, you know.'

He looked at her admiringly. 'I'm no match for you in that department. I've always loved the way you look.'

Lynne gave a mock curtsey.

'Thank you kind sir,' she said and walked to the door.

Turning, she looked at him inquisitively. 'I won't be gentle with her, Francis.'

Francis responded to the unspoken question and shrugged his shoulders acquiescently, and with that she had to be content.

The new maid was called Alicia. She was petite and pretty and, at first, very uncommunicative to Caroline's attempts at conversation. She seemed afraid of being punished if anyone found out that they were friendly. It took Caroline some efforts to allay these fears.

'Look, Alicia,' she said when the maid returned after taking away Caroline's breakfast things. 'We're both new here, am I right?'

Alicia nodded, keeping her eyes downcast until Caroline tilted her chin.

'You don't have to be that way with me. I won't tell anyone and, I don't know about you, but I'm in need of a friend. I won't give you any trouble, Alicia, I know you're only doing your job, but it would be so much easier if we could talk openly together, don't you think?'

The wide grey eyes looked back at her and then were illuminated with a smile.

'Oh, thank you, miss. I . . . I would like a friend.'

'How did you come here, Alicia?' Caroline asked as the maid unlocked the chain on her collar and held out a towelling robe for her to put on.

'Same way as I've heard you did, miss, through the agency.'

'You mean Miss Summers?'

'Yes, miss. She seemed so nice and I really needed this job.'

'You've no family?'

'No, miss. I'm all alone.'

The position was becoming clearer to Caroline. The agency was obviously a respectable front for the recruitment of slaves, perhaps for more than just this house. All the girls probably shared a common lack of family and close friends. The thought made her very angry; Francis had not been exactly truthful with her. She swallowed her anger for the moment. She did not want to repeat her error with Annette. Again, she mentally thanked Francis for his concern that Annette should not come near her. She thought about Francis as she showered. Alicia had strapped the ankle cuffs on her, but this time there was quite a long chain connecting from them to the ring in the wall of the shower cubicle and Alicia waited outside.

What did she really feel for Francis? It was almost impossible for her to understand her own feelings. She was this man's slave. She had willingly consented to it and, so far, she had to admit that being Francis' slave was more exciting than she could have thought. She was allowed minimal freedom, constantly guarded and in fear of punishment if she broke one of the rules, and there seemed to be so many of those! She could not conceal, even from herself, her state of arousal whenever Francis was in her vicinity. What did that mean to him? Why was it that her inability to just walk out of this shower and out of the house was now so exciting, made her feel sexually more aware than she had ever been? She was reminded of the promised outing today. Did Francis really mean to take her outside the sheltering walls of the grounds surrounding the house while she was in some form of bondage? The idea made her nipples erect, the additional wetness between her legs having nothing to do with the cascading water of the shower.

78

Her thoughts were interrupted by the sound of a voice which formed a very rude interruption to her reverie.

'Not ready yet, slave? That's very unfortunate for you. It means that you will be punished before we go out!'

Lynne had walked into the bathroom and she was holding the whip that Caroline remembered only too well.

'Alicia, get the slave out here now if you don't want some punishment yourself.'

Alicia scrambled to obey, unlocking the chain and escorting Caroline out of the shower. She started to towel her dry but Lynne used the whip to knock the towel from her hand. 'I haven't heard your greeting yet, slave!'

Caroline kept her eyes cast downward, trembling with guilty excitement when she thought of what was to come.

'Good morning, Mistress.'

Lynne walked around the girl, trailing the whip gently across her wet body.

'Don't you think it is a very bad error to keep your Mistress waiting, slave?'

'Yes, Mistress,' Caroline managed, before the world exploded in pain as the whip struck savagely across her tender breasts.

She was given no time to absorb this pain before the whip struck her across her breasts again and again while an obviously excited Alicia was harshly told to hold Caroline still. The beating seemed to go on for ever. Caroline could not keep count of the strokes and knew she would suffer for that. When her breasts were laced with angry weals Lynne turned her attention to her bottom and thighs, lashing her mercilessly again and again until she tired and threw the whip into a corner of the room.

'On your knees, slave!'

Lynne ordered Alicia to open the zip at the front of her dress and, with trembling fingers, Alicia obeyed.

'Pleasure your mistress, slave!' Lynne ordered.

The hood of Caroline's clitoris had not been able to confine her eager bud, straining with the excitement which the beating had instilled. She eagerly leant forward and applied her tongue to her Mistress' slit, wet and slippery with the arousal that the domination of Caroline had produced. Lynne's orgasm was not long in coming but, to Caroline's disappointment, after Lynne's shudders had subsided, she pushed Caroline away with the shining toe of her high-heeled boot.

'Get her ready!' she admonished Alicia and stalked out of the room.

Caroline stood in front of Lynne and Francis who were both appraising her mode of dress. It was an unseasonably chilly day which presented them with a perfect excuse to have her dressed as she was in a full-length black woollen cape which fastened at the neck and in one or two places in the front. The cape was so voluminous that, even when she walked, it did not fall back far enough to reveal her attire underneath, which was very little indeed. She had been dressed in a black leather corset which did not cover her breasts. Her outfit included a black leather suspender belt to which were attached black seamed stockings. The cape also concealed the fact that her wrists were tied together behind her and her elbows were also tied. Lynne had tightly strapped a pair of thigh cuffs on her, linked by a short chain to restrict her from taking all but very small steps.

'Excellent, my dear,' Francis enthused. 'No one

would know that she was in any way restrained or that she is a slave, which you are of course.' This was addressed to Caroline. 'I think we must also ensure our slave's silence. I think the penis gag will make the most effective muffler.'

Lynne immediately got what was required from a drawer in the table and went over to Caroline to complete her helplessness. Caroline opened her mouth to facilitate the insertion of the gag with its attached phallus which filled her mouth and enabled no emissions to escape. Beneath the neck of the cape Caroline also wore her collar which had a long black leather leash attached to it. Lynne held it up to show the slave how well it could be concealed from prying eyes because of its colour and thinness.

'A scarf I think, to finish it off,' Francis commented and wound a thick woollen scarf around the bottom half of Caroline's face, knotting it securely and tucking the ends into the cape. 'It's a shame our niece has such a bad toothache, isn't it, darling? We'll need to stay very close to her to make sure she doesn't faint.'

Lynne gave a sharp tug on the leash. 'If she does, I'll make sure she doesn't injure herself,' she said with an evil smile. 'After all, I want to reserve that little pleasure for myself.'

'And so you shall, my love, after our outing.'

Francis smiled at Caroline, but his voice was low and heavy with menace. 'If you give us any trouble, I will not hesitate to give you over to Lynne for some lessons in how to behave. She will not have any restrictions placed on her. Do you understand?'

Caroline nodded, trembling with excitement. There was something undeniably sexually arousing about being taken out in restraints. No one that they met would realise her true state. Caroline wondered whether the thought of that or the likely severe beating from Lynne was making her so aroused. Her nipples would have shown through a thinner material and she hoped that Francis or even Lynne would give her some relief before the end of the day. She had not yet got used to the chastity belt, stopping her self-pleasure even when her wrists were not secured, which she was made to wear every night, unless she was called upon to receive pleasure from her Master or Mistress.

As all three of them got into the large, black, chauffeur-driven limousine which was waiting at the bottom of the steps when they went outside, Caroline was made to sit between Lynne and Francis. She looked at the driver whose gaze she met in the rear-view mirror, but his lascivious smile showed her only too well that he was aware of exactly what was happening. As they made their way along the beautiful driveway she had driven up with such hope just a short while ago, Caroline considered the enjoyment of her new status with surprise. She had to admit that she relished her subservient role. She was beginning to look forward to her punishments and, in fact, looked for ways to earn them. The pain of a whipping was always the precursor to previously unimagined pleasure. Now, she reflected on her current state with an arousal that cried out to be satisfied. She couldn't walk without being supported; having her hands tied behind her made her very vulnerable. She certainly couldn't run even if she wanted to, and she couldn't call for help or even make sufficient noises to awaken the suspicions of people they encountered. She thought of Francis and how clever he was being. She rightly felt that he relished this challenge, the thrill of discovery if anything went wrong and the enforcement of his position of power over her. She had never felt that more keenly than she now did as she made a few feeble pulls at her bonds. It was of no use, she was tied far too well for any escape. She felt herself looking forward to the end of this outing and a return to the house. Would she be beaten? Would she be allowed some sexual release? Her nipples were unbearably sensitive. She looked at her Master and Mistress. She had been disappointed when she had realised that she wasn't going out with just Francis, but now she acknowledged that both of them being present only increased her excitement. She noticed that the driver was continuously giving her surreptitious looks in the mirror, his eyes clearly indicating that he also found the situation intolerably exciting.

They drove to a wooded park and she was helped to alight. She stood for a moment enjoying the feel of the breeze on her face and the fact of being outdoors. A sharp tug on the leash which Lynne held in her hand forced her to walk forward. There were some children playing with a ball nearby and one of the youngsters kicked the ball towards them. As the children and a couple of their supervising adults came running over, Caroline felt a fear of imminent discovery which was in itself very stimulating.

The ball landed by Caroline's feet and she looked helplessly at it. Francis jovially picked it up and gave it to one of the adults who had run up.

'Thanks,' the man said in acknowledgement.

His glance swept over all of them but came to rest on Caroline. His gaze was puzzled at Caroline's attire. Francis put his arm around her in a deceptively firm grip.

'We're just out for a walk. Our niece is visiting us and has unfortunately developed a very bad tooth infection.'

The man nodded in understanding. 'I know what

it's like.' He looked directly at Caroline. 'Don't worry. The antibiotics will work quite quickly an you'll be fine. I've had a couple of abscesses myself and I know how bad they can be. Well, thanks again,' and with that he and his companions ran off throwing the ball to each other and laughing.

Caroline felt laughter bubbling up inside her and only the gag kept it inside. This was turning into a very enjoyable excursion. She loved the danger of possible discovery as much as did Francis and Lynne. Her aroused state was now very apparent as she looked imploringly at Francis.

'Well, my little niece. Enough fresh air for you to-day, I think. It's too bad that you couldn't behave yourself, really it is. I had such high hopes that this little test would show you the futility of attempting to escape and that you would then become suitably doc-ile.'

Caroline made protesting noises into her gag. She had been very well behaved. Francis' next words, however, immediately stilled her protests.

'I think that it's time to introduce her to the dungeons at Beech Hall. What do you think, my dear?'

This last was addressed to Lynne who smiled warmly at him, her eyes glittering with excitement.

'Oh, yes, Francis, I do so agree.'

'However, I think our slave needs a little attention first.'

Caroline felt an overwhelming relief. Francis approached her and gripped her by the arms. His voice was low and menacing, making her shiver with excitement.

'Get into the car, my darling, now!'

Caroline was roughly helped into the car. Francis threw her on to the back seat and looked at her cold-ly, his eyes glittering with some unnameable desire.

'Lynne and I are going for a walk. Carl will take care of you!'

Francis joined Lynne and they walked away from the car. Caroline felt a small jolt of fear which only served to exacerbate her sexual excitement as Carl, the uniformed chauffeur, appeared in the doorway of the car. He was holding a short leather tawse.

'Good afternoon, slut!' was his greeting.

Caroline was pushed on to her stomach on the large, leather-covered, back seat. No further words were spoken as a leather blindfold was pushed tightly into place over her eyes. She felt the cape being lifted, felt the cool air of the late afternoon across her backside and tried to ready herself for what she knew was coming. The tawse made a loud thwacking noise as it connected with her bottom. Caroline welcomed the pain. In her aroused state, she knew that it would quickly turn to pleasure. She rubbed herself against the leather of the seat as she tensed for each stroke of the tawse. After several strokes, she heard the tawse being thrown on to the seat, then felt warm insistent fingers oiling the tight little hole between her cheeks, oiled fingers being inserted into that hole, stimulating her almost beyond endurance. Suddenly, she was aware of perfume, Lynne's perfume, she'd smelled it often enough! Then fingers were stroking her clitoris, but whose fingers? Lynne's, Francis', the chauffeur's? Suddenly, she didn't care, as long as someone was inside her giving her what she craved, what she needed.

Suddenly, the fingers were removed and she was turned onto her back. The scarf was untied and the gag was removed from her mouth, to be replaced by someone's penis. Was it Francis or the chauffeur? Caroline didn't care, because the fingers had returned to her clitoris, more fingers pushing into her anus as her mouth slid greedily up and down the unidentified penis. Hands were on her nipples, kneading and squeezing, sometimes hurting, sometimes giving pleasure, all, all of it building to a huge orgasm that went on and on, even as she tasted the saltiness of the spunk which, as a dutiful slave, she knew she must swallow.

Chapter Five

When they returned, Caroline was pushed up the steps. Lynne was holding her arm very tightly.

'Thank you, Francis,' she said. 'I've been looking forward to getting this little slut into the dungeons.'

'My pleasure. She has obviously learnt very little and you have my permission to teach her in the way you think best. In fact, I think I will change and join you. I could do with some entertainment.'

Caroline was forced downstairs by her captor and thrown against a stone wall when they reached the dungeon.

Her blindfold and other bonds had been removed during the return journey and now the cape was taken from her. Caroline was able to see that she was indeed in a dungeon. The walls were of cold, grey stone with flaming torches in sconces throwing flickering shadows. There was a small cell in one corner with black iron bars and metal loops at various points on the bars, the imagined purpose of which made Caroline shiver with excitement. In another corner, there was what could only be described as a rack, exactly as she had seen depicted in history books. There were also various wooden and metal posts around the room with ropes, leather straps and chains suspended from them. It was truly a medieval style dungeon!

Lynne dragged a heavy chain from an iron ring in

the wall behind Caroline and padlocked it to the ring on her collar.

'The Master has shown a distinct fondness for you but he will always put me first. Don't expect any mercy to be shown by him and certainly not by me.'

Lynne used the toe of her high-heeled boot to lift Caroline's chin.

'I think a few days down here will break your spirit and make you behave like a true slave. I shall particularly enjoy introducing you to the delights of our dungeon.'

She knelt down beside Caroline and looked at her for a few moments showing all the jealousy and spite in her eyes, yet unable to conceal the undeniable desire and excitement she was feeling.

'I don't like the sound of too much screaming,' Lynne said, and with that she pulled the scarf from around Caroline's neck and tied it over her mouth. With amazing strength she tore a long strip off the discarded cape and tied this tightly over Caroline's eyes. Caroline could now see nothing but she heard the hissing of Lynne's voice and her hot breath on her cheek as she felt the fire of this woman's jealous wrath.

'I want you blindfolded, my dear, because that will make you feel the pain so much more acutely, and I do want you to feel pain, lots of it. I'm going to use the bull whip on you. Francis has said there are no restrictions. I can do what I like.'

Lynne smiled at the way her slave was shivering, mistaking this for a display of fear. Caroline did indeed feel fear at her Mistress' words, but it was a fear that increased the flow of her juices and made her clitoris almost unbearably sensitive. Her nipples were hard and prominent, demanding attention. The satisfying clink of metal against metal as she moved reminded her of her subservient, yet powerful, position. She was making this woman jealous, this strict dominatrix was in fact at *her* mercy. *She* was making this woman feel jealousy and extreme desire. The feeling of power surged through Caroline and she knew that she liked being a slave, wanted nothing more than for her captors to want to use her body with an intensity of need that put them in her power.

Lynne twisted Caroline's nipples, unaware that she was answering her slave's needs.

'What I like is to give you pain, intense pain, pain that would make you beg if you could speak, beg for mercy,' Lynne whispered as her fingers found Caroline's slit.

Lynne was almost angry when she discovered how very wet Caroline was, an anger that was tempered by her own excitement.

Francis' cool voice interrupted them. 'I see you have been making our guest comfortable,' he said pleasantly.

Francis had changed into black leather trousers and tall riding boots. His chest was bare and the flickering torchlight reflected off the metal rings in his pierced nipples.

'Can we start soon, darling?' Lynne could barely control her excitement.

Francis walked over to where Caroline was chained and crouched down beside her.

'In a moment. I want a few words with our guest first. Get me some nipple clamps, I like to see her in those.'

Francis leant closer to Caroline and stroked her breasts gently before Caroline felt the pain of the nipple clamps he was using on her.

'Poor little slave,' he said, again stroking her now tortured nipples. 'What a lot you have to endure, but it's worth it. One day you will submit to my sexual pleasures willingly. You will bring me the ropes to tie you with and the whips to beat you with, but not yet. First you have to learn.'

One of them, she knew not which, was trailing a feather over her labia, tickling her clitoris, which made her squirm with the exquisitely maddening sensations it evoked. She strained against her bonds but could not even loosen them, not that she wanted to. The reminder of her helplessness increased her excitement. Her legs were spread out to either side and tied to two of the metal rings in the walls. She could not close her legs and was reduced to helpless wrigglings and whimpers into her gag. She wanted . . . needed . . . satisfaction.

'Doesn't she squirm delightfully?' Francis asked and Lynne's laugh answered him.

If only she could see who was doing it to her, it might help, but her blindfold did not admit even a chink of light. The soreness in her nipples had become numbness and she knew it was going to be the source of a lot of pain when the clamps were removed. She felt the ropes that bound her arms and wrists cutting into her flesh as she struggled, but this only further exaggerated the exquisite torture of the feather. Suddenly, the tickling stopped and she felt something very hard and large being inserted into her vagina, the buzzing sound it emitted identifying it as a vibrator.

Francis said very quietly, 'Don't orgasm, will you, my pet. I haven't given you permission and, if you do, Lynne will punish you.'

At these words she heard a loud cracking sound as the whip lashed down to the floor near her head. Now she really had to concentrate to avoid being whipped.

The vibrator had a cunning attachment that massaged her clitoris as well as her vagina and it was almost impossible to stop the inevitable climb towards an orgasm. She knew Francis well enough to know that he would know when she had orgasmed and that would bring the whipping she feared, yet guiltily admitted she desired. She twisted her head from side to side in her anguish, which brought delighted chuckles from Lynne who loved to see her helpless struggles.

'Oh, Francis, she is delightful. Increase the speed on the vibrator, will you?'

There was an answering increase in volume as this was done and Caroline knew she was lost. She could not control the orgasm that flooded her. Lynne jumped up and down, clapping her hands like a child, as she realised what had happened.

'Oh, you little darling, thank you.'

Caroline lay limp and exhausted after the orgasm, weak with the sense of triumphant defeat. She knew what must now follow. She felt her wrists and arms being untied and then her ankles, before the chain was released from her neck. She was dragged to her feet and forced towards two wooden posts. When she was between them her arms were raised and secured into two iron rings, her legs being similarly treated. The vibrator that had been removed was now reinserted, as was another, smaller one, in her anus. A thick rope was bound around her waist and then looped down between her legs before being drawn up and secured at the waist again. Both vibrators were now securely tied to her, although she tried to struggle as much as possible while this was being done, thereby awakening her to new desire. There was a pause. She heard Lynne panting with . . . what? Exhaustion or, more likely, excitement, for now was her moment. The brief respite ended all too soon as Caroline jumped within her tight bonds at the incredible pain that filled her as the whip struck her across her back.

'Easy, my dear,' came the restraining voice of Francis. 'We don't want her marked on her back, now do we?'

The next stroke was across her bottom and this was even more painful. Caroline was almost choking on her gag, tears streaming from beneath the enveloping blindfold. Yet, why was her clitoris awakening again from its exhaustion as desire stirred within her, desire for the vibrators to bring her to orgasm? The pain was reminding her of her submissive state and that, in turn, was urging her on to another climax. She twisted helplessly in her bonds, but only succeeded in making the ropes bite deeper and the knots tighten.

The next few strokes caught her between her thighs making her juices increase to an extent where she felt the trickle of liquid begin its slow journey down her legs. Her gag was soaking wet now with tears and saliva, but it still filled her mouth, blocking her screams and pleas for mercy ... the mercy of being allowed to relax into her body's screaming desire for sexual release. There was to be no mercy for her. She did not know it, but it was now Francis who was wielding the whip, expertly marking her thighs and buttocks, never using the same mark twice, but always laying fresh ones until her bottom and thighs were covered with a network of angry red weals, raised up from the skin. Then, with only a moment's hesitation, Francis struck her on her labia, giving her such pain that she almost forgot her urgent need; almost but not quite. Francis' excitement made him want to throw the whip down and replace the anal vibrator with his cock, which was straining against

92

his leather pants with its own urgent need. With great self-control Francis repeated the process, until even his iron will could not hold out and he threw the whip down, pushed aside the rope between Caroline's legs and, tearing at his zip, freed his impatient cock and rammed it into Caroline's most secret place, causing her to gasp into her gag as she relished the feel of his hard, demanding rod as it thrust into her. Francis' hands were on her breasts, impatiently removing the clamps, feeling the weight of Caroline's breasts in his hands as he spunked inside her. The pain in Caroline's abused nipples as feeling returned to them, together with her excitement and the insistent buzzing of the remaining vibrator, pushed Caroline into a series of orgasms, peaking in a huge flood of sensations, almost unbearable in the intensity of the pleasure which consumed her.

Caroline awoke to feel a wonderfully soothing ointment being rubbed on her bottom and then she became aware of the pain from her marked and abused flesh. Alicia's voice spoke gently to her.

'It's all right, miss,' and as Caroline struggled up, 'They've left you to my care.'

Caroline realised she was lying on her stomach in her own room. She caught sight of her wrists and winced as she saw the deep red indentations of the rope marks. She guessed those marks would be repeated on her ankles. She still wore her collar but no other restraints. The rope around her waist had also been removed, as had the dildo. She remembered the pleasurable feelings that had been evoked by her treatment, even as she was tied between the posts. Now she was only aware of the soothing lotion that was being administered, despite her wincing from time to time as Alicia's gentle fingers encountered a particularly deep weal.

'It's already bruising, miss. I don't think they'll be punishing you for a day or two.'

There would be more, she felt sure, more pain and more bondage. She impatiently suppressed the stirring of feeling in her clitoris at this thought. She needed rest at the moment, not stimulation. Alicia gently turned her on to her back.

'This needs treatment too, miss,' she said, as she gently massaged the cream into her bud. 'It'll soon feel better, don't you worry.'

Caroline relaxed beneath Alicia's ministrations and did indeed start to feel better. She thought of what had happened. Francis had been so cruel to her. Caroline did not know that it was Francis who had beaten her sex, but she thought he had allowed Lynne to do it. The clamps might have been removed, but the soreness remained in her nipples. She winced as she felt the gentle wetness on them and opened her eyes with pleasure as the soreness turned to pleasurable feelings, and then was truly surprised when she saw Francis licking her nipples with his warm tongue.

'Francis!' she gasped but he put his hand over her mouth.

'Ssh, my sweet, I sent Alicia away and said I'd tend to you. I love looking at your abused body, love the marks that we made.'

She knew she should be angry at his remarks but, she couldn't deny it, she was glad to see him and the feelings he was exciting in her bruised body were undeniable. He took his hand away from her mouth and gently kissed the rope marks on her wrists. 'I love marking you. You gave me so much pleasure in the dungeon. The way you struggled and squirmed, the way you pulled at the ropes binding you, the way your poor little bottom looked after the whipping you had. I'm sorry, my darling, does that shock you?'

94

She just stared at him unsure of what to say.

'It's the way I am. I love bondage and giving out discipline. I love tying you and beating you. I'm sorry you were hurt, but there was no other way. I am your Master and you will obey me. I am determined that you will submit to me. You are so very desirable.'

He raised her to a sitting position and smiled to see her nipples harden as she saw the length of rope in his hands. He tilted her chin.

'I want to tie you, my sweet. Will you let me?'

She searched his face with enquiring eyes. She wanted to tell him that her wrists were still so sore, but she knew that he knew that. This was some sort of test.

'Will you, my darling? Will you let me tie you? I won't force you this time. You have the right to say yes or no.'

This was amazing to Caroline. Francis had said that she would be offered no further choices once she had made the decision to stay.

After a pause, during which they continued to look at each other, Caroline put her hands behind her back and smiled at him.

'Thank you, my darling,' Francis said, and went behind her. He tied her wrists tightly and then helped her to stand. 'I want you to kneel in front of me, my little slave, will you do that?'

In answer she knelt in front of him. Francis looked down at her with gratitude as he stroked her hair. With his other hand, he was unzipping the front of his leather trousers and the grip in her hair tightened. When he withdrew his cock from his trousers, she realised his true intention. Francis was already erect at the sight of the bound girl before him. His voice changed and became rough.

'Take it in your mouth!' he ordered. Caroline knew

what was required from her and kept her lips obstinately closed, delighting in the game as much as Francis did. He said again with more force, 'Take it in your mouth now and pleasure me!'

She opened her mouth and did as he ordered, nearly choking at the thickness of it. He forced her to work his cock with her mouth, sliding up and down as he forced it ever deeper into her mouth. When she showed signs of resistance, he growled, 'Take it, all of it!' When he was close to his climax, his movements became more violent, thrusting into her mouth until she gagged. At last it was over. He held her head pressed hard into his body as she felt the hot liquid of his come fill her mouth. He pulled at her hair, hurting her.

'Swallow it, bitch, every drop. You will be whipped for every drop you spill!'

That was enough to make Caroline ensure that she did indeed swallow every drop, until Francis was satisfied and released his grip on her hair. He smiled at the yearning in her face, knowing what she needed.

'That's excellent, my dear. You see how you are learning. The threat of the whip is now enough to ensure your submission to me.'

She looked at him accusingly as he straightened his trousers with a satisfied smile on his mouth.

'I thought . . .'

'You thought I was going to pleasure you as well, didn't you?' Francis tweaked one of her nipples, smiling broadly. 'You are the slave and I am the Master!' This was said almost as if Francis needed reaffirmation of this fact. There was an underlying seriousness in his voice.

He moved to the door.

'I will leave you tied up until dinner I think. You will be released then. You've had a long day and you should get some rest. We have guests for dinner to-morrow night and I want you to serve them. You know the penalty for failure I'm sure.'

He came back to her and gently lifted her back on to the bed.

'I do like you, Caroline, more than I should, but you are my slave and your training is my first priority.'

He reached down and inserted a finger in her cunt. 'You are wet, my dear. I'm sorry that I haven't time to bring you off. I don't think I want you to pleasure yourself either. I think I will get Alicia to fit you with your chastity belt.' Francis reached down and kissed her gently. 'I'm sorry if that will leave you feeling frustrated but I am the only one who is allowed to pleasure you. I think I might have Alicia insert a dildo into you before she straps you into the chastity belt. Cheer up, my sweet, that will give you some pleasure.'

With that he turned and left the room, closing the door gently.

The night seemed very long to Caroline. Alicia had come in, full of apologies and, on Caroline's assurance that she knew she had no choice, inserted the thick dildo into Caroline's vagina and switched it on. She had first of all been allowed to use the toilet, with Alicia's assistance, as she was under orders not to remove Caroline's bonds until the chastity belt was in place. Caroline wryly reflected that she was getting used to being embarrassed as she relieved herself under Alicia's watchful eyes.

'I'm sorry, miss, but they've told me I have to watch.'

They wanted to embarrass her, Caroline realised. They wanted her humbled and humiliated so that she would more easily accept her slave status. Worse was to come, as Alicia had to lick her clean as Lynne had done, thereby embarrassing them both. Alicia helped her back to the bed and then inserted the dildo. This done, she strapped the chastity belt into position. It fitted snugly and allowed Caroline or anyone else no contact with her cunt or anus as both were covered with leather which was strapped tightly into position securing the dildo in place. Alicia was then able to untie Caroline's wrists, enabling her to eat her dinner which she had placed outside the door. When she had retrieved the tray, she sat opposite Caroline and watched her eat.

'I'm sorry I had to put the belt on so tightly, miss. The Master said he would check it later and I would be punished if it wasn't on tight enough.'

Caroline smiled at her.

'It's all right, Alicia. I know how difficult it must be for you. We are both slaves here.'

She paused thoughtfully.

'Do you have much freedom?'

Alicia shook her head. 'I'm chained to my bed at night just like you are, miss, and I'm never allowed to go out on my own. There's always someone with me.' Alicia lowered her eyes and smiled away her embarrassment. 'I like being supervised and all that. I like to be reminded of who and what I am. Do you understand, miss?'

Caroline nodded, almost absent-mindedly. It was not easy to eat the meal with the dildo buzzing away inside her, producing feelings she could not ignore, no matter how hard she tried. After dinner, Caroline was again chained to the bed by her collar, but not otherwise restrained, for which she was grateful. Her aching limbs needed to be stretched and relaxed without restriction. When Alicia had gone after turning out the light, Caroline's thoughts turned again to Francis. She could not deny that she had feelings for him, but he could change so suddenly, from concerned lover to strict Master. She could not understand him. She had enjoyed the look of gratitude he had given her when she had allowed herself to be tied, but he had left her knowing her needs were unfulfilled.

The man in question was spending an equally restless night. He threw back the covers of his bed in exasperation and went to the small drinks cabinet in his dressing room. Pouring himself a large whisky, Francis slumped into a deeply padded armchair and contemplated the situation, which he knew was of his own making. He recalled the scene with Caroline earlier when he had caressed her body with such gentleness, before again abusing her. Why? He was angry at himself because he had never been in this situation before. He found her fascinating. He wanted to nurture her as a companion rather than a slave. Impatiently he finished his drink. Of course that wasn't true. She was his slave and that's all she would ever be to him. He closed his eyes and tried to shut out the memory of those tear-drenched and puzzled eyes looking at him. She had needed satisfaction and he had known that, but had chosen instead to remind her of her slave status. He would just have to be crueller with her to suppress these unwanted feelings of tenderness she was exciting in him. Francis felt better after having reached this decision and smiled a welcome as Lynne entered.

'I'm sorry,' she said as she walked into the room. 'I saw your light and . . .'

'It's OK, my dear, you are welcome. I couldn't sleep and could do with some diversion. You fit the bill nicely. You are looking rather delicious tonight.'

And indeed she was. Lynne was wearing a black leather, tightly laced basque, which trimmed down her waist to an even slimmer silhouette than usual. Her long hair was loose and brushed her waist. She wore tiny, black leather panties which concealed her luxuriant bush and made a fitting companion to her black latex-clad legs. The five-inch heels she wore set off the whole outfit beautifully. Francis again felt the thrill of pride in his partnership with this lovely woman.

'Are you feeling restless?' Lynne asked, moving towards him.

In answer he reached out and grabbed her, pulling her down on to his lap. He needed her right then. His mouth hungrily found hers and he felt his cock stiffen as her tongue probed his mouth with equal passion. Suddenly, Francis threw her off him on to a deep pile white carpet which covered the floor of his dressing room. He tore off the belt of the robe he wore and, grabbing Lynne's hands, he tied it very tightly around her wrists, securing them together above her head and then tying the ends of the belt to the legs of a stout chair which was against a wall.

'Francis,' she said uncertainly, 'what's wrong? I've never seen you like this . . . not with me.'

'Shut up!' Francis said coldly and, suddenly, Lynne felt a thrill of fear. She was a dominatrix. Francis knew that. This was the way *she* treated people. She wasn't used to this sort of treatment herself. She tried to assert herself.

'Francis! I don't know what game you are playing but it's gone far enough. Untie me at once!'

'No, my dear, not this time. I want to remind you that I am the Master here over everyone . . . including you!'

Francis reached down and pulled the leather panties down her legs and off her feet. Lynne was kicking frantically with her legs, trying to stop him by the only means she had now that her arms were restrained. Lynne was a very strong woman, in personality as well as bodily strength, and she would not take this sort of treatment without extreme resistance. Francis laughed coldly.

'That's right, my dear, fight me! That's how I like it!'

'You bastard! Get off me!' Lynne yelled.

'Not yet, my dear!' Francis had wadded up the panties and stuffed them into Lynne's mouth which she had opened prior to pouring out some very vituperative words. Francis looked around feverishly and then grabbed a scarf which was lying on a dressing table. He used this to tie over Lynne's mouth, securing the panties in place. Her enforced inability to speak calmed Lynne somewhat and she looked at Francis with genuine fear yet also felt the stirring of her sex. This was a side of him she had never seen directed at her before. She didn't know what the problem was but she knew that she was going to suffer for it and that that thought excited her. She didn't like the feeling of helplessness she was used to administering, not enduring. She was a very dominant person and enjoyed her dominance. Now that was turned upside down as she was forced into the role of a submissive and she didn't like it one bit . . . did she?

Her eyes widened with fear as she saw the riding crop in Francis' hands. It was the thin one which hurt the most. She knew because she had used it with great enjoyment on a number of occasions. She moaned desperately into her gag, her eyes pleading with Francis to let her go.

'I'm going to hurt you, my dear. I feel you need to be taught a lesson. Lately you've been treating me with less than the respect I deserve. Perhaps this will remind you that I am in control in this house!'

With that, and with no regard for the pain he knew he was inflicting, he grabbed Lynne and roughly turned her over on to her stomach, increasing the tautness of the belt around her wrists. He tore his robe off and used it to tie around Lynne's kicking legs to minimise the damage she could cause. Then, without further hesitation, he swung the riding crop and landed it with a cracking blow on Lynne's buttocks.

She yelped into her gag and made a bucking movement with her body. Francis ignored this and lashed her again and again with the crop, trying to shut out the sight in his mind of Caroline's pleading eyes. Just as suddenly, Francis threw down the riding crop and flung himself full length on Lynne's back and, with no preparation, thrust his rampant cock into her anus. Suddenly Lynne felt a huge surge of sexual excitement, but that couldn't be. She was a dominatrix, not in the least submissive ... or that's what she had always thought. There was no denying the growing excitement, though, as Francis pounded into her, the whole length of his cock up her arse. He gave Lynne no consideration and she realised she didn't want any. As he quickly reached his climax, pumping his sperm into her abused bottom, Lynne felt her own unbelievable orgasm shake her. When he was finished, Francis lay quietly on top of Lynne, bathed in sweat and exhaustion, before rolling off her now inert, but satiated, body.

Francis went to the windows and threw them wide, letting the cool night air dry off the sweat. His face was set and grim. What had that achieved, apart from momentary satisfaction? Caroline's accusing eyes were still before him and now he would have to watch Lynne like a hawk. He knew she would try to take her wrath out on Caroline and he would have to protect her. Swearing at his own foolishness, he walked over to Lynne and, kneeling down, untied her legs and wrists. For a moment, he gently massaged the weals he had inflicted on her bottom, feeling the raised ridges on her skin with some regret. He expected an explosion of swear words at the very least as he turned her over and untied the scarf from her mouth and removed the panties. Instead, she just lay there looking at him, then she swung her right arm with all her might and slapped him. He knew he had deserved that and so he just sat there, again looking at her. Hesitatingly, he bent his head and gently brushed her lips with his own. For a moment, Lynne passively accepted his kiss, then her arms went round his neck and she pulled him down to her. In spite of his exhaustion, Francis responded. He was still excited by the earlier scene and he could sense that, amazingly, Lynne was also excited.

Francis thought he had felt her orgasm, but had told himself he was mistaken. Now, as she thrust her tongue in his mouth and her hand grabbed his balls, massaging them expertly, he knew that he had not been. Francis moved further down and sucked and stroked her nipples, while one hand found the wetness of her cunt. Her bush was soaking! Moving further down, he probed that wetness with his tongue until it entered the warm moistness of her slit. He could taste the juices of her excitement and could feel his cock again becoming erect. Lynne jerked under him as her climax peaked and then rolled over so that she was on top of Francis. She lowered herself on to his cock easing herself up and down on him as she fucked him, playing with his ringed nipples as she did so. Francis' orgasm was explosive and prolonged. He was still in its throes as Lynne moved off his cock and sat on his face.

Without hesitation, he responded to her unspoken plea and sucked and licked her until she climaxed again.

Satiated, they lay on their backs on the floor, letting the cool night air from the open windows dry their bodies.

'Why?' Francis asked. 'When I abused you so unforgivably, why did you respond to me like that?'

'I don't know why you did what you did but, after the initial shock, I have to admit I found it exciting, but not as a regular thing!' her voice warned him. 'It obviously helped you to ease whatever tensions you were experiencing and I was determined that you were not going to be the only one to enjoy yourself! I needed some release too after your treatment.' And she turned to him and smiled to ease the sting of her words.

Francis, responding to her mood, propped himself up on an elbow and gently stroked her breasts.

'Lynne, while you're in this forgiving mood, I would like to ask you a favour.'

Lynne sat up and circled her knees with her arms.

'Ask away, my Lord and Master,' she said mockingly.

'Caroline,' Francis said uncertainly and he saw Lynne's back stiffen. 'Don't take it out on her.'

Lynne turned to face him and looked probingly into his eyes.

'Are you forbidding me to touch her?'

'No, I need you to train her in your own inimitable way,' Francis rejoined, but his levity was not matched by Lynne who narrowed her eyes as she looked at him. 'I just don't want her to live in fear of what we might do next. I think she is developing sexually and I want her to discover the pleasure that can be obtained through pain. She is already experiencing a little of that, I think. I know she liked being tied. She is a natural submissive.'

'Are you training her to replace me?'

'No one could replace you, Lynne, but you are a dominatrix and she is a submissive. Yes, I would like to have a partner who is also my slave. She's very intelligent and, when she's trained, I will enjoy showing her off, but that's in the future.'

'You think that we can all live together in cosy domesticity?'

Francis sighed.

'I don't know what's going to happen, Lynne. I have a great respect for you and we work well together, but it's more of a business arrangement and you know it is. We don't love each other, Lynne. You prefer your own sex and I would like to have a partner who loves me as a Master and as a man. Can you understand that?'

Lynne reached out her hand and stroked Francis' cheek.

'After what's just happened, Francis, that could happen.'

'With you, you mean?' Francis stood up, shaking his head. 'Lynne, you know that we can't change what we are inside. You might try for a while, but it goes completely against what you are and what you really want. Think about it and you'll know I'm right. I care for you, Lynne, but I know what I want and I think you know what you want as well.'

Francis gave her his hand and helped her to stand. They stood together, holding each other for a while. Then Lynne looked at him and sighed.

'I guess you may be right. As to the favour, I promise I won't be unduly cruel to your little protégée, but I must know what limits you're setting.'

'Treat her as a slave, humiliate her if necessary, but teach her to love the whip not to fear it. Whip her, by all means ... I want you to ... but teach her to orgasm whilst being whipped.'

105

'As you command,' Lynne said, and gave Francis a mock curtsey. 'I think, however, training her to orgasm while under the whip may be a trifle redundant.'

Chapter Six

Caroline stood nervously in front of Francis as he strapped the leather cuffs on her wrists and then joined them together with a short length of chain. He used longer lengths of chain to attach the cuffs to a leather belt she wore around her waist. A chain went from the wrist cuffs to her cuffed ankles, which were linked by a much shorter length of chain.

'Don't try any fast movements, my dear. You will surely fall over if you do,' Francis warned her.

He picked up the black rubber ball-gag which lay on a table.

'Is that really necessary?' Caroline asked in a small voice.

'Yes, my dear, it is,' Francis said as he pushed the gag into her mouth and buckled the straps tightly behind her head. 'Our guests may want to fondle you as you serve them and I do not want them to be offended by any negative comments you might want to make. Now, let's look at you,' Francis said as he walked further back.

She did look enchanting, he decided. She was wearing her slave collar and a black leather bondage bra, leather straps encircling her breasts but leaving them free for probing hands to enjoy. She wore no panties but a black rubber suspender belt held black latex stockings in place. The hobble-chain at her ankles was not really necessary as Lynne had padlocked a pair of five-inch high-heeled shoes on to her and she was finding it difficult enough to walk in those.

'I think our guests will be very pleased with this servant,' Francis said and, walking back to her, kissed her on the cheek. 'Don't worry, my dear, I won't let any of my guests use you without my being present.'

With these far from comforting words, Francis left her and moved to the door to greet his guests.

The guests who entered eyed her appreciatively. There were three men and two women. The men wore dinner suits while the women all wore very expensive designer gowns. None of the guests seemed the least surprised to have their drinks served to them by a servant who was chained and gagged. Several of the guests pinched her nipples and bottom as she served them. Initially, Caroline shied away from their touching of her, but Lynne was watching her and rewarded such evasive movements with a sharp crack of the short whip she carried tucked into the belt of her black rubber Mistress dress. Each time she chastised Caroline in this way, she was accorded the approbation of her guests who alternately applauded and murmured approval. Caroline's face was crimson with embarrassment as she walked around serving the guests in this way. It wasn't long before the bruises and weals of her earlier experience were supplemented by freshly laid marks on her bottom. Occasionally, she caught Francis' eyes but he only answered the pleading in hers by a shrug of his shoulders, indicating that he would not intervene.

After the guests were seated and dinner had been served by Caroline and Alicia, who suffered much the same treatment, Caroline was ordered to remain in the room and to sit in a straight-backed chair. She felt curiosity as Francis removed the chains from her wrists and removed the handcuffs. Her unspoken question was answered when Francis pulled her arms roughly behind the chair and tied them tightly together at wrists and elbows, tying the rope around the chair so that she couldn't move. When he had finished, he moved away to survey his handiwork and pick up a black scarf from the sideboard. Returning to Caroline, he bound the scarf over her eyes.

Returning to his seat at the table, he announced: 'Ladies and gentlemen, after the meal, you are welcome to sample the delights of my newest slave. You will note that I have suitably restrained her for this purpose. She is there for your pleasure.'

There was a murmur of approval before the meal resumed. Caroline was aware of her nipples responding to her burgeoning sexual excitement as she contemplated the fingers and hands that would shortly be exploring her body, further arousing her and the guests. She couldn't struggle at all. Francis had tied her too tightly and too well. She held her breath when, some time later, she felt hands at her ankles removing the ankle cuffs and chains. Those same hands drew her ankles to either side of the chair where they were tightly bound to the chair legs. Her thighs also were bound to the chair, which was a solid one and could not easily be removed. Then, suddenly everything went quiet. The laughter and chattering diminished and Caroline waited, alert with anticipation, for what was to follow.

The first thing that happened was the gentle brushing of her nipples by long fingernails. She tensed and was rewarded with a stinging stroke of the whip across her breasts. There were suddenly more fingers probing her breasts and her increasingly wet slit, and more lashes with the whip as she strained against her bonds, increasing the flow of her love juices. One of these lashes caught her nipples and caused exquisite pain, but there was no escape from the incessant fingers and later the tongues that licked her nipples and probed between her thighs. But whose fingers? Whose tongues? Were they male or female? Caroline smelled perfume but there were several people around her. She was being alternately caressed and beaten. It became apparent that Lynne or Francis, or perhaps both, were watching her very carefully and whipping her at any sign of resistance, no matter how small, but it was so hard to keep still. These unknown fingers that were probing her were far from unpleasant. Caroline had to admit that being blindfolded increased her sensitivity to touch. She began to relax and enjoy what was happening to her. After all, she reasoned, she was helpless, bound and gagged and at the mercy of all these people, so why not enjoy it. Even when her movements of pleasure were also punished by the whip she learned to ride the pain because she knew it would lead to pleasure. She abandoned all reasoning and gave herself up to the pleasure of what she was experiencing. Even when Francis leant close to her and whispered in her ear, 'Don't orgasm, my dear, I forbid it!' she was unable to obey, because, by then, her excitement had built to an unstoppable level and Francis saw this.

'The slave has orgasmed without permission! Beat her!' he instructed Lynne in a commanding voice.

Lynne was only too happy to obey and Caroline climaxed through the strokes that were being administered to her, pulling against her tight bondage as she did so and enjoying the restrictive feeling of the ropes.

They allowed her time to recuperate from the strength of her orgasm. The flow of conversation resumed and she became aware of what was being said.

'She's exquisite, Francis,' a man was saying. 'I must have her.'

110

To her horror, she heard Francis say, 'What are you prepared to offer, my friend?'

'I will give you £40,000 for a night with her, if I can do what I want with her.'

The figure quoted stilled all other conversation. Caroline held her breath as Francis considered the offer. Surely he wouldn't, not after what he had said.

The reply was spoken slowly.

'£50,000 for a night with her but she is not to be marked. You are to keep her blindfolded at all times and she is to be returned, alive and well, to this house by 9 a.m. tomorrow.'

There was an agonising silence while this counter-offer was considered. Caroline felt her heart pounding so that everyone must hear it. She would not admit to herself that she relished the fact that Francis and this unknown man were prepared to deal for her as if she was a precious commodity.

'You strike a hard bargain, Francis, you bastard, but she's worth it. You've got yourself a deal!'

Francis asked everyone to go into the drawing room while he spoke to his slave.

'You won't change your mind I hope, Francis?' The voice of the man who had bargained for her came clearly to Caroline. Although she was still in shock from Francis' relinquishment of her, even for one night, she could appreciate the tone of the cultured voice that had addressed him, a voice which was firm but also had an intrinsic warmth which seemed to wrap itself around her.

'No, my friend, my word is my bond as you well know. I just want to prepare my slave for you, tell her of your little predilections. She is a novice and I want this arrangement to be part of her training. Who knows, she may even enjoy it. I'll order your car brought round when I'm ready, in the meantime please avail yourself of my hospitality.'

As Francis spoke he inclined his head towards Alicia who was standing by the door with her head bowed in submission to his will. The man smiled his thanks and beckoned Alicia to follow him. When the room was deserted except for himself and Caroline, Francis untied the scarf from Caroline's eyes and removed the ball-gag. Before she could say anything, he held a glass of water to her lips.

'Drink this,' he said gently, 'I'm sure your throat's dry.'

His kindness was too much for Caroline, and tears streamed down her face as she drank the water. She didn't want to leave him; she felt more for him than she had dared to admit. When she had finished, Francis used his handkerchief to dry her tears and untied her from the chair.

'Why?' Caroline demanded. She was confused. It seemed that Francis could let her go so easily when she had thought he cared for her. Perhaps he was just like all businessmen, it was money to him. That was the important thing.

When she was untied, Francis gently massaged her arms and legs.

'Why did you agree to it? You said you wouldn't let anybody use me unless you were there and now you've sold me!' Caroline was overwhelmed with crying again and Francis gently picked her up and carried her to an easy chair. He sat down with her and waited until the storm had subsided before he began gently talking to her.

'Caroline, Caroline, what am I going to do with you? You are my slave, you have no rights to decide what you will or will not permit. I hadn't intended anything of the sort, but I want to show you that I will be obeyed in all things. If that means giving you away – or in this case selling you – to someone else for a short period, that is my prerogative and that is what I will do when I want to. I think it will be good for you. I have stipulated that you are not to be hurt and that you are to be returned to me safely. It's only for one night. Liam is a good friend and he would not want or dare to upset me in any way. He knows that contravening my wishes will do just that and he will not risk it. He is a rich and powerful man, but he's also a realist. He needs my friendship and I actually trust him. Come now, darling, stop crying, it will be all right.'

Francis tried to stifle the thought of how adorable she looked when she was so upset and in need of his protection and he did feel protective. He had indeed wanted to use this exercise as another part of Caroline's training, but he was already regretting the alacrity with which the agreement had been concluded.

'Listen to me, my pet, Liam is OK. After what you have already experienced, this will seem like a gentle interlude to you. I meant what I said to Liam, you may actually enjoy it.'

He put his hand over her mouth to still her protests.

'I said I wanted to tell you about Liam's predilections and I do. Liam, like myself, is a bondage fan, but Liam is an artist in this area. He takes extreme care in what he does and is proud of his work. He likes giving a slave pleasure and he will take that care with you. He will return you to me tomorrow and I will be glad to see you. I hope you will tell me about your experience, because that's what this should be to you, Caroline, an experience. You are my slave and I believe you have come to accept that, so why not enjoy your situation. I feel I have come to know you a little in these past few days.'

Caroline thought with amazement that it had, indeed, only been such a short while. It seemed so much longer.

'I believe you have the makings of a true submissive and I welcome that.'

Caroline realised that it was true. She had for some time been fascinated by the idea of S/M. She had always been too afraid to let it be more than just an interest, a curiosity. Now she felt that she fitted in here more than anywhere else. She felt as if she belonged in this strange new world: a sense of belonging she had been searching for and that had eluded her for a long time.

There was no time to ponder further on these feelings as Francis was talking to her again.

'I do care for you, Caroline, and I know that what you are experiencing in this house is peculiar and strange to you. My sexual desires are . . . shall we say . . . somewhat unusual, although not as much as you may think. Many people find pleasure in the ways that I do. Believe it or not, I want you to be happy, but you have to learn what being a slave really means. Your main duty is to pleasure your Master and it pleases me to sell you in this way for the night. Liam is a very wealthy man and the amount he is paying is peanuts to him – and to me, if it comes to that – but it is what the bargain actually means that is important, not the giving and receiving of money for you. Will you at least try to understand?'

For long moments, Caroline and Francis looked at each other, then, very slowly and almost shyly, Caroline nodded.

'Good,' Francis said. 'Now, I have to get you ready and I'm afraid you'll have to be tied.'

Francis moved her forward a little on his lap and was gratified when Caroline slowly and without being told put her hands behind her back. There was a pause while Francis felt a surge of satisfaction and something else he could not name, before he started tying a length of rope around those slender wrists. As he tied the knots tightly, he knew Caroline must be able to feel the hardness of his cock. He helped her to stand and went to get a couple of scarves, one of which he tied over her mouth. He stood behind her holding the other scarf with which he intended to blindfold her but, instead, gave in to his instincts and need and held her in his arms, pressing his cock against her bottom. He felt her pressing back against him, giving her consent. He released his hold on her and went over to a table, returning to her with a tube of cream in his hand. He unzipped his trousers and then stood in front of her seeing the look of acquiescence and excitement in her eyes. Moving behind her he spread some of the lubricant on to his palms and fingers and also his cock. He gently massaged her bottom before inserting one and then two fingers, feeling the tight little hole opening for him as she bore down to accept him.

'Thank you, my darling,' he whispered, as he moved his fingers gently within her.

Caroline whimpered with pleasure into her gag as the fingers were replaced with the more persistent pressure of his cock. He was careful with her and took his time, easing his cock in gently, stopping at any sign of distress and then proceeding more cautiously. Caroline closed her eyes and gave herself up to the pleasure, for that was what it was, of giving her Master what he most wanted and needed from her.

He massaged her clitoris with one hand and, with the other, fondled her breasts. As the pleasure mounted,

Caroline thought of this man who had tied and gagged her and was abusing her anus, who could be gentle with her at one moment and be whipping her the next if she disobeyed or displeased him. Caroline knew that she was enjoying her situation immensely. She didn't have any choice anyway, she told herself. Deliberately, she struggled against the ropes that bound her, relishing the feel of their restriction, moving her head to try and loosen the gag. She felt Francis' hand move to cover her mouth; he seemed to know what she was doing and how to excite her still more.

His voice murmured against her ear, 'Oh, no, my dear. There is no escape for you. I won't let you get away and if you try I shall whip you very long and hard, you know that, don't you?'

As he said these words, the words she needed to hear, Caroline felt her climax overwhelming her as Francis, knowingly, increased the pressure over her mouth, further delineating her helplessness.

Seconds after her orgasm, Francis also stiffened and his hands reached to grip her breasts as his own pleasure enveloped him. He sagged against her, sucking in deep breaths to steady the pounding of his heart.

'Thank you,' he whispered over and over again.

It was some moments before Francis withdrew from her, further time still before their emotions had steadied enough for them to be able to look at each other. When Francis turned her head towards him, he pulled down the scarf that covered her mouth and gently kissed her.

'It's time for you to go, my love. Let's get you ready.'

Caroline felt her nervousness return as she stood in the hallway. Francis had replaced the scarf over her mouth and added another over her eyes. Only her wrists were bound, but there was a chain leash attached to her collar. She was wearing a white semi-transparent plastic cape to give her some protection from the cool night air and this buttoned at the neck. The folds of the plastic had felt cold against her skin when Francis had first put it on her, but now, with her body heat, it was providing the desired protection. More than that, the material also had a distinctly erotic feel as its slippery smoothness enfolded her. The feel of the material and her bondage served to enhance her feelings of arousal which her fear of what she might be expected to endure this night did nothing to assuage. Indeed, it was a fear laced with heady anticipation. She felt a slight tug on her lead and became aware that Francis had passed control of her over to Liam.

'She's beautiful, Francis, you can be sure I will take very good care of her,' Liam said, and then tugged on the leash again to indicate that Caroline should follow him.

With those parting words Caroline became aware that they were outside as she felt the cooler night air and could smell the fragrant flowers in the garden. She was guided to a car, whose engine was running, and into which she was helped. She could smell the leather of the seats as she sank into their softness and felt someone get in beside her. Then they were off and driving away from Beech House, which suddenly seemed to be a refuge to her. She struggled to get away – she had no idea where – and felt strong hands gripping her and keeping her still. To her surprise, the scarf around her mouth was pulled down and a warm firm mouth was covering hers, kissing her deeply. Caroline could feel her body responding as his tongue probed her mouth and her own tongue intermingled with his. The kiss went on for a long time and Caroline could not repress the irresistible urgings within her as she strained towards Liam, wanting to feel his tongue exploring her bud. The arms that held her felt warm and strong, even though they held her prisoner, or maybe because of that, she couldn't be sure. She couldn't see which man it was who had ownership of her for the next several hours and found herself wishing that she could. She wanted to see which guest was the owner of that wonderful voice, but she remembered the warnings of Francis to Liam that she was to be kept blindfolded. Why? What was it that Francis didn't want her to see? She had a sudden flash of intuition that the reason that Francis was so insistent that she be kept blindfolded was to stop her seeing someone she might like, might desire more than she did Francis.

The kiss ended at last and she felt a strong hand over her mouth as Liam's other hand massaged her body through the folds of the cape. She felt her clitoris responding, her nipples straining against the erotic texture of the material. The sensual feeling aroused by the plastic being massaged over her body was incredibly exciting. She found herself relaxing into Liam's arms, no longer struggling, no longer fearful. The hand across her mouth was relaxing slightly. Caroline opened her lips as much as she was able to and let her tongue slide over and between Liam's fingers, letting him feel her arousal, her excitement. Not for the first time, she wondered at herself at what she was becoming. Only a short time ago she had been crying because she was leaving Francis, now she found herself a willing prisoner to this unknown man whose face she couldn't see, but whose body excited a desire in her that was overwhelming and which she couldn't conceal, a desire she knew that this man would recognise and which put her totally at his mercy. It wasn't all one-sided though, Caroline acknowledged. Liam had paid £50,000 for this night with her, a very large sum of money indeed. She felt a sense of pride that she had excited such a desire in him and, yes again that wonderful sense of power that caused her juices to increase in such a marked way.

For a few moments, Liam said nothing. The strength of his feelings surprised him as did Caroline's undoubted response. When he recovered enough to speak he whispered to her gently, even though his chauffeur could not hear him through the closed panel between his seat and the passengers.

'I felt such excitement when I first saw you. I knew I had to have you no matter what the price. Francis is a fool!'

He felt her stiffen.

'Ah, so there's more going on between you than at first sight. Well, I shall have to see if I can alter that.'

He increased the pressure over her mouth as he felt her resistance, a resistance she acknowledged to be almost a duty. It certainly wasn't something she wanted.

'Yes, Francis is a fool because I would have given him £100,000 for you. My darling, we have the whole night ahead of us and maybe more. I may not give you back to Francis. I haven't decided yet.'

He held her closer to him and then whispered to her, 'I'm going to remove your blindfold. To do that I need both hands. I know Francis' knots! If I take my hand away, will you promise not to scream?'

Caroline knew that screaming was the last thing she wanted to do. The sexual attraction between herself and this faceless man was undeniable. She desperately wanted to see him. She nodded.

'Good girl,' Liam said and released his grip on her

mouth. She felt his hands behind her head and then the blindfold fell away. She blinked to accustom her eyes to the dim light in the car and looked into the deepest hazel eyes she had ever seen. She felt a surge of emotions she could not identify as she looked at her new captor. He was gorgeous ... there was no other word for it. He was a well-built man with wavy brown hair, slightly receding on top but this did not detract from his good looks; rather, this enhanced them. He had regular features and she guessed he was quite tall.

Liam was looking at her with equal enthusiasm. Gently, he rubbed his handkerchief at the mascara which the blindfold had smudged.

'You are beautiful. Even with your blindfold, I was sure that you would be when I saw you briefly at dinner. No wonder Francis captured you ... and now you're mine.'

'You can't keep me,' she faltered, still struggling with the unnamed emotions. 'Francis will come and get me.'

'Francis will do nothing of the sort. Oh, my little girl, you didn't believe that he would give away such a prize as you, did you?'

'Sold!' Caroline retorted.

Liam waved his hand.

'The money means nothing. It's just a cover!'

'He'll go to the police. He knows where you live and –'

Liam's hand covered her mouth again.

'Go to the police!' Liam laughed. 'And say what? My friend has kidnapped my slave? I think not. Francis knew this might happen. We have a sort of an arrangement. If I decide to keep you, he will get one of my slaves to replace you. A gentleman's agreement, you might say.'

Liam looked at her.

'My dear, I think you are shocked. Francis and I have been doing this for a long time, training slaves and exchanging them sometimes. Anyway, enough of that, let's talk about you.' But instead of talking, his mouth covered hers again and she felt her traitorous body responding to his kiss.

Almost as though he didn't know what to say or do next in the light of that second kiss, Liam pulled the scarf back over her mouth.

'I think I'd better keep you gagged until we get inside the house. You are still a slave, my dear, except that now you are mine.'

Caroline made a muffled protest into her gag, not because of what he had said, but because she wanted to feel his mouth on hers again. The rest of the journey continued in silence, until the headlights picked up the sweep of a gravel drive which ended in front of a sprawling, chalet-style, house. The car stopped and Liam turned to her.

'Before we go in, my dear, a few things you should remember. You are as much a slave here as you were at Beech House. You will be used sexually as and when I decide. You will be obedient and respectful at all times. I won't be cruel to you unless that seems to be the only way to extract your total obedience. You will not at any time resist me sexually, no matter what I desire of you. I will take you by force if necessary. Do you understand?'

Caroline nodded, knowing that this man would never have to use force to take her. As Caroline was helped from the car she thought of Francis with regret, but this man – her new Master – was someone with whom she knew she would go willingly, anywhere he chose to take her.

* * *

121

Francis paced up and down in his study. He was cursing himself for a fool and cursing Liam. He had deliberately blindfolded and gagged Caroline at the dinner party and it patently hadn't worked. Liam had been attracted to her at once and Francis had not been surprised by the offer Liam had made for her and he knew he had to accept. At least he had screwed another £10,000 out of the bastard but that didn't make up for the loss of Caroline, his Caroline. He thought of her with the depth of feeling that usually comes when one is deprived of a previously undervalued possession.

Francis had got ready for bed but had been unable to sleep. Lynne and Melanie, one of the female guests, were still very active in Lynne's suite of rooms, he thought without jealousy. He remembered Caroline, the way she had looked when Liam took her, the trust she had placed in the lies he had told her. He remembered, too, the thrustings he had made with his cock into her anus. It hadn't been planned, and now he missed her, missed her like hell. He swore savagely.

'Come in!' he growled at the timid knock on the door. Alicia stood there uncertainly, balancing a tray.

'I thought you might like some coffee, sir,' she whispered.

'I'd rather have a whisky!' he growled, and then waved her in as she made to leave. 'Coffee will be fine. Put the tray on the table, Alicia.'

Alicia did so and Francis watched her appreciatively as she walked over to the table and bent over to place the tray. She was wearing her maid's uniform which revealed her pert little bottom as she bent over. She turned and curtsied to him and went to leave, but Francis stopped her.

'I need some entertainment, Alicia.' He looked at her. She couldn't have been more than eighteen.

'If it pleases you, sir,' Alicia responded.

'Yes, it does please me, it pleases me very much. Bend over that table.'

Alicia did as she was told, quivering with anticipation as she knew what would follow. She felt Francis' hands on her bottom, smoothing and patting her. She knew the pats would turn to smacks and the smacks would turn to some form of corporal punishment and she felt the excitement in her. It was not long in coming. The first part of the spanking was fairly restrained.

'Have you been good, Alicia?' Francis asked her as he continued to spank her.

'I try, sir, but . . .'

'But?'

'Sometimes I'm not very good, sir.'

'Have you been bad today, Alicia?' Francis asked.

'Yes, sir, I'm afraid I have,' Alicia admitted.

'Do you think you need punishing?'

'Yes, sir, I do.'

'Good girl. How many strokes of the cane should you receive?'

'Twelve, sir.'

'Good! Excellent! Should I be severe with you or not?'

'I think I deserve your severity, sir.'

'Good. Stay there.'

Francis went to the cabinet where he kept the canes and, with a connoisseur's eye, selected one. Returning to Alicia, he instructed her to pull up her skirt, which she did. He brought his arm up and then down with severity on her backside, the cane making a resounding crack as it landed. Alicia whimpered and couldn't help moving away in fear of the next stroke. Because of Caroline, Francis' enraged temper erupted. Furiously, he grabbed Alicia's hands and pulled them behind her, using the strings of her apron to tightly tie her wrists.

'I didn't give you permission to move!' he snarled.

Before Alicia could protest, he ripped the white cap off her head, scattering pins over the floor, and stuffed the cap into Alicia's mouth.

'I'll teach you to disobey me, you little bitch!'

Francis was out of control as he laid into Alicia in a frenzy with the cane, but it was Caroline he was striking, Caroline who had left him and who must be punished! A strongly restraining hand on his arm stopped the cane descending again and he heard Lynne's calming voice: 'It's not Caroline, Francis, this is Alicia!'

At the sound of her words, Francis calmed down and came to himself. Lynne was soothing a sobbing Alicia.

'Melanie, take Alicia to my room. Untie her and use some salve on her bottom. She may stay the night with you if you wish.'

Lynne had removed the cap from Alicia's mouth and she sobbed her thanks as Melanie helped her from the room.

Lynne turned to Francis and took him in her arms, soothing him as she had soothed Alicia.

'How did you know?' Francis demanded. 'How did you know that I was punishing Caroline?'

'I know you, my love, remember? For whatever reason that little bitch has got a firm hold on you and you can't let her go. Do you think Liam will keep her?'

Francis sighed and rubbed his face wearily.

'He might. She means a lot to me, Lynne. I've really let this one get to me. I've got to get her back.'

Lynne put her arms around him. She knew what he needed.

'If you'll promise not to flay my hide off, let's go upstairs. I've got my leather panties on if you'd like to stuff them in my mouth again!'

Caroline stood in the hallway of Liam's house. From the outside it had seemed deceptively small. Inside, the reality of the size of the house amazed her. The hallway was more like a ballroom, with a flagged stone floor and polished pinewood panelling on the walls. It was brightly lit and she looked around her, appreciating the beauty of the house. She imagined that the large windows would let in plenty of light in the daytime and she looked with awe at the polished pine staircase that ascended to the upper floors in a grandly sweeping fashion. Descending the stairs was a slim but well-muscled man in his late thirties. His features were a little too sharply etched to be described as handsome. His black hair was cut short and he wore a well-cut black suit. It was his movements, however, that held her. He moved with a fluidity that suggested a well-oiled machine, utilising total economy of movement, as though not a step was taken which had not been previously well thought out, its usefulness and necessity having first been fully taken into account. Caroline felt an interest and . . . yes . . . an excitement which surprised her. She had watched him walk down the stairs with a fascination she could not easily comprehend. She felt confused by her feelings. So much had happened this evening. She wasn't sure who or what she was any more. Caroline found herself moving closer to Liam, who put a reassuring arm around her.

'Clive! Good to see you arrived safely.'

By way of explanation, Liam turned to Caroline.

'Clive's an old friend of mine who's come down here from the wilds of Scotland to help me with some of the problems that I have with the estate. Did you have a good journey?' he asked Clive as he moved forward to shake his hand.

'Very good, thank you. I see you have a new acquisition.'

His eyes roved over Caroline, not so much admiring as assessing her.

'This is my new slave, Caroline. Sorry she can't say hello at the moment,' Liam indicated the gag still tied over her mouth, 'but you see the problem.'

Clive laughed and walked over to Caroline.

'Well, Caroline, I hope you'll be happy here.'

It was his eyes, Caroline decided. They were very black and very direct. As Clive looked at her, she felt that she held no secrets from him. It wasn't so much that his eyes undressed her – there was, after all, not much that needed undressing – but they seemed to see into her brain, almost as though he was working out whether she was worth his interest or not. Clive looked from Caroline to Liam, his eyes considering the real situation that existed between them. Caroline felt drained by his scrutiny and could not repress a shiver.

Liam saw the shiver and moved to place his arm around her.

'Now, Clive, you're frightening my slave. Come, darling, I think we'd better get you properly settled in for the night, don't you? Where's . . . oh, there she is. Hello, Mrs Davies. This is Caroline and I would welcome your assistance to get her settled in.'

Mrs Davies came forward into the light. She had appeared in the doorway of a room off the hallway. She was in her fifties, Caroline guessed, with greying hair and fairly stern-looking features. Her black eyes were very alert in her heavy face. She was not overweight, but looked very strong and capable. She wore an apron over her nondescript dress which, together with very sensible shoes, gave her a matronly appearance.

'It will be a pleasure, Master,' she said, looking at Caroline as if weighing up how much trouble she might give her. 'Is she to be kept in restraints?'

'Yes, for the time being anyway. I'll leave her in your capable hands, Mrs Davies.'

'Come along then, my dear,' Mrs Davies intoned in her lilting Welsh-accented voice. 'You won't give me any trouble now, will you?'

She laid stress on her words by the firm grip she placed on Caroline's arm and Caroline had no choice but to follow her.

Liam shouted after them, 'I'll come up to tuck you in, my darling.'

Caroline was led upstairs, having to pay very careful attention to keeping her footing on the polished pine staircase, and into a room on the first floor at the back of the house. The curtains were drawn over the windows and there was a fire burning in the grate to alleviate the chill of the night, but Caroline was not allowed time for an appreciation of her surroundings as, once they were inside the room, Mrs Davies pushed Caroline up against a wall and grabbed her leash, twisting it painfully until she brought Caroline's face close to hers.

'I'll warn you now, don't give me any trouble. I have the Master's permission to discipline new slaves and I won't hesitate to beat you if you give me cause. Do you understand?'

Caroline nodded, wondering how long she was going to be left alone with this woman. Satisfied, Mrs Davies pushed her into a chair. In the room, there was a single bed which Caroline was facing. Mrs Davies pulled back the covers to reveal thick black leather straps all the way down the bed on either side. Mrs Davies indicated that Caroline should stand by the bed and then took the plastic cape off her, nodding approval at the way her wrists were tied.

'Mr Francis is good with his knots. I think that you can stay tied for the moment until the Master's seen you and told me what he wants.'

She pushed Caroline on to the bed and fastened the middle strap over her, pulling it tight. As she buckled the strap, Caroline could see that she was enjoying what she was doing and felt an unexpected stirring in her clitoris. Was it the thought of Liam coming to see her and 'tucking her in' as he'd promised, or was it Mrs Davies' obvious pleasure as she renewed the proof of Caroline's helplessness? Perhaps it was a bit of both.

Mrs Davies moved to the door.

'Don't even think of attempting to escape. You wouldn't get far if you did and I'd enjoy punishing you. I think I'll enjoy that anyway.'

She went out, closing and locking the door. Caroline wriggled to test the strap, which, as she had expected, held firmly. There was nothing she could do until Liam came to her and then what? She felt a growing frustration. She wanted Liam to fuck her. She was revelling in her enforced confinement. It was only the thought of Clive which filled her with apprehension and she shivered at the memory of those coldly calculating eyes sweeping over her. And what of Mrs Davies? Caroline knew that Mrs Davies would look for every opportunity to inflict punishment on the new slave. The way she had looked at her when she was strapping her to the bed! Those narrowed eyes alight with excitement as she studied Caroline's bound body. She had to admit that she had felt excitement as she realised that she would be

Mrs Davies' slave, maybe as she had been Lynne's. She knew that she could look to Liam for protection but she didn't know to what sexual excesses he intended she should submit. Her thoughts turned to Francis. Did he know the sort of people to whom he had entrusted her? Did it matter anyway? He had lied to her, even as he fucked her. He had planned to continue lying to her so that she wouldn't give him too much trouble. He didn't, couldn't care for her if he treated her in this way.

She heard the key in the lock and looked almost with hope at the door as it opened. Was this Liam? Would he remove her gag and let her ask him all the questions to which she needed answers?

She somehow wasn't surprised as she saw Clive walk into the room and close the door behind him. He walked over to the bed and looked down at her, smiling in that oddly speculative way she had noticed earlier.

'I've just come to make sure that Mrs Davies has you safely tucked in,' he said.

He had the faintest Scottish burr, Caroline thought inconsequentially, and then struggled against the restraining strap as she felt him pushing two fingers into her vagina, smiling as he felt her wetness. It was the smile of the curious scientist.

'Hmm, just like a bitch on heat. So you like this treatment, do you?'

Clive pushed another finger into her. Caroline could feel herself responding, wanting those fingers in her, wanting him to fist-fuck her. She was so frustrated after her encounter with Liam, so confused by her strange fascination with this man, that she felt her sex straining towards Clive's undoubted sexuality; if he could only give her what she needed.

'You like it rough, don't you, slave!'

Clive's change of tone – the addition of a threatening hint – was unexpected, but exciting. It reminded Caroline of all those fantasies she had had, when it was perfectly safe in the comfort of her own bed to imagine herself at the mercy of a strong man, whose very strength was dangerously exciting. This was real, yet she felt her body responding to her fantasy man.

Clive removed his fingers and unzipped his fly, freeing his rampant cock. He knelt on the bed with his knees on either side of Caroline's head. He pulled down the scarf that had gagged her and placed his penis between her lips.

'Suck it, bitch!'

As he said this, he reached backwards and inserted his fingers once again into her slit and, with his other hand, twisted one of her nipples between his fingers.

Caroline did like it rough. She liked the feeling of being at this man's mercy, liked the feel of his fingers in her cunt. She only wished it was Liam who was doing this to her, but she needed release, desperately needed to orgasm. She sucked at Clive's cock, tasting the semen that was already escaping from its tip. Caroline felt somehow privileged that this man, whom she felt did not do anything which he thought was a waste of his time, considered her worth his attention. His hand moved from her breast and twisted in her hair. As he rammed himself into her, she steeled herself for the inevitable rush of spunk that filled her mouth. The hand in her hair twisted again forcefully. It was a pain she welcomed.

'Drink it, bitch!'

She swallowed, feeling tears escaping through her closed lids as her orgasm shook her, fuelled in its strength by the brutal way that Clive withdrew his fingers.

Clive got off the bed and replaced his now flaccid

cock in his trousers. With a surprising gentleness, he used his handkerchief to wipe the dribbles of his semen from Caroline's mouth before replacing the gag, knotting it tightly.

'Don't go telling tales after school,' Clive warned her, almost as if he were doing her a favour. 'I will deny it and punish you if you attempt to tell anyone. Do you understand?'

Caroline nodded, without taking her eyes off him. He was not threatening her, merely explaining to her what would happen if she disobeyed him. She could not repress the stirring in her clitoris as she wondered what sort of punishment Clive might have in mind for her.

Clive went to the door and looked back at her, that speculative look again in his eyes.

'When I need to, I'll use you again.'

He smiled at her, confirming his words. Caroline knew that he was well aware of her feelings. Her eyes had supplied him with the unspoken acknowledgement of his total power over her, to which she had no choice but to submit.

Chapter Seven

Liam O'Neill was a successful entrepreneur who had made his fortune by more or less legal means several years ago. He had been married twice before, and he had two children, both living with their respective maternal parent. The marriages hadn't lasted because Liam, coming from a very happy childhood, believed in the sanctity of marriage and entered into it enthusiastically and at far too young an age. After the failure of his first marriage he had unthinkingly entered into another such relationship shortly thereafter. Both marriages had fallen victim, in the first instance, to his devotion to the exclusion of almost everything else, to his work and secondly, and more importantly, to his inability to encourage his partners' interest in the darker side of his sexual desires.

Liam was a very dominant person, in his work and his relationships and, although one of his wives had professed an interest in that side of him as the reason for her attraction to him, she had not been prepared to explore much more than Liam's taking the leading role in their sexual relationship. They had had many rows, because of his then wife's inability to experiment and his own inability to keep his fantasies as just that. Liam remembered the fearful row that had erupted when he had held his wife down, which previously she had seemed to like, and asked her if he could tie her hands before they had sex. She had refused, calling him a pervert and even threatening to call the police. Liam did not abandon his efforts and even tried to sit down with his wife and talk about his sexual needs and desires but, although she had sympathised, she had made it clear to Liam that she would never consent to that sort of sex and certainly did not want to be forced. The argument had ended with Liam informing her coldly that he had no intention of forcing her and wanted a willing and adventurous partner. They parted not long afterwards, with regrets on both sides but a recognition of the inevitability of their splitting up in the circumstances. Since then, Liam had had several girlfriends who were attracted to him by his looks and money. Some had even consented to be tied up, but they had treated it as a game and Liam soon tired of their attitude. He had met Francis, firstly as a business acquaintance, and then they had become friends. It was as if they recognised in each other similar aims and desires. The got talking and soon had no secrets from each other. Liam well remembered the day when Francis had invited him to dinner at Beech House, when he promised an especially entertaining evening for his friend.

Liam had arrived in a mellow mood, but he was also curious. What had Francis and Lynne arranged for his entertainment? Liam was alone, having just finished another unsatisfactory relationship. He sighed as he parked the car and walked up the steps to Beech House. There must be a woman out there somewhere who could relate to his needs and desires, but where was she? He rang the bell and, as he waited, looked appreciatively around the expansive gardens, smelling the unmatchable mixture of the scent of sweet flowers and the tang of freshly cut grass. The door was opened by Annette, whose bottom Liam pinched playfully as he walked into the hallway, to be greeted by Francis and Lynne. He shook hands with Francis and embraced Lynne, holding her slightly longer than was necessary. She always excited his interest in fetish dressing by the clothes she wore, and he loved the feel of the tight black latex dress she was wearing on this occasion. He knew that Lynne was a dominatrix and understood the relationship that existed between herself and Francis, but he also knew that Francis, like himself, was looking for a submissive to be his partner.

After dinner, which was, as usual, excellent, Liam was invited to accompany Lynne and Francis downstairs to their special room, which room he had never seen before. Liam could not believe his eyes when he was shown into their dungeon, complete with flaming wall torches and discipline equipment.

'Something I haven't told you about, my friend, is my other "business" interest,' Francis said, leading Liam to a cell in the corner of the dungeon.

Liam gasped, for in the cell sat a pretty young girl, with long dark hair and beseeching eyes. She wore a maid's outfit which had a very short skirt and she also had her hands hand-cuffed to the bars of the cell.

'One of my newest acquisitions,' Francis explained. 'Unfortunately, this one is very badly behaved and needs to learn some discipline. I thought you might like to watch or maybe even partake in her training.'

Liam could not believe his good fortune and he eagerly accepted Francis' offer. Lynne unlocked the cell door and released the young girl, who was led out to stand in front of Francis and Liam.

'She is yours to do with as you wish. Tie her and beat her or do whatever you desire. Lynne and I will leave you alone with her. Take your time, my friend, and come upstairs when you're ready.'

After Francis and Lynne had left, Liam resumed his inspection of the girl. He had been presented with an opportunity to live out one of his fantasies. Before he did anything, he went to the girl and put his arm around her trembling shoulders.

'Don't worry, I won't hurt you. I just want to have some fun with you.'

Liam then took off his jacket and threw it on to a chair. Looking around, he realised it was a well-equipped dungeon. There were restraints of every sort ranged around the walls, as well as some evil-looking furniture which could be used for punishing a recalcitrant slave. Liam selected some lengths of rope and returned to the girl who had stood, frozen with fear, watching him. He genuinely had no desire to hurt her but he wanted to explore some of his dominant fantasies and she could help him. As if on cue, the girl screamed and started to run towards the stairs. Liam caught her easily – indeed, she hadn't seemed to be running very fast – and clamped his hand over her mouth as he held her in a strong grip.

'That was silly, wasn't it. There's no escape for you, little one, and you've just made it harder on yourself.'

With that, Liam quickly and very expertly tied her wrists behind her back. Because this necessitated the removal of his hand from her mouth, the girl continued to protest and verbally abuse him. Once he had got her wrists tied tightly, Liam pushed her to the floor and pulled her panties roughly down and off her kicking legs. Wadding them up into a ball, he stuffed them into her mouth and used her handkerchief to tie them in place.

'That's exactly what a handkerchief was intended for,' he commented, as he tied another length of rope around her ankles to restrain them from kicking out, then stood back to admire his handiwork.

'I think you should be more tightly secured than that, don't you?' he asked pleasantly, and proceeded to tie her elbows together, and then went to work on her legs with more lengths of rope, tying her thighs, knees and calves together. Liam was now thoroughly enjoying himself and, after studying her again, proceeded to rip the bodice of her maid's dress off her, exposing two small but beautifully formed breasts with their dark nipples which looked very hard. He paused to examine them. The hardness of her nipples encouraged him to push two fingers into her cunt. He looked into eyes that had turned liquid with desire.

'You are very, very wet, my dear,' he said as he probed her. 'I think you are enjoying yourself.'

She didn't shake her head and he knew that Francis had indeed given him an evening's entertainment. This girl enjoyed being tied up. Her whole body was arching towards him with desire. He reached down and sucked those inviting nipples and then, with a long piece of rope, he bound each of her breasts, squeezing them into prominence.

'Beautiful,' Liam said as he stroked and squeezed them.

The girl moaned into her gag with unmistakeable pleasure and struggled against her bonds, but Liam now knew that this was only to increase her feelings of pleasure. He got some more rope and tied it around her arms and then replaced the handkerchief with two tightly tied cords to hold the panties securely in her mouth. Liam then used the redundant handkerchief to tie over her eyes. When he had finished, he surveyed his work and knelt down beside the girl.

'You look beautiful, my dear. You are truly my helpless little prisoner, bound and gagged, available for me to do with as I choose and you can do nothing whatsoever about it.'

Liam's erection could no longer be contained and he removed his trousers impatiently, kicking them aside. He took the helpless girl in his arms, feeling a great amount of erotic pleasure from his dominance over her.

'I'm going to fuck you, my dear, again and again.'

He knew from her high state of excitement that she was very aroused. He did not need to worry about lubrication as he entered her, and thrust greedily into her as his excitement built and matched hers. They came together, fused into each other with their lust and matching sexual desires. Liam had never known such a orgasm. The realisation of his fantasy was so much better than he could have hoped and he knew that he was truly home. He had found his true self and did not want or need to deny it any longer.

They lay, spent, for a while and then Liam took off her blindfold. He wanted to watch her eyes this time and, as his cock ravaged her for a second time, he saw gratitude in her eyes. The moans she made into her gag were not moans for mercy or release, but pure desire. She was as eager as he and daylight was breaking outside before they both fell asleep, lying on the floor, too exhausted to be concerned about that. For safety, Liam had removed her gag before they slept but her answer to his whispered question as to whether she wished to be untied being in the negative, she remained tied up through their rest. When Liam awoke, pushing aside some hastily grabbed blankets, he saw his 'prisoner' still tied up and waiting for him and he did what any gentleman would have done and woke her with a kiss, thrusting his tongue urgently into her mouth until she responded. Liam moved over her until he was able to thrust his erect penis into her mouth, which she sucked at greedily until he filled her mouth with his spunk. She swallowed without hesitation, smiling at him as she did so.

Liam felt the remembrances of that pleasurable evening, making his cock stiffen as he stood looking down at Caroline. Unable to resist, he leant down, pulled down the scarf that still gagged her and pushed his tongue between her unresisting lips. He felt her immediate response and knew that, if she'd been able to, her arms would have wrapped themselves around him. Liam straightened almost regretfully and then unstrapped her and helped her to sit up.

She smiled tremulously at him and gratefully drank some of the water from the glass he held to her lips. Liam could not repress the thrill he felt at being so important to Caroline. With her hands still tied, she could not even hold the glass on her own but needed Liam to provide for her needs. He liked the feeling this gave him, he liked the sight of his new bound and submissive slave, her eyes demurely lowered as she drank.

'I'm sorry I didn't come and tuck you in last night, my darling. Something came up. Now, would you like some breakfast?'

Caroline nodded and moved back a little, indicating that she had slaked her thirst sufficiently.

Caroline watched as Liam left her and walked out of the room, closing the door behind him. She still felt his warm tongue probing her mouth. She struggled against the ropes that bound her wrists then wished she hadn't, as her futile attempts to gain freedom reminded her of her helplessness, making her nipples harden and the wetness become apparent between her legs. She wished that Liam would come back, take her and use her in whatever way he wished, as long as he satisfied this incredible yearning that she was discovering was always produced in her by being tied. She remembered her encounter with Clive and became thoughtful. Was she really such a slut as she seemed to be? Any man, no matter how afraid she was of him, seemed able to produce a need in her. Perhaps it was the bondage, perhaps Francis was right and she was a natural submissive, yearning for pain and pleasure, most of all for pleasure. She had felt afraid of Clive when she'd first met him. There was no attraction there, it was just that he had seen her at her most vulnerable. She remembered his cock pushing forcefully into her mouth and knew that she had revelled in it, loved feeling his fingers inside her as she fought against her bonds.

Impatiently dismissing all attempts at self-analysis, whilst waiting for Liam to return she used the time to study her surroundings. The room was quite lovely, large and airy. Its size dwarfed the single bed to which she had been strapped. The walls were panelled in a smooth pinewood. The furnishings were also of pine, tasteful as well as utilitarian. The drapes at the windows were of a rich dark brown, complementing the panelling. With some difficulty, because she was unable to use her hands, Caroline got off the bed and walked to the window. Her high-heeled shoes had been removed, enabling her to accomplish this small task without any difficulty. The deep bay window looked out on the well-tended gardens. Large oak trees spread their branches proudly across the lawns. How much had they seen, Caroline wondered? They seemed like wise old men, sheltering the house with their protectively lush foliage.

Did she belong here, like the trees? Caroline wondered. She hoped so, as she thought about Liam and the overwhelming sensual passion he aroused in her.

* * *

As Liam carried Caroline's breakfast tray, his thoughts drifted once again to that first time at Beech House.

After he had released the girl and locked her back into the cell, he felt, although satiated, yet more stirrings of excitement as he handcuffed her to the bars of the cell, as she had been when he had first seen her. Liam had exchanged deeply pleasurable farewell kisses with her before retrieving his clothing and going back upstairs where he discovered Francis, freshly showered and shaved, reading the papers.

'I would imagine, by the length of time you have been, that the evening was successful?'

The question was rhetorical and Liam furnished the answer by slumping, exhaused, into an armchair.

'Thank you, Francis. I'm in your debt.'

'That could be just a sample for you, Liam. Lynne and I have, for the past few years, used Beech House for the training of slaves.'

'Where do you find these slaves?' Liam asked, without surprise. Francis always got what he wanted.

'We place requests for staff with agencies and always interview here. We assess the applicants to see if they meet our rather exacting requirements, in other words if they seem to have the right attitude for slave training, and then employ them.'

'"Employ" them?'

'We only see applicants who are basically alone in the world. We give them a good home and they are well looked after. We tell them what we want and give them a day or so to reach a decision as to whether it's what they want as well.' Francis smiled.

'We are rarely wrong. The applicant is given various tests before the offer is made to ensure that she is the right . . . material. Most are usually retained by us here and the rest are sold on.'

'Sold?'

'To discerning friends and business acquaintances. We vet all of our slaves' prospective owners. We do reject unsuitable ones. For instance, we abhor violence for its own sake. When it is used in the training of a slave, that is different, but if we suspect that prospective owners merely want to ill-treat the slaves, we don't do business.'

Liam chuckled.

'Francis, you have such a strange morality!'

'You don't approve?' Francis queried, raising a sardonic eyebrow reflecting on how Liam had just spent an entire night keeping a girl prisoner, albeit a willing one.

'I didn't say I didn't approve,' Liam said with an answering grin.

'Then, would you like to join the team?'

It was an offer that did not need to be made twice and Liam had since spent many happy hours at Beech House assisting with the training of slaves, giving free rein to his dominant desires. He had even bought a couple of slaves from Francis, as he had bought Caroline.

As Liam approached Caroline's room, he saw Clive walking towards him. Liam was a man who didn't waste words.

'Touch Caroline again without my permission and I'll kill you!'

Clive recoiled in obvious shock. He was an intelligent man and cursed himself for forgetting that all the rooms where the slaves were kept had hidden cameras. Liam must have seen everything! Being a pragmatist, Clive quickly recovered himself, making his tone ingratiating.

'Come on, Liam, I was only welcoming her to the house. I didn't mean anything by it. She's only a new slave, isn't she?' As he spoke, Clive's eyes narrowed, the speculative look that Caroline had noticed once again in evidence.

'Caroline is more to me than that, although that was my first intention when I saw her. I told you about my activities because I thought you could be trusted and you showed a definite inclination to take part.'

'Which I've always respected and thanked you for! Look, Liam, I'm sorry, I was in error and it won't happen again! Let's not let a single incident like this destroy our friendship, please!'

Liam relented. He knew he was probably over-reacting to the film he had watched in his own room last night and, let's face it, he had enjoyed wanking himself to a very strong orgasm as he had watched.

'Of course it won't. We'll say no more about it.'

Liam held out his hand and Clive shook it warmly and with relief.

'But I'm warning you, Clive, stay away from her.' Liam's voice held the tone of menace he used to discourage business opponents.

'Understood. We'll have a chat about the estate later, OK?'

'Yes, I'll see you at lunch.'

With that dismissal, Clive watched as Liam turned the handle of the door to Caroline's room and walked inside, closing the door firmly behind him. Clive's mouth tightened as he walked down the stairs, meeting Mrs Davies, who always seemed to him to be prowling about the house.

'Everything all right, Mr Clive?' she asked her favourite house guest.

Clive nodded but he had a brooding expression on his face.

Intuitively, Mrs Davies, who had seen Clive

coming out of Caroline's room, asked: 'Not trouble between you and the Master over that little slut upstairs, I hope?'

Clive looked probingly at Mrs Davies and smiled in recognition of the kindred spirit.

'Nothing I can't handle, Mrs Davies. Keep a watchful eye on Miss Caroline! I am of the opinion that slaves are here to be used by all who so choose, don't you agree?' Clive raised enquiring eyebrows, at the same time directing his hypnotic eyes at Mrs Davies, eyes that held the promise of so much.

Mrs Davies smiled in an almost girlish fashion at Clive.

'I do indeed, Mr Clive. You know that you can always count on me to assist you in any way you require. Any way at all.'

Clive smiled, indicating an acceptance of the implied flirtatious behaviour.

'I may well hold you to that, Mrs Davies. I think we could make a good team when it comes to disciplining that little bitch and, perhaps, in other ways.'

Clive let his voice trail off seductively and watched the pathetic eagerness with which his hint was grasped. Mrs Davies almost orgasmed with delight. Only his imposing demeanour prevented her from offering herself to him then and there. She temporarily satisfied herself with what she considered to be a sexy sidelong look at him as she hurried off down the corridor.

When Liam returned to Caroline's room and sat down beside her on the bed, he spent a long time talking to her, explaining his problems with relationships in the past, the realisation of his fantasies when he was at Beech House and his subsequent relationship with Francis.

'I was very eager to see his new slave but, when I saw you at the house that night, I knew I wanted you and would pay any price to get you. Francis knew that I was not going to return you after one night, but he will expect me to return you eventually.'

'Will you?'

'Caroline, I don't know. I know that I don't feel about you as I did about others I've bought from Francis, but I just want to see how it goes for a while.'

Liam paused and frowned slightly.

'You won't have any more trouble with Clive, by the way.'

Caroline looked at Liam in surprise. Knowing nothing about the cameras constantly monitoring her, she could not imagine how Liam knew about her encounter with Clive. Quickly, her mind replayed that earlier scene. Had Liam seen her enjoyment, the strength of her orgasm? She felt colour flooding her face. If he had, what must he think of her? She wanted to explain but couldn't imagine how she would do so. She hadn't satisfactorily unravelled the confusion of her feelings about Clive and, if it came to that, her feelings about everything that had occurred since she had left what now seemed to be the comparative safety of Beech House. However, intuitively judging that Liam did not want to discuss that particular matter any further, she decided not to pursue it.

'What about you, Caroline? How do you feel about your new situation?'

Caroline sighed.

'I don't know what to say, Liam. It's so difficult. You know I am attracted to you, but the fact remains that I'm still your slave. I'm not free to come and go as I please.'

'We'd never have met in any other way.'

'We might have done, but that's not the point.'

Liam looked at Caroline, feeling the stirrings that refused to be ignored. He took her in his arms and knew she was aware of his desire.

'Caroline, I've told you what I'm like. I've spent many years of personal unfulfilment and now that I've acknowledged what I am and what I want, there's no going back. I'm happy with myself now and it's taken me a long time to come to terms with that. I want to dominate you. Is it to be by consent or by force?'

Caroline stared at him for a long moment.

'You won't need to force me, Liam, you know that.'

Now it was Liam's turn to be silent, acknowledging the feelings that undoubtedly existed between them. Caroline was his willing slave, but he wanted to be sure she understood his desire to play out the dominant side of his persona to the full.

'As my slave, you will do anything I say, without question?'

Carolone nodded, feeling renewed stirrings of arousal. Liam reached behind her and untied the rope from her wrists, at the same time bending forward and taking her right nipple between his teeth, biting it playfully and then more forcefully, making Caroline gasp with the pleasurable pain.

'I like playing games with my slaves, particularly one as beautiful as you. You do not object?'

Caroline wondered how he could contemplate her refusal when feelings of arousal surged through her with such strength as his fingers slid under the hood of her clitoris, stroking the bud within. Liam could barely control his own growing excitement but, taking her silence for consent, decided to play the Master to her slave.

'Mrs Davies!' Liam yelled in a very loud voice as he stood up, bringing Mrs Davies scurrying into the room.

'Get me some more rope and something to gag her with and bring me the riding crop!'

With a knowing smile in Caroline's direction, Mrs Davies hurried to locate the items requested and brought them to her Master.

'You can go!' Liam ordered as she hesitated in the doorway.

Reluctantly, she went out, closing the door behind her. On the landing, she met Clive.

'I don't think you need to worry, Mr Clive,' she said, smiling intimately. If she had been a cat, Clive reflected, she would surely have rubbed herself against him, purring her pleasure. 'The Master is in a very bad mood and he's tying the slut so that he can beat her. I don't think she's behaving herself.'

'Well done, Mrs Davies. Keep me informed.'

Mrs Davies basked in the approbation, waiting expectantly for a further exchange of confidences. Clive, however, merely lifted a sardonic eyebrow, clearly expecting her to leave. With ill-concealed disappointment, Mrs Davies turned and walked down the stairs.

Clive watched her go, before walking to the window at the end of the corridor. He stared at the sloping, flower-filled lawns without really seeing them. His was an organised and clear-thinking mind. He possessed a business acumen that had led to his relationship with Liam – a business relationship which Clive hoped to turn into something more.

Clive had first discovered that he was bisexual at boarding school, surviving the sometimes embarrassing encounters with his more adventurous fellow pupils, his coolness and confidence more or less intact. At university, he had enjoyed relationships with both sexes, moving from one to the other with equal ease. He had had no difficulty in finding partners, the sexual confidence he was rapidly developing making it necessary for him to also become adept at mind-games, playing one off against another, making the lies he had to tell with increasing frequency sound believable. He found that he enjoyed all this, enjoyed his bisexuality. If you swung both ways, it meant you didn't have to take decisions. Clive just took sex where and when it was offered, providing the person concerned met his exacting criteria. This had never given him any problems until he met Liam.

He had been strongly sexually attracted to Liam, but it was made perfectly clear to him that, whilst Liam accepted and welcomed his friendship, that was all it was ever going to be. Their business partnership proved to be extremely profitable to both men and Clive had pretended to accept that the relationship was going to be just one of business and friendship, but he didn't like losing. Clive was a winner and refused to accept that there was a concept known as defeat. That was something for other people to endure. Then Caroline was added to the equation. When Clive had first seen her, dressed only in that plastic cape, which had merely served to outline the seductive curves of her body, gagged and with her hands very obviously tied behind her, he knew that he wanted her. He wanted to possess her, in mind as well as body. Clive enjoyed control. It was a supremely sexual stimulant to him.

He wanted Caroline for two reasons: to possess her for himself and also because Liam wanted her more than he had ever wanted any of the others. Clive knew all about the slave-training that went on in the house. In fact he sometimes assisted in that training. He liked to see women tied up and helpless, already controlled. He had liked to see Caroline tied up, had enjoyed the fear and desire that had intermingled in her eyes when she had looked at him. This was the sort of game Clive relished. He would make Caroline want him, want him so much that it became obvious to Liam. If it didn't make Liam turn to him – and Clive was too much of a realist to hope for that – it would satisfy his bruised ego to see the hurt in Liam's eyes.

Clive moved away from the window, striding purposefully and confidently down the hallway, giving no more than a perfunctory glance at Caroline's door as he walked past. Enjoy yourself, Liam, he thought, while you can.

Liam had tied Caroline's wrists and elbows together and had stuffed into her mouth the scarf that Mrs Davies had brought and tied it tightly in place with some more rope. He threw her onto the bed and tied her ankles to either side of it, leaving her very vulnerable and open to him. When he had finished, he tore off his own clothes and climbed on top of her.

Putting his face close to hers, he whispered savagely, 'You'd better learn, my girl, and learn quickly. You are my slave! Resist me all you want, that excites me! This is how I like having you – tied and completely at my mercy.'

Liam felt from the wetness of her cunt that Caroline was aroused. She was very wet, and he inserted three fingers into her.

'This is what you like, isn't it?' he whispered to her. 'Perhaps I should let Clive have some more fun with you!'

Caroline wanted Liam inside her, not Clive. She made protesting noises into her gag.

'Oh, you don't like that idea?'

Caroline was struggling so much that Liam was

almost dislodged. With an oath, he grabbed one of the leather straps and secured Caroline to the bed, making her whimper with excited pain as be buckled it into place.

'That's the sort of treatment you can expect, bitch!'

Liam bit none too gently on one of her nipples and then looked at her again, enjoying her helplessness as she stared back at him, pleading with her eyes for him to take her. In answer, he rammed his cock into her, making her scream into her gag. He was rough with her, but she acknowledged again that this was how she liked it, her juices oiling Liam's penis as he pounded into her.

Liam's orgasm took him by surprise because of its force, but even then he wasn't satisfied. The level of excitement in him had not abated and he unstrapped Caroline and forced her onto her knees in front of him. Because of her tied elbows and wrists, this position was far from comfortable for her, but her own orgasm could not long be withheld and she was not averse to whatever Liam had in mind. She didn't have long to wait.

Grabbing her by the hair he untied the ropes that secured the scarf and removed it from her mouth. Caroline fantasised that Liam was a stranger – a handsome and exciting stranger – who had tied and gagged her and, now that she was in his power, was using her sexually. She was helpless and at his mercy. These imagined images sharpened her excitement and she deliberately tried to hold back her orgasm. She wanted to keep the sexual tension high for as long as she possibly could.

'Francis tells me you're very good at this. Show me how good you are!' Liam's voice held an urgency, but also a strength born from the recognition of his own power over Caroline.

She was forced to take his cock, still dripping with

his come, into her mouth. She sucked and licked it, wanting to pleasure him and, still fantasising, knowing she had no choice.

Liam came with an unexpected forcefulness, making him press Caroline's head hard into his groin while she drank the spunk, feeling her orgasm clamouring for release. Liam waited until the shudders from his climax had subsided before turning to Caroline, coldly watching his spunk running down her chin and into her hair. He picked up the riding crop and then grabbed her by her arms and forced her to stand. Throwing her onto the bed on her stomach, he used all the straps to secure her. Her bottom was invitingly visible between two of the straps and he knew he was going to greatly enjoy beating it. Liam lost count of the strokes, taking pleasure from seeing the weals laid with increasing density on her bottom.

Caroline was moaning with the waves of orgasm that she at last allowed to sweep over her, seemingly unending as Liam paused occasionally in the beating to insert one or two fingers into her slit and sometimes into the tight little hole in her bottom, using her own juices as lubrication. When he judged her orgasm to be at its peak, he stopped the beating and, stuffing the scarf again into her mouth, massaged Caroline's clitoris and anus, bringing her inexorably to another orgasm.

Liam was unprepared for the strength of his feelings and, without a word, left Caroline to recover from her exertions and almost staggered out of the door, closing it behind him. Liam took a few minutes to lean back against the wall, taking in great gulps of air to calm himself, before walking unsteadily to the stairs, heading for his study.

Mrs Davies had been watching her chance and, seeing Liam come out of the room and go downstairs, she went into the bedroom, locking the door behind her. Caroline lay still and exhausted, not apparently noticing that she was no longer alone. Mrs Davies stood at the foot of the bed and admired her Master's handiwork. Then, very gently, she ran one finger over the weals on Caroline's bottom. She felt Caroline jump and then lie still again. Caroline thought that Liam had returned and was showing her how sorry he was for his treatment of her by being very tender.

The gentle finger moved downwards until it stroked her clitoris. In spite of her throbbing backside, Caroline moaned with pleasure into her gag. She wanted to show Liam how ready she was to forgive him. With difficulty she raised her head and looked back. She made a moan of protest as she saw Mrs Davies. It was Mrs Davies whose finger was massaging her clitoris, making her damp in spite of herself, Mrs Davies who smiled coldly at her and moved the finger with another to her slit and entered her there.

Mrs Davies was crooning to her. 'That's right, my dear, get nice and wet. I can be kind as well as nasty.'

She smiled approvingly at the wetness she had found at the slave's clitoris and, for a moment, stopped the stroking to sniff her fingers, breathing in the smell of Caroline's sex. Mrs Davies sat on the bed by Caroline and, while one hand stroked her hair, another stroked the tight little hole that was the entry to her anus.

Mrs Davies did not know what she had intended to do when she came into the room, but now she wondered why she should not taste the delights of the new slave as well. Master Liam had always welcomed her help in the past in dealing with his slaves, so why not this one? Mrs Davies had not always had lesbian tendencies, but there was something about being put in control of these helpless female slaves, all tied up and just waiting to be looked after, so why not?

Caroline was also thinking quickly. All her instincts warned her to fight and struggle, make as much noise as she could, but there was a shard of common sense making itself felt, despite her natural desire to struggle and resist. What good would it do to make an enemy of this woman? She had the ability to cause Caroline a great deal of trouble and also the ability to make things much easier, maybe even pleasant, for her. What did it matter that this woman was sexually attracted to her? She knew it would not be very difficult pretending to be acquiescent, not necessary at all to pretend to feel sexually aroused. Mrs Davies' stroking fingers were definitely doing that! No one was about to let her go and it was in her best interests to make things as easy as possible for herself.

She did not trust Clive. There was something about him . . . about his eyes . . . that unnerved her. When Clive looked at her, she felt the dominance of his personality, felt that his eyes could see into her mind, that he knew what she was thinking. Even though Liam had said Clive would not bother her again, or maybe because she could not trust herself, she would perhaps make Mrs Davies want to keep Clive away from her, because of jealousy. She could try and keep up a pretence with this woman, at least until she could gain Liam's confidence and talk to him about her. Caroline took as deep a breath as her gag would allow and smiled at Mrs Davies, who immediately bent towards her and brushed her hair with her lips.

'That's my good little girl,' she said softly, as she covered Caroline's mouth with her hand. 'We'll have such fun whenever the Master is busy. I'm afraid I'll have to keep you tied up, but we can still give each other a great deal of pleasure. You know, I thought you didn't like me when we first met, but I can see now that you were just trying to delude the Master. Well, that's all right, I won't tell him.'

She brought her finger to her mouth and wetted it before inserting it into Caroline's anus.

'Just a little extra juice, eh, my darling? Softly, my dear,' she cooed, as Caroline could not suppress a sudden movement as she felt her anus being penetrated, eliciting a surge of pleasurable feeling. 'I won't hurt you' – she kissed the blonde hair again then added, in a menacing tone – 'unless I have to.'

Chapter Eight

Liam sat in his study, stroking his penis into erection as he recalled the pleasures he had just enjoyed with Caroline.

The phone rang at his elbow and he picked it up, stifling his annoyance at the interruption. He wasn't surprised to hear Francis' voice at the other end of the line.

'Hello, Francis,' he said wearily. 'What can I do for you?'

'I think you know.'

'I'm sorry but I don't.'

'I think we should meet. We need to talk.'

'That's fine with me, but what about?'

'I want her back!'

'Francis, we had a deal. The transaction was carried out in front of several witnesses –'

'Damn the witnesses! I want her back!'

'Francis, you may get her back when I've finished with her, but the timing of that I don't know about at the moment. Come and see me if you like, but I'm not promising anything.'

'All right. When?'

'Let's see, it's Friday today, how about Monday?'

'Why not now?'

'Francis, I don't want to fall out with you. Monday after lunch. Take it or leave it.'

'I'll see you then.'

* * *

Francis banged the phone down. He had known Liam would be difficult but he wanted Caroline back and he would go to any lengths to get her. He wondered how she was and whether Liam would let him see her on Monday and, more importantly, whether Liam would let him take her back. Could he, Francis, come up with something of sufficient import to persuade Liam to part with the prize. For prize she was. He recognised that now. Lynne knew how he felt and had agreed to do anything she could to help get Caroline back, and he would get her back, somehow or other. He would!

Liam replaced the receiver into its cradle and sat deep in thought. The call had not surprised him. What had surprised him was the brevity of time between his taking Caroline and the request for her return. But she was special, he told himself, he already knew that. If this was a competition, which seemingly it was, he had to win Caroline over before Francis arrived on Monday to stake his claim. He wondered how Caroline was feeling now. He wanted to see her, but he was supposed to be the Master, *her* Master. He was not really behaving like that, more like a love-sick calf, he told himself angrily. Then his mouth hardened. Maybe it was time she learned a lesson or two. He knew she wanted him, but perhaps he should let that need grow until she was begging him to take her.

Liam leant back in his chair and absently fondled his cock, remembering with renewed excitement Caroline's struggles, her immediate participation in the game and with what pleasure he had tied her so tightly. He took his cock into his hand again, holding it firmly as he moved his hand up and down the shaft. How she had struggled though, forcing him to throw her on the bed and strap her down and afterwards, when he had forced her to suck his cock as he had fucked her mouth. He could feel her lips on his cock as his hand movements became faster and faster. He had thrown her back on the bed and strapped her down so that he could use the riding crop on her. It should have been the whip, but that would come later.

Liam allowed his imagination to formulate images of how that implement could be utilised to discipline Caroline. He would use it to beat her breasts and her thighs and buttocks and then the insides of her thighs. That's where it really hurt! He'd have to gag her before he whipped her! Liam cried out as his semen spurted all over his trousers.

Later, as he cleaned himself up, Liam realised how much pleasure he had derived from the pictures in his mind of Caroline's helplessness. He was a dominant and he wanted her to be his submissive. She had shown no aversion to that idea and he smiled as he thought of the many fantasies she could help him to realise, maybe even some of her own.

Mrs Davies freed Caroline from the restraining straps and, turning her on to her back, after admiring the weals that Liam had inflicted on Caroline's white skin, sat beside her.

'I want us to have a little talk.'

She was, however, scrutinising every inch of Caroline.

'You have beautiful breasts,' she said as she gently stroked them.

Caroline used every ounce of energy she possessed to suppress the rising shudder. The soreness in her bottom helped Caroline to concentrate her mind. She needed to be careful in order to win this woman over to her side.

Mrs Davies ran her fingers over the ropes binding Caroline. She was obviously enjoying the fact that Caroline was tied. She smiled at her.

'My name is Carol, like yours, but I'm not called Caroline, so you must call me Carol . . . or Mistress. Yes, I think that might be better, because that's what I am to you of course. I have control of you and you must do everything I say.'

Mrs Davies got up and moved to the table to pick up more rope.

'I think we'd better have your legs tied, don't you? I wouldn't want you to try to run away, because then I'd have to hurt you.'

She smiled at Caroline and, because Mrs Davies was busy tying her ankles, Caroline was able to wonder at the sexual urgings she felt at those softly spoken words, at the sensations generated by the tightness of the bindings.

'There, that's better.'

She sat back on the bed. This time she used her mouth on Caroline's breasts and nipples, kissing and sucking them. Then she moved upwards and Caroline felt the woman's lips on hers: the gently insistent lips which made her part her own and allow Mrs Davies' tongue to fill her mouth. Caroline forced herself to remember that she must put up with this and, she acknowledged, it might not be all that bad. In any event, she must pretend to be in agreement. She must pretend to want this. Despite her reluctance, her clitoris was making such a pretence unnecessary. With a greater effort than she knew she could make, Caroline pushed her own tongue into Mrs Davies' mouth and Mrs Davies' excitement increased immeasurably at the sign of Caroline's willingness to give in to her demands. To Caroline's surprise, the ending of the kiss proved to be a disappointment; she knew that she wanted more, wanted Mrs Davies to probe her clitoris with her tongue and fingers.

'That felt so good. None of the other slaves ever responded like this,' said Carol Davies.

She gently pushed Caroline back on to the bed and started to remove her own clothes, all the time never taking her eyes off Caroline.

'I'm going to suck you off, my darling, and then you can do it to me, would you like that?'

Caroline's answer was to urge her bound body towards Mrs Davies, not fully believing that her unspoken desires were going to be met.

Mrs Davies stripped off her clothing and proved that the lumpiness she always seemed to display was caused more by her clothes than her body. Caroline watched her as she went to the table. For her age, Mrs Davies had a good body. She was well built and muscular, not overweight. She had large breasts with dark brown nipples, which were erect, denoting her excitement. She returned to Caroline with some more rope and a scarf.

'I'd better gag you, my dear,' she said as she climbed back on to the bed, 'but not before another delicious kiss.'

Caroline again felt the intrusive tongue in her mouth and again responded as before, realising that her body was dictating her actions much more so than her mind. After a long moment, Mrs Davies looked up and gently ran a finger along Caroline's lower lip.

'You know why I must gag you, don't you, my darling?'

'Yes, I do,' Caroline responded, wishing Mrs Davies would get on with it. At least, if she was gagged, she wouldn't be expected to kiss the woman and her bodily urgings could, she hoped, be dealt with without too much more prevarication.

'I think you even like it a little bit, don't you?'
Carolie nodded. 'Ask me, then.'

Caroline frowned in puzzlement.

'Say, please Mistress, please gag me.'

'Please, Mistress, please gag me.'

Mrs Davies clapped her hands with glee and
pressed a kiss on Caroline's reluctant mouth.

'That's my good little girl. Open wide.'

Caroline opened her mouth so the wadded-up scarf
could be pushed in. Mrs Davies wound the rope a
couple of times around Caroline's head and secured
the scarf in place. She then cuddled Caroline and
said, 'Once the Master has gone to bed, I'm going to
give you a little present, but now I'm going to give
you a lot of pleasure.'

Caroline reflected on both the mysterious present
she could expect and the pleasure she was supposed
to receive right now. Mrs Davies ran her tongue all
the way down Caroline's body to her cunt and, once
there, she pushed her tongue into Caroline's slit. At
the same time, she used one finger to play with Caroline's clitoris. Caroline twisted in her bonds, pulling
against the ropes that tied her so tightly and moaning
into her gag. Later she would ask herself how it had
happened. How could this woman, whom she feared
was not quite normal, be giving her such exquisite
pleasure? Her sex responded with extreme wetness
which Mrs Davies lapped up with enthusiasm, continuing to massage her clitoris in a way that was
driving Caroline inexorably towards orgasm. As she
came, Mrs Davies lapped at her juices and her lips
were gleaming as she looked up at Caroline, who
could only stare back at her in confusion at this
woman who had expertly brought her off.

'My turn now,' said Mrs Davies, moving up to
Caroline and removing her gag.

'Thank you so much, Mistress, but I would beg you to please let me rest. You have pleasured me so well, I'm exhausted.'

That much was true. Mrs Davies looked at her uncertainly, but Caroline smiled so sweetly at her that she was completely taken in, mostly because she wanted to be. She bent and kissed Caroline gently.

'All right, my darling, you get your rest. I'll see you after the Master has retired. I've got to give you your present, haven't I, and perhaps,' as she spoke her words became heavily underlaid with menace, 'perhaps you'll feel more able to bring me off then?'

'Oh, yes, Mistress, and thank you,' Caroline said with very sincere feeling.

'I'll just pop this back in,' Mrs Davies said as she forced the scarf back into Caroline's mouth and re-tied the ropes. 'After all, I don't want you giving pleasure to anybody else, do I?'

Liam did not see Caroline until after she had been allowed to shower and have her dinner, always supervised. At dinner, she wore a black leather collar around her neck and leather cuffs on her ankles with a short hobble-chain linking them. Another chain went from this one to a metal ring in the table leg. Apart from these and a pair of high-heeled shoes, she was naked. After dinner, she was taken to Liam's study, where her chain was again linked to a metal ring inserted in the chair in which she was told to sit.

Caroline had dined alone and been glad of that. She wanted to think. She wasn't a lesbian, she knew that, but there was no denying her body's responses to Mrs Davies' expert ministrations. She thought about the coming night and Mrs Davies' promised visit. Could she persuade Liam to stay with her, she wondered. She shook her head impatiently. She didn't even know how he was going to react when he saw her again. He had left her so abruptly.

She looked up as the door opened and Liam walked in. His face was set and he sat in the chair behind his desk and looked at her for several minutes, saying nothing.

'Liam, I want to say I'm sorry.'

Liam looked at her with unfeigned surprise.

'Really? About what?'

'I like you, Liam, at least, I feel something for you, and I'd like to make the best of things, but you left so suddenly. I can only think that I must have upset you . . .'

Liam rose and came over to her. Sighing, he crouched down beside her. Taking her hands, he looked at the rope marks on her wrists, marks that stirred him sexually, then he looked at her.

'I left you because I couldn't handle the way you make me feel. I am supposed to be . . . I *am* . . . your Master. You make everything seem so right, I don't have to worry about being different, trying to change the way I am, because the way I am is OK. You make it OK. As a Master, I am always supposed to demonstrate control, of you, of our situation, but most of all of me. When I'm with you, I'm not sure I'm in control, it feels more as if you are. I just have to re-assess the situation, see if it can work . . . if I can make it work. It's not you or anything you've done. You are perfect, exactly what I've been looking for. I just need time to adjust . . . will you give me that time?'

Caroline could only nod, overwhelmed by what Liam had said, but she knew that she could say nothing about Mrs Davies yet. Liam did not need a further problem to add to the equation. Caroline genuinely wanted to feel a closeness with Liam as she had started to do earlier, but her main concern was the coming night and Mrs Davies' promised visit and what she would be expected to do.

'Liam, get the ropes now! Tie me up! I want to show you that it's all right. We can make it work. Please spend the night with me!'

For a moment, she could see he was tempted, but he was still unsure about how he wanted the relationship to go.

'No, Caroline, not tonight. Maybe tomorrow, I don't know, but not tonight.'

He got up and rang the bell for Mrs Davies.

'I care for you, Caroline. I just need to sort my thoughts out, see where we're going.'

Liam looked up as there was a knock at the door. 'Come in,' he called.

Mrs Davies stood there looking at Caroline and her eyes were gleaming.

'Mrs Davies, Caroline is in your care tonight. I want her suitably restrained when she goes to bed. You are in charge of her.'

'I won't let you down, Master. She won't get away from me, that I promise you.'

Mrs Davies went over to Caroline and unlocked the chain that was restraining her. She helped Caroline to stand.

'Good night, Caroline. I'll see you tomorrow,' were Liam's parting words as Mrs Davies attached a chain and leash to Caroline's collar and led her towards the door.

Caroline gave a despairing look backwards, but Liam was already sorting through some papers on his desk. Mrs Davies tugged harder on her leash and forced her into the corridor, closing the door behind them. She forced Caroline up the stairs and into her room. Once there, she pinned Caroline against the wall and kissed her.

'What a stroke of good luck that the Master didn't want to use you tonight! I've put your present in here and we have the whole night in front of us. Oh, my darling, we're going to have such fun!'

Mrs Davies led Caroline to the bed. 'You can have your present if you please me, my darling.'

She sat down on the bed pulling Caroline down with her.

'You are so pretty, my dear, so very pretty.' She ran the chain of the leash through her fingers. 'Now I want you to kneel down in front of me, my darling. Go on.'

Remembering her determination to get this woman on her side, Caroline obeyed, kneeling in front of the bed. Mrs Davies got off the bed and went behind Caroline.

'Hands behind your back, my darling,' she said, and again Caroline obeyed.

She felt, not the expected ropes, but a chain being wound around her wrists and then, as she felt her head jerked backwards, she realised that Mrs Davies had tied her hands with the chain of the lead. Mrs Davies tested the security of the chain before she moved her hands to Caroline's neck to check the collar was secure, but not too tight.

'Now, my darling, my advice to you is not to struggle, because the more you do, the tighter the collar will become around your neck as you pull on the chain. Do you understand?'

Caroline nodded and felt the tightness of the collar increase as her movements pulled on the chain. Satisfied, Mrs Davies took off her dress and stood before Caroline. She was naked beneath the dress. She placed her legs on either side of Caroline's head and ordered her to suck at her sex. Caroline shut her eyes and tried not to think of what she was doing as she

163

sucked at the proffered thick labia, the engorged clitoris obscenely protruding from its hood between the
puffy lips.

'Lick me, bitch!' came the angry command from
Mrs Davies.

Caroline licked and sucked at Mrs Davies' cunt
and swirled her tongue around the swollen bud of her
clitoris.

'Put your tongue in me. Do it now!'

Caroline's tongue entered Mrs Davies, her own reluctant excitement growing, and she sucked at the
plentiful juices she found there.

'Oh, that's good. Yes! Keep going!'

Fortunately for Caroline, Mrs Davies had been sufficiently aroused by tying her up in the cruel way that
she had as to not require much further encouragement before she came. As Caroline nibbled on her
clitoris she felt warm juices trickling into her mouth,
which made her more aware of her own need. Mrs
Davies cried out as she came and then immediately
grabbed Caroline's face.

'Swallow it, you bitch, swallow it!'

Caroline had no choice but to do so and tried to
calm her agitation as Mrs Davies collapsed on to the
bed, sated.

When she had sufficiently recovered, she went to
Caroline and kissed her on the lips.

'Thank you, my darling, you did well.'

She unclipped the lead from Caroline's collar and
unwound the chain from her wrists. She kissed her
again.

'Now for your present, my darling. Let me just
settle you in a chair while I get everything ready for
you.'

So saying, she helped Caroline to rise and made her
sit in a chair. Caroline did not know whether she was

more curious or fearful as she contemplated the identity of this mysterious present. What on earth could this strange woman have got for her? She wriggled in the chair to try and ease the throbbing of her clitoris. As she did so, she felt her arms being drawn behind the chair and rope being wrapped around her wrists, drawn through the bars of the chair and tightly knotted.

'Just a security measure, my darling. We can't have you running off now, can we?'

To Caroline's amazement, Mrs Davies stripped off the bed and went to a drawer in the table. From this, she drew some plastic sheeting, which she proceeded to lay on the bed as if it were a real sheet. She tucked in the corners and then retrieved some other items from the drawer which she placed on the bed, before returning to Caroline to release her from the chair.

'On to the bed with you, my sweet, we don't want mummy's little baby getting cold, do we?'

Caroline approached the bed, curiosity and sexual excitement mingling with the slight fear she felt. She was made to sit on the bed.

'Hands behind you, darling.'

Caroline felt rope biting into her wrists as she was tied tightly. In spite of the discomfort, she felt her now familiar and immediate bodily response to the bondage.

'That's a good little girl, now lie back.'

Caroline winced at the coldness of the plastic sheet and hoped she was wrong about the woman's intentions, but knew she wasn't when she was told to lift her bottom and felt a piece of material, the texture of which resembled a towel, place under her.

'This is your present, because I know you've been a naughty girl before.'

Caroline tried not to think too much about what

was being done to her as she felt the nappy, for that's what it was, being folded and pinned on to her. Next she was forced into a pair of plastic pants. When this was done, Mrs Davies stood over her with satisfaction.

'I'd better not find you've wet your nappy when I change you in the morning. Now, good night,' and she bent over to kiss Caroline again. 'Oh, I almost forgot! Open wide.'

When Caroline did so, a large baby's dummy was pushed into her mouth but this dummy, unlike the usual sort, had a leather strap which Mrs Davies buckled behind her head. She then used the bed straps to secure Caroline and, blowing her a kiss from the doorway, snapped off the light before leaving the room, locking the door behind her.

Caroline spent an extremely uncomfortable night. She felt humiliated by her predicament, but strangely excited too, an excitement tempered by her frustration from her unfulfilling encounter with Mrs Davies. She had done what the woman wanted her to do, but she had hoped that her exertions might be rewarded by some reciprocal pleasuring. Instead, she was tightly bound, unable even to so much as touch herself, let alone bring herself off, and she also had to try desperately not to give in to the urgings to relieve herself, which was always closely associated, for her, with sexual arousal. When she realised, during the night, that these urgings were becoming irresistible, she gritted her teeth and determined that she was not going to give in. She was not going to let Mrs Davies have the pleasure of humiliating her further. She determined that she wouldn't sleep and was almost grateful for the tight restraints that held her, as it meant she could not move and cause her overladen bladder further irritation. She alternately dozed and thought with excitement of her experiences and her earlier encounter with Liam. What conclusion would he reach in his deliberations?

The curtains had not been drawn and she was able to see the shadows of the trees on her window as their branches gently waved in a slight breeze. The night looked beautiful. Caroline reflected gratefully on the fact that Mrs Davies had not blindfolded her. She also thought of the irony that, under other circumstances, she could have been happy in her situation here, with Liam. She wanted to share with him in the fulfilment of even his wildest fantasies. A mischievous thought occurred to her. What would Liam say if he could see her now? Was this one of his fantasies? Would he like his slave as an adult baby? Or would he sympathise with her humiliation? The nappy felt thick, but oddly comforting, between her legs. The dummy's teat tasted of rubber, but she found this strangely sensual as well. It was uncomfortable lying on her bound wrists, but the strapping was not too bad. She revelled in her restrictions as she had always done, but her concern grew that, as her sexual excitement increased, she would not be able to avoid using her nappy.

Thoughts of Francis immediately intruded. OK, she thought, let's be logical. Francis had a wife with whom he seemed perfectly content. She thought of Lynne and shivered, cursing herself as she did so, feeling the answering urge for relief from her bladder. She could not imagine herself living happily as part of a *ménage à trois* with that one as part of the triangle!

She remembered Liam's kisses. There was no doubt that she had enjoyed them. Even now, they generated a stir of erotic feelings, which caused her further complications in her determination not to give in to her natural desires. Could she, though, live as a slave with equanimity? Would he ever come to trust her enough to allow her her freedom and, if she had that freedom, would she not want to return to her ordinary life? Caroline would have laughed aloud at that if it had not been for the dummy. What life? No job and no home, no close personal friends or emotional ties. She would have to start all over again and she wondered if she could or even wanted to return to her original normality after what she had experienced since her voluntary entry into slavery. She had had a taste of a very different way of life . . . yes, in part it had been frightening, painful and humiliating, but it was also exciting. She knew that she had never before felt so sexually alive. Francis had been right when he had sensed her enjoyment of being restrained.

She thought back to childhood games when she had been tied up and had enjoyed it so much that she had never minded being the 'victim', and had often volunteered for that role. Even at that age, she remembered her feelings of guilt because of her enjoyment. Surely it wasn't normal to feel that way? She had experienced a lot of, then unidentifiable, sexual feelings when she had been tied up. In her teenage years, she had experimented sexually like any other normal girl, including having crushes on other women, and she grew into full womanhood believing herself to be totally, acceptably, normal in the sexual arena. That had all been knocked aside by her Masters and Mistresses. She could not deny that she liked having sex when she was restrained. It added something indefinable to her pleasure and, because she was being forced to submit, she didn't need to give credence to any feelings of guilt. She was a slave and had no choice in the matter, did she? Being forcibly restrained by Francis and Liam, wasn't that just a bit exciting? Caroline shook her head impatiently. Of course it was! The little voice of truth would not let her get away with it. When Francis had used her, she had felt the excitement, had wanted to struggle, as much to exacerbate her own excitement as to genuinely protest. When Liam had forced her, wasn't that just as exciting? She remembered his cock being forced into her mouth while she knelt in front of him, helplessly tied. But what about last night? She knew she was not a lesbian, then why had she come so forcefully when Mrs Davies had brought her off so expertly? She was confused and did not appreciate the fact that she was becoming much more sexually aware. Her body was demanding satisfaction, whoever gave it. There was, however, no doubting her initial distaste at the thought of bringing Mrs Davies off. But, said the little voice at her ear, hadn't she secretly enjoyed even parts of that, being tied in the way she had been, and being forced to submit?

Caroline would not countenance that. Again, she refused to acknowledge a further truth, the truth that intuitively Francis had seen at the interview. She was a true submissive but, as yet, had not quite accepted this. As for Clive . . . no, she did not want to think about that dark and sinister, yet undeniably sexually attractive figure. She wouldn't think about him being in this room, making her feel so excited in spite of her fear – or maybe because of it. No, she wouldn't think about that, because it was making her so aroused and she couldn't deal with that . . . not now.

Streaks of morning light were making their first appearance in the black sky when Caroline faced the inevitable. She was going to have to allow her bladder some relief. She knew she could not hold it in any longer and, in spite of her fears of the humiliation and other, as yet unknown, consequences, she sighed with relief as she relaxed and wet her nappy.

After relieving herself Caroline slept surprisingly well and did not wake until she felt Mrs Davies feeling her nappy. The fear returned with a great rush. She watched as Mrs Davies brought her fingers to her nose and sniffed. She looked at Caroline and shook her head.

'You have been a bad girl, haven't you!'

Caroline tried to mumble apologies but they just came out as muffled noises.

'We know what to do with naughty little babies, don't we?'

She was undoing the straps as she spoke and then, sitting on the bed, pulled Caroline over her knees and, peeling off the plastic pants and soaking nappy, proceeded to spank her long and hard. Caroline found it hard to breathe as her face was pushed into the plastic sheeting and she was still gagged with the dummy, but felt renewed excitement as her bottom warmed. She wriggled as best as she could but, with her hands tied, it was a futile effort. Her bottom was now very painful, but still the relentless hand came down and down on her buttocks, stimulating her arousal. She became conscious of her increasing wetness and her bottom seemed to strain towards the punishing hand and not away from it. At last, Mrs Davies had had enough and pushed Caroline on to the bed, ignoring her mute pleas for some sexual release. To Caroline, the withholding of such release was the greater punishment.

'Naughty little baby! Mummy is very angry with you!'

Mrs Davies showed no interest in Caroline's plight, playing the enraged 'parent' to perfection.

'Naughty little babies must learn a lesson when they've been so bad,' Mrs Davies said and removed the dummy.

Before Caroline could mumble her apologies, the soaking wet nappy was tied around her nose and mouth, loose enough for her to breathe but impossible to dislodge as Mrs Davies firmly knotted it behind her head.

'This is what happens to naughty little girls who wet their nappies!' Mrs Davies told her as she forced her into a chair and tied her to it.

Caroline was now breathing the smell of her own piss and it was making her stomach heave. She tried to call out to Mrs Davies and beg her to let her go, pleading that she was sorry, but opening her mouth wide enough to scream her pleas only resulted in Caroline taking in large drops of her own urine, so she closed her mouth again to mitigate the worst of her situation. Breathing became difficult with her mouth closed and she had to open it periodically to take in gulps of air. Mrs Davies did not release her until she had finished putting clean sheets on the bed and making it up properly. When at last she untied the sodden nappy and dropped it on the floor she looked at the distressed girl and smiled.

'Perhaps you'll think twice before you are so naughty again, yes?'

She untied Caroline who, after her experiences, was not as sexually aroused as she had been. She offered no resistance when Mrs Davies took her into the bathroom and, still treating her like a child, soaped her in the shower. Caroline welcomed the feel of the clean, hot water cascading over her body and tried to shut out of her mind the feel and smell of that dripping wet nappy tied over her face. After the shower, Mrs Davies towelled her dry, then dried and brushed her hair. She gave Caroline some make-up and watched as she applied it. Caroline was still trembling slightly from her experience but, when she was finished, Mrs Davies beamed her approval.

'Would you like some breakfast, my dear?' she asked as she kissed Caroline's forehead.

'Yes, please, Mistress.'

Mrs Davies smiled. 'I'll go and get you some. I'll just make sure you're nice and secure first.'

She tied Caroline's hands and then tied her to the chair.

'That's a good little girl,' she said as she patted Caroline and then left her to get the breakfast.

Caroline realised that, in spite of everything, she was hungry and did full justice to the delicious breakfast that was brought to her, even though Mrs Davies had decided not to untie her and insisted on feeding Caroline as though she were indeed a child. This reminder of her helplessness reawakened Caroline's clitoris to pulsating life, hardening her nipples.

After breakfast, Mrs Davies untied Caroline from the chair and, her hands still tied behind her, she was made to sit on the bed. Mrs Davies talked for some minutes, not really to her but more to herself, giving Caroline some ideas about why this woman behaved as she did.

'It's so nice having a little girl to look after again. I won't let this one go . . . not like the other.' She turned and stroked Caroline's hair. 'She had lovely hair too, nice blonde hair like yours. She was a very good baby, though, not like you, my dear. She didn't give me any trouble and I really loved her, would have given her anything but . . . she left me.'

'Where did she go?' Caroline ventured to ask, not wanting to disturb this woman's reminiscences, but curious in spite of herself.

'She left me. Went off with some man. I told her he wasn't good enough for her but she wouldn't listen and now she never writes to me, never lets me know how she is.' She turned and stared at Caroline. 'I don't even know if she's all right!'

Suddenly, she threw her arms around Caroline. 'You won't leave me though! You won't go away! I won't let you!'

She pulled away slightly after a few minutes and smiled, an odd and sinister smile. 'I'm going to make sure you don't leave. I'm going to make sure you can't get away.'

Caroline didn't know what to say. She felt a real foreboding. This woman meant what she said. Caroline fervently hoped that Liam would want to spend the nights with her in future and yet, strangely, she felt safer from Clive's attentions, because of how Mrs Davies behaved with her now. Caroline knew she had to encourage that, no matter at what cost to herself.

Summoning up her courage, she smiled winningly at Mrs Davies. 'I won't leave you, Mistress. How could I?' Caroline closed her eyes as Mrs Davies kissed her.

'Now, I have to get you ready for the Master. He's got someone coming to see you and has told me how he wants you prepared.' Mrs Davies was obviously excited. 'He's going to have you marked.'

'Marked?' Caroline asked in alarm. 'What do you mean, Mistress?'

'The Master wants you to be marked as his property and that's what's going to be done today!'

Caroline struggled to rise off the bed, but Mrs Davies forced her down until she was lying on the bed. Quickly Mrs Davies strapped her in, using all the straps so that she was firmly restrained.

'Now, don't give me any trouble, you silly girl.'

173

Mrs Davies sat on the bed beside her and gently stroked her heaving breasts.

Caroline was thinking quickly. Whatever Liam had in mind for her, she did not believe he would want to really hurt her. He had hit her with the riding crop and that had hurt, but it was a pain she had welcomed, a sensual pleasure-pain. It was the sort of pain to which he knew she acquiesced.

Mrs Davies smiled at her as she drew the final strap over her. It was one that had not been used on her before and Caroline felt her deepening arousal as it was buckled into place. The strap had two uses, it held her head still and covered her mouth.

'Easy, my dear. It won't hurt much and it will look very pretty on you, you'll see.'

She resumed her stroking of Caroline's body.

'You look so pretty all tied up like that.'

Her hands stroked further downwards until she was pushing her fingers into Caroline's cunt.

'Nicely wet, my darling. It's a pity I haven't got time to deal with you now, but perhaps later.'

She continued stroking and probing, enjoying Caroline's feeble struggles against the restraining straps. Caroline fought against the feelings of arousal that were enveloping her. She wanted to know how she was to be marked and by what. Mrs Davies was now stroking her clitoris, which was hard and very responsive to her touch. Mrs Davies seemed to remember something and moved away, returning with some rope. She undid the straps from Caroline's legs and forced each of Caroline's ankles to the corners of the bed where they were tightly tied. She resumed her strokings and laughed at herself.

'Silly me, I almost forgot because I was so enjoying strapping you down, but the Doctor needs unrestricted access to your labia.'

So that was where she was to be marked. Caroline's curiosity grew. She wondered how she was to be marked, but overwhelming her mental questioning was the desire she had to feel Mrs Davies' probing fingers inside her, bringing the relief she craved.

'Don't worry, my dear. I'm here and everything will be all right.'

She used Caroline's own wetness to lubricate the pulsing clitoris. Caroline strained against the straps, feeling the welcome pressure of her bonds, the unstoppable build-up to her orgasm.

'Did you enjoy the smell of your own piss, my darling?'

Caroline barely heard the words as her orgasm shook her. Mrs Davies, in any event, treated the question as purely rhetorical.

'I think that's why you wet your nappy because you knew I'd do that, you naughty little girl.'

She closed her eyes for a moment and swayed back and forth on the bed as she continued to stroke Caroline.

'I think I'd like you to drink my piss – would you like that, my dear?'

Caroline was in that languid half-conscious state, between satiation and exhaustion, that often follows on the heels of an orgasm. Her drifting reverie was only interrupted by the opening of the door. Liam stood there accompanied by a much shorter man who was wearing a white coat and carrying a black bag. He was younger than Liam and smiled in a friendly fashion at Caroline as he placed his bag on the table. He ran a critical eye over the way she was tied and nodded approvingly at Mrs Davies.

'Well done, Carol. Your usual efficiency.'

Mrs Davies inclined her head in acknowledgement of the compliment.

'Just the labia, Liam?' he asked, inspecting Caroline's cunt with professional disinterest.

'For now, yes.'

'Then I'd better get to work.'

So saying, he extracted from his case a selection of instruments.

Seeing Caroline's widened eyes, the doctor smiled at her reassuringly.

'My name is Steve. Don't worry, I've done this thousands of times. I'm going to freeze your labia which will make the area numb. I promise, you won't feel a thing.' He smiled. 'Do you trust me?'

Caroline nodded as much as she was able to.

'You know, you're a lucky girl that Liam cares enough about you to do this.'

Caroline looked at Liam, who met her gaze and returned it with such a warm smile that she felt her uncertainty dissolving.

Steve moved further down the bed and began his work. Caroline felt a slight shock as the cold spray found her labia, but found that Steve was right; by the time he started the piercing she couldn't feel anything.

'Don't worry,' Steve smiled at her. 'The numbness will quickly go and you'll be surprised at how speedily you heal up.'

She couldn't move at all as the piercing progressed. The whole thing was over in a matter of minutes. Caroline had felt nothing. With some excitement, she wondered what had been done to her and what it looked like.

Steve was collecting his instruments and returning them to the case. Peeling off his rubber gloves, he smiled at Caroline.

'You see, I told you it would be OK. Perfectly sterile and painless.'

176

Liam expressed his gratitude and offered to show Steve out. When the door had closed behind them, Mrs Davies admired Steve's handiwork and smiled at Caroline.

'You really do belong to the Master, now. You belong to us. You'll never be allowed to leave here now. Never!'

Chapter Nine

When Liam returned, he dismissed Mrs Davies and removed the straps and ropes from Caroline himself.

'Sorry about that,' he said, as he removed the strap from her mouth. 'It was important that you didn't move while Steve was working on you because you might have injured yourself. Do you want to see the result?'

Liam helped her to sit up and she looked down at herself. There was a small steel ring through her labia which had some sort of catch on it. Suspended from the ring were two tiny letters: Liam's initials.

'You are truly mine, now, Caroline. The ring and initials cannot be removed except by unlocking the catch and I am the only one who has the ability to do that.'

He sat beside her and tilted her chin. 'You are my slave and I have marked you as such. Francis or anyone else cannot lay claim to you.'

She looked at him. 'As your slave, what is my position in this house?' she asked. She needed to know. She needed to know how much she could tell Liam about Mrs Davies and what she had done to her and planned to do to her.

'You are a very precious possession to me. As such, I will see to all your needs and allow you certain freedoms. This is conditional on you accepting your position.'

'What about my contract?'

'Contract?'

'The one I signed when I accepted "my position" with Francis and Lynne. Francis told me that the contract would run for one year, after which time I could stay or leave as I chose.'

Liam smiled.

'I suggest we utilise the same terms in your new contract.'

'Francis didn't mention that the terms of my contract also included his right to sell me whenever he chose!'

Liam silenced any further words of Caroline's by kissing her deeply, pushing his tongue into her mouth and being rewarded by feeling her tongue joining with his. Pushing her down on the bed, Liam fondled her breasts, feeling the hardening nipples, which almost seemed to have a life of their own as they strained towards him. Liam's finger dived into Caroline's slit, finding it, as he suspected, slippery with her juices. His cock was insistent, demanding for release from his trousers. He felt a thrill of ownership as Caroline's fingers unzipped him and extracted his rampant penis, already oozing secretions from its tip as his excitement grew. Caroline pushed the tip of his penis into her cunt, ignoring the slight soreness in her labia. Liam was considerate and gently pulled Caroline onto her side as he rolled with her, easing the pressure from her newly pierced labia. They both felt a thrill as they heard the initials jangling as they touched.

Caroline stretched her body sensuously and managed to join her hands together behind her back. As Liam thrust into her and she felt her orgasm building, she looked submissively at Liam. Understanding the gesture and what it signified, Liam felt a deep rush of passion and placed his mouth firmly over hers, their tongues mingling as they probed each other, seemingly unable to get enough, both wanting to explore every part. Liam wrapped his arms around Caroline, imprisoning her with his passion. Caroline felt unbelievable waves of pleasure enveloping her as the precursor to her orgasm. These incredible feelings were further fuelled as she felt Liam wrapping one of the bed straps around her arms. From their relative positions, he couldn't buckle the strap but that didn't matter, it was purely symbolic to both of them. As Liam spunked into her, Caroline's own orgasm refused to be kept back any longer, so that they shuddered together in tremendous mutual gratification.

Caroline knew that she must persuade Liam to come to her bed regularly, that she must use every endeavour to avoid the ministrations of Mrs Davies and her desires, but she also knew that she felt an urgent longing for Liam just for himself.

'I want to be tied,' she whispered. 'Kiss me, Liam, please.'

Responding to the urgency in her eyes and the excitement that her words were occasioning, Liam bound her wrists together, tying the knots tightly. Caroline revelled in the now acknowledged and welcomed increase in her sexual excitement that the bondage produced in her. She was still lying on her side and Liam went to the opposite side of the bed so that he was behind her. He gently trailed his tongue down her spine, making her squirm with pleasure. When he got to her bound wrists, Liam drew his tongue in and kissed her instead, trailing warm wet kisses down over her bottom. Reaching the cleft between her buttocks, he used his tongue to probe gently at the tight little opening of her anus, slipping the tip into the delicious little hole before continuing to trail his tongue down her thighs and calves. Liam straightened a little and bound her ankles together, knowing from the moans of pleasure emanating from his helpless slave that she was enjoying the feel of the ropes constricting her limbs. Wetting his fingers, he inserted two into her anus and, as she gasped with pleasure, lay on the bed behind her and covered her mouth with his free hand.

'You are my slave, my darling. You must do as I say or you will be beaten into submission. You must let me fuck you in whatever way I choose. You can fight me if you want to, that really excites me, but it means I will have to tie you up when we have sex.'

His words excited her almost as much as his gently moving fingers within her. Was this what she wanted? She didn't know anything any more except for the growing sexual arousal that needed to be quenched. The fingers were now gently removed and she felt the head of Liam's cock pushing gently at her anus until it was moving deep within her. He kept her mouth covered and used his other hand to massage her breasts and nipples.

'Oh, that feels so good, my darling, so very good,' Liam said, holding her more fiercely as his excitement increased.

Caroline responded to him, opening her anus by bearing down and moving backwards and forwards in a way that she knew would increase the feeling for him as well as for herself. She peaked just before he did, screaming into the hand that covered her mouth and then moaning a little with pain as his grip tightened as he came, jerking against her spasmodically until the effects of the orgasm lessened. He released his hand from her mouth as he lay against her, sated. Caroline lay with her eyes closed. She felt good and she knew it. She had enjoyed what had happened and, for the first time, was prepared to freely acknowledge it. Her wrists and ankles were still tied and Liam was gently stroking her breasts and belly, almost meditatively. Occasionally, he squeezed Caroline with pleasure and gratitude. She had given him so much and he was aware of her own pleasure. Perhaps this could work after all.

Caroline was busy with her own thoughts. She did care for Liam, as she had cared for Francis, but this time there was no Lynne to take into consideration. She burrowed happily into the protective circle of Liam's arms around her. She would build up his trust and maybe they could be happy together. Did that mean she wanted to be a slave? Caroline could see that there were ways she could come to terms with that. She knew she could not tell Liam about Mrs Davies . . . not yet. That would shatter whatever trust he had in her if she complained about his staff. She had gathered that Mrs Davies had been with him for many years and was a trusted employee. No, she was just going to have to deal with Mrs Davies as best as she could, until she felt she could reveal everything to Liam and know that he would believe her when it came to a question of who he was to trust. She wouldn't think about Clive at the moment, Mrs Davies could help her there in any event. Caroline sighed inwardly. She had her work cut out but she believed it could be done.

Liam stirred and sat up.

'I'm sorry, my darling, but I have to leave you now.'

Her eyes widened in alarm and Liam laughed softly and kissed her.

'Not for long, I have a business meeting, but I'll only be gone for a couple of hours.'

'Liam, will you stay with me tonight?' Liam looked at her pleading eyes. 'Please?'

He kissed her gently. 'Of course I will, but right now I have to go.'

He untied her wrists and massaged them gently. He repeated this procedure with her ankles, sucking on her toes and smiling at her moans of desire.

'I'll send Mrs Davies to you to help you dress for dinner tonight. I want you to look beautiful for me.'

She was about to protest but remembered her resolution and simply smiled at him. At least he would be with her tonight.

After he had gone, Caroline lay on the bed and thought about her life with Liam. Now that she was thinking more clearly, she could see that Liam did care for her – she remembered what Steve had said about how lucky she was – but she also knew that he enjoyed her status as his slave. She realised that that thought didn't bother her, not any longer. She liked being held captive by the man she was coming to care about more and more. She questioned her own depth of feeling that could seemingly so easily be transferred to Liam from Francis in such a short time, but pushed the thought away impatiently. Francis had sold her, thereby surely proving the lightness of his own feelings, so she should not concern herself with that. She sat up and looked again at the mark of ownership Liam had put on her. The soreness was still there but she felt a tinge of pride in the knowledge that she was owned by someone like Liam who would not easily let her go. She went to the bathroom to use the toilet, revelling in her freedom to do so and, before she went back to the bedroom, poured herself a glass of water, drinking it thirstily. She realised that she had made no move to run to the window, throwing it wide and glorying in her unexpected freedom. She didn't want to. Instead, she strolled over to the window and opened it, smelling the fresh, cool air and admiring the expansive grounds she could see spread out before her. Smiling, she closed the window and turned back into the room, just as the door swung open.

The smile froze on Caroline's face as she saw Mrs Davies standing there. She held out what was unmistakably a gymslip. She also carried some other items of clothing and a vicious-looking cane. She smiled at Caroline.

'Time for my little girl to go to school,' she said, flexing the cane.

Caroline tried not show her fear as she smiled at Mrs Davies.

'Is that the outfit the Master wants me to wear tonight?'

'Oh, no, you stupid girl! The Master has gone out and won't be back for a couple of hours, so I thought we could continue with your training. You obviously need it as you were such a bad girl this morning.'

Mrs Davies moved into the room, closing and, more ominously, locking the door behind her. She slipped the key into her pocket and ordered Caroline to put on the clothes she had brought her. Caroline, realising she had no choice and remembering her resolution to deal with Mrs Davies in a friendly way until she could safely talk to Liam about her, put on the navy-blue school knickers and the white knee-length socks. Mrs Davies watched approvingly as she buttoned on the white school shirt and pulled the gymslip over her head. It fitted her perfectly and she wondered if these clothes had once belonged to Mrs Davies' daughter. Mrs Davies knotted the tie around her neck, pulling it unnecessarily tight. Then she stood back and looked at her approvingly before grasping the cane in her hand and asking her in a sharp voice why she had not done her homework. Caroline looked at her in a startled fashion, before realising that this was a game and she had better play it properly.

'I'm . . . I'm sorry, Mistress, really I am.'

'I don't know what I'm going to do with you! I think I've been far too lenient with you in the past, my girl, and I'm going to teach you a lesson this time! Bend over that chair!'

Tremblingly, Caroline obeyed. The chair was a very solid wooden one with wide arm rests.

'Put your arms out!'

Caroline laid her arms on each of the rests and winced as Mrs Davies bound them tightly to the chair arms, before tying her ankles to the chair's wooden legs. Caroline was thus forced to lean forward as her arms were tied and her bottom was most appealingly presented. As before, the bondage excited her and the fear added rather than detracted from that excitement.

'You will count each of the strokes I give you. If you make a mistake, I shall start again! Do you understand?'

'Yes, Mistress.'

Mrs Davies stood behind Caroline and then jerked down her knickers until they were around her legs. She then spent a few minutes smoothing her hand across Caroline's bottom which still bore the marks of earlier punishments, before slipping one wetted finger into Caroline's slit eliciting a gasp of surprise from her captive. Caroline felt her juices begin to lubricate her clitoris.

'We don't want you making any noise now, do we?' Mrs Davies asked and stuffed the ends of Caroline's tie into her mouth. 'Pity about the counting, but I think I can ensure you are properly punished in any event. I'll just add a few strokes for the mistakes in counting that I'm sure you would have made, don't you agree?'

Effectively gagged, Caroline could only continue to play along. She was imagining the pain that was to come to her already abused bottom and wondered at the sexual tension this thought generated in her. She felt Mrs Davies' hot breath as she put her lips close to Caroline's ear.

'This is for your own good, my girl. You know you deserve it, don't you?'

Caroline nodded her head, playing the penitent to perfection, and Mrs Davies ran the cane down her bottom and legs, making Caroline shiver in anticipation, although Mrs Davies took this to be a sign of fear and smiled cruelly to herself while continuing her probing of Caroline's cunt. Caroline knew she was becoming very wet and hated the knowledge that this would undoubtedly impart to the woman who was about to beat her. The confirmation of this was not long in coming.

'You really are a naughty girl! You're very wet. I'm afraid that will earn you some more strokes!'

Caroline felt the fingers being removed from her vagina and tensed for the expected first stroke of the cane. Instead, she felt something else probing her and realised after a few minutes that Mrs Davies was fucking her with the cane. She struggled against the ropes that held her, making useless muffled sounds, more of pleasure than of protest. She couldn't help responding to the feel of the cane inside her as it was expertly manipulated by Mrs Davies, who was again whispering at her ear.

'It's so amazing, isn't it, that something that can give so much pleasure can also bring so much pain?'

Caroline was only capable of incoherent mumbling through the tie that obstructed her mouth. She knew that she was going to come and that Mrs Davies would surely know it.

'Is my little girl enjoying this, eh?' she quizzed.

Very carefully, amazingly mindful of Caroline's recent piercing, Mrs Davies' fingers found her clitoris and massaged it gently in concert with the cane moving within her. Caroline could not stop herself and, as her climax exploded, the cane was swiftly withdrawn.

As she leaned against the chair, grateful for the restraining ropes that prevented her from falling, Mrs Davies brought the cane down on her bottom with a swishing sound, followed by a vicious crack as it connected with the soft skin of her buttocks. Caroline yelped into her gag and pulled against her bonds, desperately trying to escape the pain. The first stroke was swiftly repeated, causing her to buck against the chair until Mrs Davies held her by the hair, pulling on it sharply. The feel of the cane on her bottom was like no other pain she had thus far experienced. It had its own distinctive and excruciating level, causing waves of stinging that did not immediately abate, but seemed to go on and be joined by others as Mrs Davies caned her repeatedly. Caroline's bottom showed the increasing number of double thin red lines, slightly raised on the surface of the skin and like miniature tram-lines, so characteristic of the cane, the kind of marks that would cause her pain when she sat down and which would remain for several days. Caroline could not believe it when the pain gradually became pleasure and she found herself arching her bottom up towards the instrument, wanting more. Mrs Davies took a great delight in her handiwork, keeping a firm grip on Caroline's hair as well as swinging her arm enthusiastically as she dealt each blow. Caroline felt her second orgasm building, or was it just a continuation of the first. She didn't know or care, but gave herself up to the exquisite pleasure she was feeling, wanting the cane to continue beating her buttocks and legs, riding the tidal wave until at last it came crashing down.

Eventually, Mrs Davies seemed satisfied and stopped, also releasing Caroline's hair from her grip. Caroline was sobbing with the extreme soreness of her bottom, which felt as if it were on fire, and the tingling sensitivity in her scalp which had resulted from having her hair pulled repeatedly, but also from the force of her orgasm, the pleasure of which left her weak and gasping.

Mrs Davies allowed her time to recover and then she started to untie her.

'There, that wasn't so bad, was it? Has my little girl learned her lesson?'

Caroline nodded, realising that her nipples and clitoris were incredibly sensitive as Mrs Davies pulled the tie from her mouth and finished untying her. Caroline caught a glimpse of her bottom in the mirror and saw the network of red lines, a sight which thrilled her.

Her ordeal was, however, far from over. Mrs Davies ordered her to remove all her clothes, which she did, wincing with pain whenever any material brushed her bottom. When Caroline was standing naked in front of her, Mrs Davies went behind her and started to gently massage her breasts. The nipples of Caroline's small breasts were surprisingly large and rubbery. Now those same nipples became quickly erect under Mrs Davies' expert ministrations.

'You were very good, my darling, but now that you've received your punishment, we still have plenty of time before the Master comes back,' she said.

With renewed feelings of fear, which still had an

element of sexual excitement, Caroline wondered what Mrs Davies had in mind, but merely smiled and nodded. They were both facing the mirror and she could see Mrs Davies' hands on her breasts. She knew that the deceptively light touch could turn to a grip of steel if she showed any resistance. Mrs Davies saw Caroline's smile and beamed approval. She moved one hand up to cover Caroline's mouth and her other arm gripped Caroline around her waist, imprisoning her arms, as Mrs Davies told her exactly what she had in mind for her.

'I want to relieve myself, my dear ... right over your face!'

Caroline struggled helplessly in Mrs Davies' grip. She knew she should show willingness, but the enormity of the idea of this woman's piss in her mouth was something she could not easily passively tolerate, even though the very fact that Mrs Davies was holding her so tightly, that she knew herself to be indeed truly in this woman's power, was making her sexual juices leak onto the insides of her thighs. Mrs Davies' voice hissed into her ear.

'That's right, my dear, struggle, struggle all you like. It won't help you.'

Mrs Davies dragged her over to the table, from the drawer of which she extracted a scarf. She removed her hand from Caroline's mouth and shoved the scarf into it, cutting off the partially born scream for help. She thrust Caroline into the chair over which she had earlier been bent for the caning, and tied her to it. Caroline knew that her own struggles were exacerbating her arousal, knew that she struggled deliberately to increase it.

'You are a little handful, aren't you? I'm really going to enjoy this,' Mrs Davies said as she tied a piece of rope around Caroline's mouth to keep the scarf in place.

'No blindfold, I think. I want you to see exactly what is going to happen to you! Now, I must get things ready. Can't have the room all messed up, can we?'

She went to the drawers and extracted a couple of plastic sheets, one of which she spread over the floor. Watching Caroline's struggles intently, she went to the door and unlocked it. Before she opened the door, she turned back to Caroline.

'I won't be long, but I'm going to need some assistance and I know just the person to ask.'

She blew Caroline a kiss and went out, again locking the door behind her. When she had gone, Caroline struggled desperately against her bonds, but the chair was a stout one and she was tied tightly to it. Nevertheless, she continued to struggle, feeling her orgasm building, until she heard the key in the lock again and, as the door opened, she saw Clive standing behind Mrs Davies. When they were both in the room, Mrs Davies relocked the door. Was it her imagination, or did Mrs Davies look slightly put out, Caroline wondered. She was given no time to reflect on this as the man she had been so desperate to avoid crouched down in front of her.

Clive was dressed in a black turtle-neck sweater and black trousers. He looked at her with those dark, unfathomable eyes and stroked a pitying hand across her hair.

'Good afternoon, sweetheart. I hear you've been a very naughty girl,' he said.

Caroline looked from Clive to Mrs Davies.

'Carol has decided to let me take care of your discipline this afternoon, isn't that right, Carol?'

'Yes, Master Clive,' Mrs Davies responded, with a look of pure hatred directed at Caroline.

'Thank you, Carol. I won't be needing any further assistance.'

'Master Clive, I can help you. I won't get in your way. Please let me stay.'

Caroline couldn't believe it. Mrs Davies was nearly in tears as she begged Clive to allow her to remain. Clive got up and went to Mrs Davies, putting a deceptively gentle arm around her shoulders.

'Now, Carol, I thought we'd agreed. You know how good I am at disciplining the slaves and you know how Master Liam relies on my assistance. He would want me to spend some time alone with this slave. It's one of the reasons I am here. You know that, don't you?'

'Yes, but –'

Caroline's eyes widened in disbelief as Clive gently turned Mrs Davies to face him.

'Carol, are you listening to me?'

With his index finger, he tilted Mrs Davies' face upwards until she had to look at him, sullenly pouting like a recalcitrant child.

'Yes,' she mumbled.

'Then be a good girl and run along. Later, perhaps . . .'

Clive touched his lips suggestively to the pout, changing it immediately to a girlish smile. Mrs Davies looked up at him adoringly as he propelled her towards the door.

'Yes, I do have a lot of things to do, Master Clive.'

'Please, call me Clive,' he said as he ushered Mrs Davies out of the door.

'I'll see you later then . . . Clive?' Mrs Davies hesitated on the threshold, her eyes yearning for his confirmation.

'Maybe and, Carol, thank you.'

Clive closed the door and leant against it momentarily, trying to dismiss the memory of an unpleasant conversation before turning back to Caroline. When he did so, he resumed his crouching position in front of her, tracing her features with a gently insistent finger.

Caroline's mind was in a turmoil. She had witnessed Clive's power over Mrs Davies, power he was now exercising over her. She didn't struggle. The ropes binding her to the chair were unnecessary. If Clive had untied her, she couldn't have moved. His very presence seemed to freeze her into stillness. She tried to think of Liam and of how much she wanted him, tried to block out Clive and what he was doing. She couldn't even seem to control her thoughts. Even when she shut her eyes she still saw Clive, felt his power.

'You are so beautiful, such a perfect slave,' he whispered.

She became aware that Clive was untying her, removing the gag from between her lips, replacing it with his warm mouth. His tongue mingled with hers, his caressing hands stroking her nipples. Caroline fought desperately to think of Liam. She wanted to pretend that it was Liam kissing and caressing her, but Clive wouldn't let her. He was so different from Liam. Unwillingly at first, her arms went around Clive's back, pressing him into her. She wanted him. She tried to tell herself that it was only gratitude. He had stopped Mrs Davies from doing what she had wanted to do to Caroline. She was only showing how grateful she was.

Clive broke the embrace, moving back from her.

'I want you, Caroline.'

Her eyes answered him, gave her consent. Clive smiled, feeling the surge of power that control always brought.

'Will you let me do what I want?'

It was a rhetorical question and they both knew it.

Caroline was totally hypnotised by those black eyes. He could do with her whatever he liked, but she nodded because it was expected of her.

Clive picked her up and carried her to the bed, all the time controlling her with his eyes. He didn't want her to move, so she didn't. Clive laid her gently on the bed and kissed her again. His mouth trailed kisses from her mouth to her breasts. Caroline felt the urgent pulsating of her clitoris as he took each of her erect nipples in turn into his mouth, sucking gently, sometimes nibbling the teats. When he wanted to be, Clive was an expert lover, able to exercise total fascination over his willing partners, male or female. Now, as his tongue travelled downwards to Caroline's slit, he knew that she was wet and ready for him, anxious for this consumation. Clive, however, enjoyed his task and did not want to be hurried. He teased Caroline with his tongue and then stood up.

'There's no rush, my darling. We have the rest of the afternoon.'

He moved away and retrieved a small bag which he had brought into the room with him. Caroline had not noticed this earlier, she had only noticed Clive. Now he returned to her and sat beside her on the bed, his eyes devouring her, giving the promise of pleasure such as she had never before experienced. He opened the bag and took out a few items.

'Give me your hands, Caroline,' he said.

Unhesitatingly, she obeyed, putting her hands together and holding them out to him. She was used to being tied now. She expected and enjoyed it.

'Not rope this time, my darling,' Clive said as he took one of her hands in his. She looked down as she realised he was putting something that felt cold and slippery over her hand. He repeated the procedure with her other hand and she realised that it was a pair

193

of black rubber mittens which now encased her hands, making it impossible for her to use her fingers effectively. Clive strapped the mittens on to her hands and she saw that they were joined together by a short length of chain. After he had buckled them tightly into place, Clive covered her mouth with his, letting Caroline taste herself on his tongue. She responded with a strength of feeling fuelled by her excitement over this unusual form of bondage, but Clive had only just started.

'I don't want you to get away from me, my darling.'

Caroline knew that she did not want to get away from him, but her bondage seemed to be exciting Clive as well as herself. She was more than happy to go along with it. She would have said so, but there was something about Clive that kept her mute. She knew he did not want her to comment or question and, acknowledging his strange power, she obeyed his unspoken command. To her surprise, Clive assisted her to stand. She stood patiently, feeling her arousal growing stronger. Experimentally, she tried to wriggle her fingers inside their rubber enclosure. The heat from her body was already causing the mittens to stick to her hands, further restricting her movements.

Clive smiled as he heard the clink of chain that denoted her movements. He said nothing, enjoying the situation as much as he knew she was. His plan was going well, even though he was becoming more interested in Caroline than he had originally intended. He knew that she was already in his power, but he was not so sure about his own position. Caroline seemed to be exercising her own power over him and that was definitely not what he had intended. Dismissing these thoughts from his mind, at least temporarily, he took out a roll of cling-film from his bag. He had only recently discovered the restrictive advantages of this particular material at an S/M party he had attended. He knew that Caroline would look delicious with the cling-film wrapped tightly around her body. Caroline stood with growing excitement as the cling-film was wrapped around her. It was a very effective material. Clive started at her shoulders and continued to her buttocks, smoothing the cling-film sensuously, moulding it to her. He could sense her arousal, smell the heat of her as he worked. When he had finished wrapping that section of her, she was unable to move any part of her that was covered with the cling-film.

It was not uncomfortable, particularly as Clive spent a considerable amount of time stroking and massaging the parts of her body that had been bound with the cling-film. It was an indescribable sensation when he squeezed her bound nipples. She wanted to cry out to Clive that she wanted him . . . needed him. Sensing this, however, he put his hand over her mouth, silencing her. She looked up at him with eyes liquid with desire. He held her gaze as, removing his hand, he ensured her continiued silence by wrapping several layers of cling-film across her mouth. Smiling gently at her, knowing and responding to her needs, he turned her onto her stomach, spread her legs wide and secured each ankle to the corresponding sides of the bed with more cling-film. Lastly, he tied a scarf over her eyes before standing at the bottom of the bed and looking at her. This is how he had envisaged her. Bound, gagged and totally helpless. He felt the exuberance of power as he realised that he could do whatever he wanted with her and she couldn't stop him. He also knew she wanted this as much as he did.

He stood watching her for a while. He would take his time. She was not in control . . . he was.

Eventually, Clive took his clothes off and lay on the bed, taking the sensually bound figure in his arms. He sensed her need, his probing fingers assured him of that. His cock was hard, as it had been during the whole course of the bondage. For a moment, he was tempted to thrust his cock in that little rosebud of a hole he had deliberately left uncovered. He wanted to explore that opening . . . make it his. He wanted to make Caroline realise that this part of her body belonged to him, to abuse as and when he chose. At that moment, revenge against Liam was far from his mind. He revelled in his power over this beautiful creature, loved the taste and feel of it. Moving slowly, he used her own juices to lubricate the entrance to her anus. He felt her slight tensing and whispered to her, 'You can refuse me nothing, Caroline. You know I can do with you whatever I like, don't you?'

She nodded, the cling-film rustled as she struggled a little, telling him that she was ready for him. She couldn't see anything, she could only feel. She wanted Clive whichever way he wanted to take her. She wanted to feel his cock in her and, if he wanted to take her anally, that was OK. She just wanted the relief her body had been craving for since Mrs Davies had tied her to the chair. She felt Clive's fingers in her vagina, knew he was lubricating those fingers for another purpose. She felt him withdraw, then felt one, two, three, maybe more, fingers being inserted into her anus. She bore down, welcoming them. She was disappointed when they were withdrawn, but then felt Clive's cock pressing for entry, which she willingly gave. Clive's expert fingers manipulated her clitoris as he moved within her anus. She wanted to scream out her pleasure, but the cling-film only allowed small moans to escape. Clive answered her with increased thrusts and more pressure on her clitoris. She knew he was approaching orgasm, tried to hold off on her own to make his more rewarding. Clive was the one who screamed out as he came, the force of his orgasm making him tangle his fingers in her hair and pull her head up with the strength of his tugging. She didn't mind, welcomed the pain in her scalp as the ignition to her own orgasm which made her buck under the weight of Clive's now inert body.

Nothing was said between them as Clive removed the cling-film, mittens and scarf. He did not need to tell her to put her hands behind her back so that he could tie her wrists. No communication was needed as he tied the scarf over her mouth, needlessly gagging her. Just an exchange of looks was the only conversation they required. Clive paused in the doorway before he went out and gazed wordlessly at Caroline. The encounter had shaken them both. Neither knew what should happen next or indeed what they wanted to happen. Clive had done what he had intended to. He had total power over Caroline. He also knew that, by her very submissiveness, she was exercising her own control over him.

Chapter Ten

By the time the day of Liam's meeting with Francis had arrived, he had decided not to meet Francis at his own house but to go instead to Beech House and meet with him there. The reason, which he found it hard to admit to himself, was that he didn't want Francis encountering Caroline. In any event, he knew that Francis would ask to see Caroline if he came to the house and there was no point, therefore, in just locking her in her room. Was he afraid of the renewal of the very obvious attraction that had existed between Francis and Caroline? Perhaps. Francis had certainly accepted the change in venue for their meeting with very bad grace. As he drove to Beech House, he frowned at the recollection of Caroline's demeanour since she had been pierced. When he had returned from his business meeting, she had seemed very subdued, although pleased to see him. Things had been going well between them and Liam was beginning to think he had found everything he had ever wanted. Caroline, too, seemed resigned to her position as his slave and sometimes almost seemed to enjoy it. There was something, though, that she wasn't telling him. When he asked her what the problem was, she just shook her head. Liam thought with concern over how she had been when she'd realised he was going to be away for the whole day and would not return until that night. He remembered how she had begged and pleaded with him not to leave her.

'Please don't leave me, Liam, take me with you!'

'Darling, I can't,' Liam had answered. He hadn't told her where he was going and had no intention of doing so. 'I have important business to conduct and you are too much of a distraction,' he'd said to her, lifting her chin with his finger. 'And not only to me.'

Caroline had ignored the implied compliment and shook her head, dislodging Liam's finger.

'I promise I'll be very good. I won't make a sound. Please, Liam, I don't want you to go without me!'

She had been so insistent that he had become angry with her.

'You're my slave and you will do as you're told! As I've already said, I have an important meeting and I do not want to be worried about you, wondering whether you're bored and whether I can trust you. Please be sensible. One day I'll be able to take you with me, but not yet. Caroline, if you persist, you will make me very angry!' he'd warned.

She had apologised then and had seemed to be a bit more reconciled to the situation, but she still tried to plead with him.

'Liam, don't go! I must tell you something! Please Liam!'

Liam was impatient to be on his way. He hated scenes. Mrs Davies knocked at the door just then and when she came in, Caroline had reacted even more strongly.

'Don't leave me with her and Clive, please!' she'd pleaded.

'Mrs Davies, would you come and take charge of Caroline for me, please. She seems to have become rather difficult and I've got to be on my way. I'm late already!'

'It will be my pleasure, Master,' Mrs Davies had said, and grabbed the struggling Caroline.

'Liam, please listen to me! I must tell you – !' Caroline had protested but Mrs Davies' hand had clamped over her mouth.

'And I thought that this slave was well behaved! You leave her to me, Master Liam, I'll take very good care of her while you're gone!' she assured him.

'Thank you, Mrs Davies, I know I can trust you. I don't know what's the matter with her. I won't be home until late tonight and I give you a free hand to teach her some discipline, which she obviously needs.'

'Yes, Master. I hope your meeting goes well.'

Thanks to Mrs Davies, Liam had eventually managed to get away. Looking back as the car moved down the driveway, he saw a resigned-looking Caroline, held firmly in Mrs Davies' iron grip, her mouth still gagged by the housekeeper's unyielding hand. Shaking his head, he turned back in his seat and considered the meeting ahead. Francis had invited him to lunch and then dinner, so they could have a good long discussion. Liam knew that he would not give Francis what he wanted but, after this morning's hassle, he wondered if he was doing the right thing. He had a lot of business interests, very important interests, which needed his constant attention. He did not relish the prospect of protracted battles with Caroline every time he had to go out.

He put his head back against the seat and closed his eyes as the car, driven by his chauffeur, sped smoothly through the country lanes. He knew Mrs Davies could handle her and he hoped to find her in a mellower mood when he returned. She had kept saying she wanted to tell him something but had seemed to find it difficult to say what. She'd appeared intimidated by Mrs Davies, but she did seem to be somewhat fanciful on occasion. Mrs Davies was one of the most devoted servants he had ever had. She had proved invaluable in the training of his slaves and in her discretion. He knew he could safely leave Mrs Davies to handle Caroline.

Caroline struggled in Mrs Davies' unrelenting grip as Liam's car drove away. When the car had turned a corner in the drive and was out of sight, Mrs Davies dragged Caroline back into the house, meeting Clive as she did so. Caroline's eyes widened as she saw him. She hadn't wanted this. She hadn't told Liam about her most recent encounter with Clive; she hadn't even evaluated it in her own mind because she would not allow herself to think about it too much. It was another addition to the equation that she knew she couldn't handle. Now, face to face with Clive, she had no choice but to think about it. She stared into those very black eyes, so deeply disturbing. Her body responded to him, wanting him. Observing her nakedness, his eyes acknowledged her arousal, but also apologised to her and she understood why as, with a quietly spoken 'Let me take her' to Mrs Davies, possession of her was transferred to the man she had hoped to avoid. It was Clive's hand pressed over her mouth, Clive's iron-hard grip, that still managed to be a caress, holding her arms. Caroline could feel her arousal growing. Clive's grip tightened, telling her that he did not want Mrs Davies to guess that they meant more to each other than either of them had ever intended.

'You don't understand, Master ... Clive. The slut was trying to tell the Master about –' Mrs Davies broke off, well aware that Clive knew nothing about her treatment of Caroline.

'About?' Clive's eyebrows rose, emphasising the question.

Mrs Davies did not seem inclined to respond. Clive let his arm slide up to Caroline's breasts.

'I am sure you have a lot to do, Carol. I'll take over the responsibility for the slave for a couple of hours, then you can have her this afternoon.'

Mrs Davies looked as though she was going to argue. Clive smiled at her.

'Don't forget that we have to spend some time together.'

The argumentative look was replaced with an expression that could only be regarded as fawning.

'Of course ... Clive. I do have some things that need doing this morning. I'd be grateful if you would look after her for me.'

Caroline watched Mrs Davies walk towards the kitchen feeling concern and a definite surge of excitement. She was concerned because she did not want her feelings for Clive to grow. She cared too much for Liam. If she had been able to, she would have told Liam about Clive and the inexplicably strong feelings she had for him, feelings that had returned with a startling force as she stared into those hypnotic eyes of his. Feelings that were exacerbated as Clive's hands roamed across her breasts and down to her clitoris. Clive turned her around so that she was facing him and his mouth covered hers. She responded to the kiss with an urgency that spoke of her body's desire for satisfaction. She felt his lips on her neck and a surge of excitement that held no fear as she heard the words he whispered against her throat:

'I want to own you. I want to possess you. We're going to my room and I'm going to teach you all about control. I'm going to show you that I do have total control over you!'

Clive closed and locked the door of his room behind them. He could sense Caroline's confusion, no less intense than his own. They had walked to his room as equals, even though Caroline was aware that the fingers curled around her own as they walked hand-in-hand could so easily become bands of steel, should she try to escape. She had no desire to escape from Clive, overwhelmed yet again by the fascination he held for her. Clive felt an incredible excitement, walking with this gorgeous woman whom he knew that he could use and abuse as he chose. He wanted to prove this to her.

Caroline took in the bareness of Clive's room. It was comfortable but everything in it was utilitarian and impersonal. There were no photographs or ornaments, nothing that revealed the guest's personality. Maybe that was deliberate, she told herself. Clive did not need to be surrounded by the little knick-knacks that to other people were comforts but to Clive were unnecessary detractions.

Caroline felt herself being gently yet insistently pushed on to the bed by hands that indicated she should lie down. She did so, wondering what was to come and how Clive intended to demonstrate his control over her. She felt no fear, only an awareness of her body's stimulation. She closed her eyes and felt gentle hands exploring her as if she was a treasured possession. She felt her nipples harden as fingers stroked her clitoris into greater awareness. She felt a tongue swirling around her erect nipples before starting its journey down her body towards her pulsating bud. Her body strained to feel that tongue pushing against her slit and gaining entry. Instead she felt the tongue pause just before it reached that desired area. She was aware of a swift movement and a firm mouth covering hers and tongues intermingling while hands kneaded breasts. She thought she heard a whispered 'Caroline' but perhaps she was mistaken. On opening her eyes, she saw Clive staring at her.

Was it confusion and uncertainty that she saw in his eyes? She couldn't be sure. Suddenly his eyes seemed to harden and he stood away from her.

'Sit up.' It was a barked command.

Caroline sat up, looking wonderingly at Clive.

'Hands behind your back.'

Caroline did as she was told, feeling rope being tied tightly around her crossed wrists. Clive moved down the bed. Just a look was enough to tell her to place her ankles together. She watched as Clive tied them, knotting the rope securely. He moved to a table and picked up a handkerchief. Wadding it up as he returned to her, his eyes commanded her to open her mouth. When she did so the handkerchief was pushed between her teeth and secured there by rope tied around her head. Efficiently gagged, she knew that she could only manage small ineffectual sounds through the cloth.

'Kneel up,' was the next order.

She looked at Clive helplessly, trying to indicate with her eyes that, bound as she was, this was going to be very difficult. Clive responded by coming close to her and tilting her chin, making her look into his eyes.

'That was not a request. That was an order,' he said.

With some difficulty, Caroline bent her knees and managed to push herself upwards, enabling her to swing her legs around and underneath her. Clive nodded his approval and then went to a drawer in the table. Opening it, he extracted a thin black riding crop. He displayed how flexible this was by bending it as he moved back to Caroline.

'Push your tits out.'

Caroline had not taken her eyes off the riding crop and could only shake her head dumbly. She felt his hand in her hair, pulling her head backwards.

'Listen, you stupid girl. I want you to do this for me. I thought you wanted to obey me.'

Wordlessly, Caroline looked at him, expressing with her eyes that that was indeed true.

'Then do as I say. Now!'

Caroline closed her eyes and pushed her chest out fearfully, knowing she was exposing her tender breasts to punishment but also knowing she wanted to do this because Clive expected it of her. She wanted to please him more than she feared the pain.

'That's better. That's my good girl,' Clive said.

Positioning himself in front of Caroline, he aimed the crop at her left breast, striking firmly. The pain was sharp, making Caroline moan and shrink away, trying to shield her breasts.

'Sit up!'

Caroline forced herself to resume her earlier position. This time, the crop found her right nipple. She struggled to keep her position, her eyes stinging with tears. She also felt pride. She had done what he wanted. She would try not to flinch away again, no matter what the provocation.

Clive looked at her silently for a few minutes. Looked at this beautiful creature, breasts out-thrust, waiting to receive whatever punishment he decided to administer . . . because he wanted it. He took a deep breath of satisfaction. Clive aimed the riding crop again and again, laying an intricate interlacing network of thin marks across her breasts. Sometimes he played with her nipples before he struck them, using the end of the crop. Sometimes, as a reward he fingered her slit, wet with her juices, until they were both enjoying the game as much as each other. Caroline's pride in bearing with increasing stoicism each blow, seemed to make the pain not only bearable but increasingly pleasurable.

Clive eventually threw down the crop, staring for long moments at the result of his handiwork, proud of the red weals criss-crossing Caroline's breasts, very proud of her for her endurance because it was his wish.

Gently, he eased her downwards, straightening her legs until she lay flat on the bed. He removed his clothes, keeping his eyes on her, exchanging glances that spoke of their mutual need. Lying down on top of her, gently stroking her abused breasts, Clive thought about removing the gag so that he could kiss her. He didn't because he liked to see her this way, tied and gagged, awaiting whatever he chose to do. The feeling of his power over her flooded through him with such intensity that he knew that this was right for him, this was where he belonged. There was no confusion about his sexuality now. At this moment, he loved Caroline, but he knew that the identity of the partner didn't matter. The power did. All he wanted and needed was the ability to exercise that power – male or female, the gender of the submissive not really important. He felt grateful to Caroline, grateful that she had proved this to him beyond doubt.

Because he owed her this debt of gratitude, with a great deal of consideration and care, he gave her the satisfaction he knew she craved.

Mrs Davies eyed them both suspiciously, as a still bound and gagged Caroline, eyes sleepy with satisfied desire, was handed over to her.

'I hope you disciplined the slut, Master Clive.'

'Oh, yes, Mrs Davies. I don't think she'll give you any further trouble.'

Clive was about to leave, but was stopped by a hand on his arm. Looking down with unfeigned disbelief at the hand on his arm, Clive looked sternly at the perpetrator, until Mrs Davies dropped her eyes with embarrassment, quickly removing the offending member.

'I'm sorry, Clive,' she saw his expression, '– Master Clive. I was just wondering whether we could spend some time . . .'

Clive was smoothness itself. 'Of course, Carol, but not right now. I have many things that require my attention and you of course have to look after the slave. Perhaps later.'

'Of course, Master Clive. I have to go out later on. Perhaps when the Master returns . . .'

'We'll see. I'm sure we can arrange something, Carol. Now, if you'll excuse me . . .'

Clive turned and left the two women, both watching him go with very mixed emotions, particularly Caroline. She forced her thoughts away from Clive and back to the immediate prospect of dealing with the housekeeper. She had witnessed Clive's rejection of Mrs Davies, something for which she felt she might have to pay later.

Mrs Davies had grasped Caroline's arm with a tight and painful grip, marching her up the stairs and into her own room without saying a word. As soon as they got into the room, Caroline was untied and thrown on to the bed. Caroline had been thinking furiously as she was propelled along and had come up with what she hoped was a satisfactory story to get Mrs Davies very much on her side. As soon as her gag had been removed she took her chance.

'Mistress, please listen to me,' Caroline begged as she struggled into a sitting position on the bed. 'I wasn't going to tell Liam about you and me, truly I wasn't.'

Caroline thought that it would be sensible to deal with this first, as she guessed that Mrs Davies was still angry about what she had thought – rightly – that Caroline was going to tell Liam. She had to use Clive's rejection of Mrs Davies for her own purposes, manipulating Mrs Davies into wanting to keep Caroline all to herself. She hoped in this way to veer Mrs Davies away from thoughts about what Caroline had intended to tell Liam, replacing that with excitement at the afternoon's prospects. Caroline knew that she would have to accept whatever Mrs Davies wanted to do to her. Anything, however, was preferable to incurring this woman's wrath further.

Mrs Davies was standing and watching her with her arms crossed. As she seemed more amenable to listening, Caroline looked at her pleadingly.

'Why would I tell Liam? I haven't told him so far, you know I haven't. I don't want him to stop us from being together, Mistress, I couldn't stand that!'

Mrs Davies was watching her intently, inviting her to carry on. Caroline swallowed and continued.

'You do see, don't you, Mistress, that if I had said anything to Liam, he would have stopped us being together and he would be jealous of the fun that we have and how we feel about each other. I wouldn't want that, please believe me, Mistress, please! I wouldn't want anyone else to stop us either.'

She allowed herself to look innocently at Mrs Davies.

'Anyone else? Who are you talking about, girl?'

Caroline allowed her eyes to widen in surprise.

'I thought you knew, Mistress. Master Clive wants me whenever the Master isn't here. He would like to keep me all to himself. He's told me so. You've seen how he is with me. That's why . . .'

Caroline let her voice trail off suggestively. She knew that Mrs Davies' imagination would supply the rest, knew that Mrs Davies would put her own rejections down to the fact that Clive wanted Caroline.

The silence seemed to be prolonged. Caroline watched the differing emotions chasing across Mrs Davies' features, chief among them the knowledge that what she had been told might indeed be the truth, that the reason for her rejection by Clive might be laid at another's door. Caroline was aware of her heart pounding in her chest as she waited for Mrs Davies to show some sign that she believed her. She had to succeed, otherwise she did not want to think about the possible consequences. If Mrs Davies believed her now, she could beg for her protection from Clive by playing on her jealousy. Caroline knew that Clive was dangerous. He was dangerous to her peace of mind and to her burgeoning relationship with Liam. She resolved that, with Mrs Davies' help, she would do everything she could to avoid being alone with Clive. She knew that she would have to gather her courage and talk to Liam about both of her tormentors . . . and soon.

'Are you telling me the truth?' Mrs Davies eventually asked. 'What were you going to say to the Master?'

Caroline threw herself before the unbending figure and clasped her around the knees.

'I wanted to tell him about Clive. How Clive keeps intervening when you are disciplining me, Mistress. You are only doing what the Master wants, after all, but he hasn't given Clive permission to come between us! Oh, Mistress, I want to serve you in any way that I can!'

Caroline hoped that Mrs Davies wouldn't analyse too closely what she had just been told. She was playing on Mrs Davies' possessiveness of Caroline that had been made apparent on previous occasions.

Mrs Davies looked down at the penitent kneeling before her. She wanted to believe Caroline, needed to believe her, but she wanted something else first.

'Ask me properly, then!'

Weak with relief, Caroline found it easy to prostrate herself on the floor at Mrs Davies' feet.

'Please, Mistress, please let me serve you.'

'You know that means I shall do anything with you that I want?'

'Yes, Mistress, I do. I welcome it!'

'Kiss my shoe,' she ordered Caroline as she extended one foot in front of her.

With only a fractional amount of hesitation, Caroline obeyed and kiseed the shiny tip of the proffered shoe. When she had done so, she felt Mrs Davies raising her and then enfolding her in a restrictive embrace.

'Oh, my darling, we will have such fun.' Her mouth set in a grim line. 'I'll just slip downstairs and tell Mr Clvie that we shall not be needing him, that I will be responsible for you in the Master's absence.' She allowed herself a smile, denoting her satisfaction. 'I'd better just tie you up first, though, just to make sure.'

Caroline sat in the chair without offering any resistance, welcoming the feel of the ropes as Mrs Davies tied her securely into it. As she watched her jailer going out, locking the door behind her, Caroline felt another huge wave of relief, on the heels of which came a feeling of trepidation as she contemplated what might lie ahead. At least Clive wouldn't be a problem, not an immediate one anyway. She would be thankful for that.

Clive was furious when he spoke with Mrs Davies.

'What do you mean, you want her for yourself?'

'It's quite simple, Master Clive. The Master has left her in my care and I am to look after her, now and in the future. I've been here a long time, Master Clive, and I intend to remain. I want the slave to be in my debt, so she won't tell the Master anything bad about me.'

'What about me?' demanded Clive.

Mrs Davies eyed him shrewdly.

'You and the Master are good friends, but he was upset with you once before over his new slave and he won't be prepared to listen to anything bad you have to say about her or me. He needs me here and, the plain truth of the matter is, he doesn't need you! I know that you've been deleting the tapes that would show what you have been up to. I always make duplicate copies of the tapes, Master Clive, particularly from the slave's room . . . and yours of course.'

Clive looked at Mrs Davies. She wasn't bluffing. Always the pragmatist, Clive acknowledged that he was – on this occasion – the loser. He would let Mrs Davies have her triumph, but Clive determined that it would be a transient one. He had never liked to lose.

'As you say, Mrs Davies. The Master did leave her in your care.'

Clive forced himself to put a gentle hand on her shoulder.

'Perhaps I've been wrong about not making time for us, Carol. I'd still like us to spend some time together. Please bear that in mind.'

She stepped away, but looked at him uncertainly. She turned and opened the door. Looking back at Clive, she wondered why her revenge didn't seem to be as sweet any more.

Mrs Davies entered the room where Caroline was waiting with equal uncertainty for her. Her eyes widened as she saw what Mrs Davies had in her hand; a collection of items, foremost of which, Caroline saw, was a pair of plastic pants. The sight of them immediately recalled the humiliation that she had experienced such a short time ago. She was in no hurry to repeat her earlier ordeal and the guilty pleasure she'd experienced when she had finally given in to her bladder's urging. It was amazing the way in which the mind called up images. Caroline well remembered the only other time she had wet her knickers, when she had been six years old. Old guilts die hard, she had ruefully reflected.

Mrs Davies laid the items on a table and went over to Caroline. She had decided not to dwell upon her interview with Clive until later, but to enjoy the rest of the afternoon. Bending down, she untied the ropes that bound Caroline to the chair and helped her over to the bed.

'You have no need to worry about Master Clive,' she informed Caroline as she indicated that she should lie on the bed. 'I have told him that the Master left you in my care and that I would carry out my duty and look after you.'

Caroline felt a wave of relief and then returned her mind to the immediate present as she watched Mrs Davies pick up a folded nappy and shake out its folds as she sat on the bed.

'Mummy is going to take baby out for a little walk in the grounds and we must get ready.'

Caroline bit her lip as the nappy was folded on to her. Mrs Davies pinned it firmly into place with a large pin and then told her to lift herself again while she pulled on the plastic pants. When she had finished, she stood back and shook her finger at Caroline warningly.

'Let's hope we don't have a repeat performance from last time. You know what will happen if we do, don't you.'

'Yes, Mistress.'

'Come now, you don't have to call me Mistress today, you can call me Mummy.'

'She looked expectantly at Caorline.

'Yes, Mummy.'

Caroline had only to look into eyes that bore the light of fanaticism to know the pointlessness of showing any reluctance to play a full part in the game. She knew that, to protect herself, it was the only thing she could do.

Caroline was ordered to sit up and Mrs Davies attached a modified version of the reins that were used on small babies, only these were definitely for restraining and controlling adults. It was a harness made of thick black leather which strapped around the body and under the arms, leaving long lengths of strap for restraining purposes when sitting in a chair or to be used as leading reins. The harness was fitted to the upper part of Caroline's body and strapped tightly into place. Caroline felt the familiar surge which any kind of bondage engendered in her, making her oddly grateful for the nappy folded tightly around her sex as she felt her juices begin to flow. If Mrs Davies saw any sign of that, she might be punished. Caroline was uncertain as to whether she feared or welcomed that prospect. Her hardening nipples made the latter more likely.

Mrs Davies tied Caroline's wrists together behind her back and pulled the straps of the harness around her arms, still leaving enough for her to use as reins. She then produced the larger version of a baby's dummy, which Caroline had been forced to wear before and which was now pushed into her mouth before being strapped tightly behind her head. Caroline's humiliation was complete and she tried to ignore the building excitement. She caught a glimpse of herself in the mirror and the sight of the straps confining her limbs did nothing for her peace of mind. The teat of the oversized dummy filled her mouth completely, the tightly buckled strap allowed for no possibility of dislodgement. Caroline knew that she was enjoying her situation. Now devoid of fear concerning Clive's participation, she gave herself up to the pleasurable pulsing of her clitoris, trapped inside the terrycloth folds of the nappy. She discovered that by rocking herself slightly in the chair, she could massage her clitoris and, by pulling against the tightness of her bonds, she knew it would be possible to bring herself off.

Mrs Davies was also visibly excited by her adult baby. Caroline could see the large nipples of her 'mummy's' ample bosom straining against her blouse, making Caroline want to take them in her mouth and suck them hard.

Picking up the reins, Mrs Davies forced Caroline to her feet and walked her to the door which she unlocked. As they went downstairs, Caroline thought how quiet the house was and how she missed Liam – not just, she realised, because of her current helpless predicament, but because she was beginning to care for him more and more, as she believed he cared for her. What would he do if he knew what she was having to undergo? Or did he indeed know? Had Mrs Davies been given a free hand in her treatment of Caroline? For the moment, these questions had to remain unanswered, but Caroline knew that she would have to talk openly to Liam as soon as he came home, so as to find out exactly what her position was as regards the other members of the household.

They went out of the front door. It was, fortunately for Caroline's naked state, a very pleasant, warm day, which held the promise of a hot summer. Despite her enforced babyhood, Caroline sniffed appreciatively at the scent of the flowers from the profusion that grew on the lawns directly in front of the house. Mrs Davies did not allow her much time to enjoy the view as she led her around the back of the house and they entered an area of dense shrubbery that opened out into woodland, thick with trees, flush with their spring finery. If her situation had been different, Caroline knew she would have appreciated being among those beautiful trees; trees that leant so closely inwards on the path they traversed that she felt leaves brushing her nipples, making them quiver and stand erect. Twigs crunched under her bare feet as she walked.

Liam's house was in a very isolated part of the country, well away from the city and not even close to a small town or village. There were none of the usual noises associated with people living their busy lives, just birds piping their greetings to one another, enjoying the beauty of the day. Caroline resigned herself to suffering whatever humiliations might lie ahead and looked forward with desperate eagerness to Liam's return that night.

The journey was conducted in silence. The dummy in Caroline's mouth had been designed for naughty adult babies and was a very effective gag. Mrs Davies seemed, for the moment, disinclined to say anything, seemingly content to lead her charge along the path. Caroline wondered if she had an object in view or if this was merely an exercise for her which would end with their return to the house. Somehow, she didn't think so.

Her thoughts were confirmed as they entered a clearing and Mrs Davies pulled on the reins, indicating Caroline should stop. Obediently, Caroline stood still and looked around her. The clearing was light and airy, as the trees were thinner here, allowing plenty of light and sunshine to penetrate. Mrs Davies led her to a large tree and, dropping the reins, used them to strap around her ankles before producing some long lengths of rope with which she tied Caroline to the tree, securing her at shoulder, waist and knee level. Caroline made protesting noises, hoping her dummy gag would be removed. Mrs Davies, understanding, smiled and shook her head.

'Baby must be patient,' and then, more sternly, 'You haven't wet your nappy, have you?'

Caroline shook her head furiously. She was going to try very hard not to let that happen again.

'Good girl. Now, let Mummy show you some of the delightful things that can be found here.'

As she spoke, she pulled a pair of thick gloves from her pocket and drew them on. Looking around, she saw what she wanted and stooped down with her back to Caroline. When she straightened she had a bunch of some sort of plant in her hand, which she took triumphantly over to the helpless Caroline.

'Look what Mummy's got for you,' she said delightedly and, when Caroline recognised the plants, she moaned desperately into the dummy. Mrs Davies held a bunch of nettles in her gloved hand. Caroline's eyes widened as Mrs Davies brushed the nettles gently across her breasts, lovingly caressing each of the defenceless nipples. Then, with a cruel smile, Mrs Davies raised her arm before bringing it down with a violently swinging movement. As the stinging plants were used to whip her breasts, Caroline struggled helplessly against the ropes that bound her, moaning into the dummy as she was stung repeatedly. Her tender and abused nipples had to suffer this treatment for several minutes until Mrs Davies seemed to have had enough and threw them down.

Caroline's breasts, already sore and abused from her encounter with Clive, now felt as if they radiated heat. She was unprepared for Mrs Davies picking some more plants and returning to her task, looking at her and smiling strangely. Mrs Davies ran her finger over the tight ropes that bound Caroline to the tree. She opened her hand and showed Caroline the dock leaves she held before pressing herself up against her captive, who moaned at the contact with her sore nipples. Mrs Davies moved back slightly and, spreading her hands which were now both holding dock leaves, she gently massaged the red and tender-looking flesh.

Caroline's whimpers of pain quickly became moans of excitement as the gently sensual motion of the dock leaves on her breasts produced relief and pleasure. Her aroused and abused body demanded attention as Mrs Davies unstrapped the dummy, thrusting it into the pocket of her dress and replacing it with her mouth and tongue. Caroline's highly charged state accepted this welcome intrusion as she opened her mouth to accommodate Mrs Davies' tongue, returning the sensual pressure with her own.

It didn't matter to Caroline that this was Mrs Davies. Her body demanded satisfaction, whoever gave it. The hands massaging her tortured breasts became more insistent. The stroking fingers, divested of the dock leaves, squeezed her nipples, the pain this occasioned being welcome to Caroline, as she urged her body towards Mrs Davies, fighting the ropes that bound her in order to get closer. It was this restrictive pressure on her limbs that triggered her orgasm, the strength of which made her buck against the bindings. The feeling of the ropes cutting into her flesh as she struggled against them made her orgasm go on and on, until she thought it would never stop.

At last, however, Caroline sagged against the tree, the ropes the only thing that forced her to remain upright, stopping her collapsing on to the ground. Mrs Davies had watched her as she threshed about in the throes of her orgasm, keeping her tongue in Caroline's mouth to prevent her crying out. Caroline's screams of pleasure came out only as muffled cries. Mrs Davies withdrew her tongue from Caroline's mouth as she felt the girl relaxing from the strength of her orgasm. Mrs Davies' own excitement was intense. She forced Caroline's head up by getting a firm grip on her hair and pulling. When Caroline was looking at her, with eyes sleepy with exhaustion, Mrs Davies smiled and put her hand over Caroline's mouth.

'Baby was making an awful noise,' she said as she withdrew a small but vicious black leather whip from where she had thrust it into the back of her belt.

Mrs Davies raised the whip and brought it down on Caroline's breasts, already tender from being beaten with the nettles.

'Naughty, naughty baby!' Mrs Davies crooned as she continued to whip her, moving her action further down to strike her across her stomach and thighs, laying a network of red lines which matched those on her breasts. She was able to apply considerable force in spite of retaining one hand over Caroline's mouth. Caroline could not believe how her sex was yet again stimulated by the whipping, how her body was responding to this treatment.

At last, the whipping was over and Mrs Davies removed the hand that covered Caroline's mouth and untied her from the tree. She was obviously very excited, her breath coming quickly, making her large breasts heave as she helped her prisoner over to a fallen log. Caroline's hands were still tied. Mrs Davies sat on the log and pulled Caroline on to her lap, crooning gently.

'There's my little girl. Bad girls have to be taught to behave, don't they?' She stared hard at Caroline, who nodded her head. 'Your poor little breasts, the nipples look so sore. Shall Mummy kiss them better?'

Again, Caroline nodded to her enquiring look, unable to prevent her nipples from hardening again. Mrs Davies cradled her in her arms like the little baby she was supposed to be and bent her head. When she first put her lips on one of Caroline's nipples, Caroline quivered with the pleasurable sensations occasioned in her. Mrs Davies undid the buttons of her blouse revealing her own naked breasts.

'Baby must be hungry,' she said as she pressed Caroline's head in towards her so that she was forced to take one of the large nipples into her mouth. 'That's it, suck it like a good baby.'

Caroline needed no further encouragement and eagerly sucked at Mrs Davies' nipples, feeling the juices of her sex trapped within the confines of the nappy and plastic pants. Mrs Davies kept up her gentle crooning but she was becoming more and more excited. When Caroline grazed a nipple with her teeth, however, Mrs Davies became taut with anger.

'Baby mustn't bite Mummy. Now she must be spanked!'

Forcing the dummy back into Caroline's mouth, she strapped it behind her head even more tightly than she had earlier, before turning her over and putting her across her lap. Pulling down the plastic pants and nappy, she brought her hand down firmly on Caroline's bottom, again and again, making Caroline's buttocks glow with the severity of the spanking. Notwithstanding this treatment, or perhaps because of it, Caroline was fast approaching her second orgasm.

As she was spanking Caroline, Mrs Davies became increasingly excited, her breath coming in loud gasps, spittle dribbling from her mouth, until she suddenly thrust Caroline on to her stomach on the log. Caroline, almost incoherent with her own sexual excitement, was only dimly aware of the scratchiness of the bark on her tender flesh and exposed pubis. Using the rope with which she had previously bound her to the tree, Mrs Davies tied Caroline to the log, tying the rope around her arms and legs. Egged on by her pulsating and demanding sex, she picked up the whip and lashed Caroline's buttocks mercilessly, the redness of the bound girl's helpless buttocks fuelling the urgency of the beating.

Somewhere during this beating, Caroline lost control and again her body bucked against the restraining ropes as she climaxed. As before, the tightly tied ropes played a large part in the strength of her orgasm. No matter how hard she twisted and turned, she could not free herself, nor indeed did she want to. Revelling in her helplessness, Caroline gave herself up to the sheer pleasure that enwrapped her, more tightly than her bonds, glad of the dummy that gagged her screams of pleasure.

Suddenly, Mrs Davies flung herself on the ground, lying with her back to the log on which Caroline was bound. She pulled up her skirt and inserted her hand between the waistband of the skirt and her pants, eager fingers pushing the pants down until she could touch the hard, pulsating button wet with her juices. It only needed some slight massaging before she felt herself caught in the waves of an orgasm that had been building since she had put the nappy on Caroline. As she climaxed, she turned and mounted the log and, dragging down the dummy, she forced Caroline to suck her juices, sending fresh orgasmic waves through her as she pressed the willing girl's head against her cunt.

Afterwards, she lay inert for a long time. Caroline was glad of the respite, feeling sexually replete. She had been happy to suck Mrs Davies off, as she had, albeit unwittingly given Caroline a great deal of pleasure.

When Mrs Davies recovered, she seemed like a different person. She unstrapped the dummy and put it into her pocket. She untied Caroline and forced her to stand up, holding her arm in a cruel grip.

'We're going back to the house,' she said as she jerked on the reins.

She stood behind Caroline, checked that her wrists were still securely tied and tightened the straps around her arms. Then she put one arm around her and pinched her nipples, twisting them viciously, muffling her cries of pain with the hand that she put over her mouth.

'I have to go out this afternoon, so you'd better behave yourself. I will make sure you are well secured before I go, but I don't want you to think that you're going to have an easy time of it until the Master comes back. I've been nice to you so far, but you've been behaving very badly with your struggling. I'm afraid I'm going to have to punish you when I get back!'

This prospect obviously excited Mrs Davies, who was already planning how she would tie Caroline and how much she would enjoy disciplining her.

Caroline felt a hard push between her shoulder blades, which nearly sent her sprawling to the ground.

'Now, get going! I don't want any noise from you! Save your breath for later on, you're going to need it!'

Chapter Eleven

Francis looked at his reflection in the mirror and was pleased with what he saw. Once again, he assured himself, the image that looked back at him wore its usual assertive and confident appearance. The past few days had been terrible for him. For the first time, he had gambled and lost. He knew that there was a risk that Liam would be difficult about returning Caroline to him, but he had not appreciated that in Liam he had a worthy opponent. Liam had agreed to this meeting, also telephoning and re-arranging the meeting to Beech House. Francis chuckled. It was patently obvious he didn't want him to ask to see Caroline and then have to produce her.

Thoughts of Caroline made him frown. Was she happy? Did he really care anyway? Yes, he did care. He had felt something different for Caroline and had felt the inevitability of the offer that Liam made for her and of his acceptance. Francis was nothing if not honest with himself and he knew that part of the problem was that he had been thwarted in his desire to keep this slave with him. He had cared for her and he felt it could have grown into something deeper, especially as he became aware of her growing enjoyment of bondage and thought as to how that might develop. Now she belonged to someone else. He wasn't happy about that, but something strange was happening at Beech House that he couldn't explain. It was, however, a strangeness he was enjoying.

Ever since he had had such savage sex with Lynne, she had seemed to change toward him, subtly at first, but lately she had become increasingly demonstrative and kinder. That seemed a strange choice of words, but kindness had never been a strong personality trait with Lynne. Being a dominatrix had somehow seemed to take over her whole outlook on life. She was strong and assertive in business as well as in the training of her slaves. Since that night when he had been so brutal with her, she had taken to knocking on his bedroom door at night and asking if she could sleep with him. He had given his permission, at first because he was puzzled by her behaviour, but increasingly because he had discovered that he enjoyed being with her, whether they slept or made love. They had always enjoyed great sex, neither making demands on the other but each taking the lead naturally, but now Lynne seemed to want him to take the strong role all the time, to show her enjoyment as he pinned her down on the bed.

As he strolled into the study to await Liam's arrival, he thought of last night and its contribution toward his feeling of well-being this morning.

Lynne had dined with him and had dismissed the staff for the evening, preferring to serve him herself. She came down to dinner wearing a very short, black pvc dress with matching elbow-length gloves. Her shapely legs were encased in sheer, glossy tights and were well set off by her four-inch high-heeled black patent shoes. Her hair had been brushed until it shone and lay across her shoulders, catching the reflected gleam of the cadelabra that had been placed at the centre of the table.

Francis had looked at her appreciatively and had

run his hands up beneath her skirt, encountering the pvc panties she wore.

'You look wonderful, my dear,' Francis said, and she knew he meant the compliment.

'You've been a little down lately. I thought tonight we could have a quiet dinner and then . . .'

'And then?' He raised his eyebrows questioningly.

Lynne wet her lips as he watched and put her hand on his trousers, feeling his erection with pleasure.

'Then it's up to you. Francis, the other night . . .'

'I'm sorry about that. I don't –' he started.

'Ssh.' She covered his mouth fleetingly with her own. 'Don't apologise. Francis, you've been responsible for sending some very confusing feelings through me. At first I was angry with you. I wouldn't let myself enjoy what was happening. I was a dominatrix and I didn't want to be dominated like that! When I thought about it afterwards, relived it several times in my mind, I realised that I had felt a great deal of pleasure. Being the strong, dominant one was what I thought I'd always wanted. I enjoyed beating the slaves, tying them up, humiliating them, but perhaps a part of me envied them too.'

'Envied?'

'Submissives have abdicated their responsibility. They can relax and enjoy what is happening to them, because they don't have any choice. You made me re-evaluate myself. Do I really enjoy being dominant? I can say, with truth, that, yes I do, but perhaps not always. There's a part of me that wants something else, that wants to be treated as you treated me, receiving what I'd only ever given out before, and I liked it.'

She sat down beside him and held his hands.

'Francis, I don't know whether this is a passing thing or whether it can work, but I'd like to try. Since

Caroline left, I've seen how it has affected you. I've felt your pain. I've felt, for the first time, an unselfish desire to make you forget, at least for a while, that pain.'

'What are you saying to me?'

'I'm saying that I'd like to try being your submissive. I'm not sure that it'll last long, I don't know how I'll feel. Perhaps the other night was a one-off, but you remember when we played that game afterwards, pretended to re-live that scene and found we enjoyed it? Well, I'd like to experiment further. I don't want you to dominate me like we do the slaves. I don't want to be humiliated. I don't think I'll ever want to go down that road, but I want to have sex with you when you've tied me up. Sometimes I want you to be rough with me, and, most of all, I want us both to enjoy it.'

She reached down and kissed him and, in answer, he slid his hands back up her legs and felt the wetness of her cunt by probing beneath the pvc panties.

'Later,' she laughed, moving away. 'Dinner first.'

She sat on his lap and fed him, as his fingers probed her cunt and her anus.

'I think you'd look beautiful with your nipples clamped,' Francis told her as he opened his mouth to accept another delicious morsel of the impressive dinner.

'You can do whatever you want with me, my darling,' she replied.

After dinner, they went to Francis' bedroom and he stripped her clothes gently from her, marvelling as he always did at the perfection of her body. He removed her panties and sniffed appreciatively at the smell of her sex before throwing them on the floor. He held her down on the bed and looked at her.

'Are you sure this is what you want?' he asked.

225

'No,' she answered with a wry smile, 'but I would like to find out if it is.'

Francis saw the light of honesty shining from her eyes and knew that, even though she had been prompted to do this with a genuine desire to make him feel better, she also had a real curiosity to try to learn the truth of her own desires.

'All right, my darling, let's see what happens and, whatever does, thank you.'

She gave him an answering smile and he bent down and kissed her, pushing his tongue, at first gently and then insistently, into her mouth. She was still pinned down, otherwise she would have wrapped her arms around him, but that was something neither of them wanted. He released her mouth and sucked at her nipples, taking pleasure in the speed with which they responded to him.

'Oh, Francis,' she whispered, but he wanted total control of her and put one hand over her mouth. Her eyes opened wide at that before she moved with pleasure beneath him, giving her consent. He replaced the hand over her mouth with a long and lingering kiss which she returned with unmistakable passion. He reached for a scarf on the bedside table and tied it around her mouth, using the pressure of his body to contain any resistance. He turned her on to her stomach and used some of the rope that was always kept by his bed to tie her wrists, which he had crossed firmly behind her. He got off the bed and returned with some ankle cuffs which he strapped to her ankles. Francis tied some more rope around her bound wrists, the end of this extra rope was threaded through the ring at the back of the collar he had tightly strapped around her neck, pulling the rope tight and forcing her tied wrists inexorably up towards the collar. He thrust her knees apart and used rope threaded through the ankle cuffs to secure her ankles to each side of the bed, tying the rope through rings which were set into the wooden frame for this purpose. He had done this so often before with his slaves, but never with his wife until now. What he was doing and to whom he was doing it really excited him, making his cock hard. He paused, after tying Lynne, to massage his pierced nipples, increasing his excitement, before reaching for the lubrication cream which he spread lavishly over her tight arsehole. To prepare her, he pushed two fingers into her, making her moan with pleasure into her gag. He replaced his fingers with his cock, pushing gently at her anus as she bore down to receive him. He lay on top of her as his cock fully entered her and he felt the tight muscles close around him, making him thrust into her even harder, at the same time massaging her swollen, slippery clitoris. She was soaking with the juices of her sexual excitement, pushing back against him to encourage even harder thrusts. He panted as he approached his climax, pressing himself on to the woman he was abusing, who wanted his abuse. His climax was prodigious and he spurted his hot sperm into her. He felt her struggling against her bondage as she reached her peak and, in spite of his own fatigue, increased his massaging of her clitoris, replacing his cock in her anus with four fingers of his other hand, driving her into a state of frenzy. She screamed into her gag as she came and he held her tightly until her paroxysms subsided.

They lay sated until mumblings from Lynne told him that she wanted to be untied. When he removed the scarf, he kissed her gently.

'That was brilliant,' she said, 'Please, can we experiment some more?'

* * *

227

Francis greeted Liam warmly, shaking hands and then showing him into the dining room where lunch had been laid out and where Lynne was also waiting to greet him.

'I hope you don't mind Lynne being here. We've both talked about Caroline and how I feel about losing her.'

Liam shook his head. He liked Lynne and he was somewhat relieved about the lightness of Francis' greeting. He was also surprised by Francis' statement that he felt sorry about losing Caroline, as though he had accepted it. Francis saw his puzzlement and smiled.

'When I asked for this meeting, I was prepared to do battle with you, Liam. I was going to tell you how determinedly and ferociously I was going to fight you on this one, but something's changed all that.'

Francis looked across the table at his wife and reached for her hand. Liam looked confusedly at the two of them. He knew what the situation was between them, had known it for years, but now?

'What happened?' he asked and they told him.

As they did so, their newly discovered delight in each other was obvious. As the meal progressed, Francis kept looking at Lynne with something akin to pride in his eyes. After lunch, they all went out on to the terrace for coffee. Liam congratulated them.

'Does this mean the end of your recruitment and training of slaves?' he asked.

He was pleased for both of them, but the situation raised many questions which, in their happiness, they were obviously prepared to answer.

'I'm not sure,' Francis said. 'Perhaps, but we are going to wait and see what happens for a while. This is all so new to both of us and we need time to assimilate the situation properly.'

Francis sighed with pleasure as he looked out over the rolling acres of his beautiful home. He was a man very much at peace with himself.

'We've always chosen to train girls that were very much inclined towards submissiveness anyway. Girls with no home and no family, no close friends. Every slave we've trained has been happy to stay with us or has settled in well with one of our friends or business acquaintances. We have never embarked upon the training of someone who we felt was not that way inclined or would not respond positively.'

'Eventually,' Liam supplied.

'Eventually in some cases,' Francis agreed. 'But there was always an inclination there in the first place even then. In others, acceptance has been immediate. Girls like Caroline . . .'

'Girls like Caroline take longer, but she's there, Francis. You felt her growing enjoyment of bondage, you felt her submissiveness well before she was aware of any part of it. She's beautiful, Francis. She's been through such a lot and she's learned from it. In a way she's stronger now and we've come to a sort of an arrangement as well. She's still my slave and she accepts that, but she also accepts that it's very possible that she will become a more than willing one.'

'I'm glad,' said Francis. 'You know how I felt about her, but I think I've found something far more precious much closer to home.'

He ran his hand lovingly over Lynne's breasts, tightly confined within a black satin basque which she wore with black leather thigh boots. As always, she looked gorgeous and Liam raised his glass in acknowledgement of that.

'It's a great relief to me knowing that we can still be friends.'

229

'As with me. Perhaps all four of us can be friends one day.'

Liam smiled his acceptance but, remembering what Caroline had told him of the part Lynne had played in her training, he thought that day could well be some way off. He looked affectionately at Francis and Lynne, glowing with happiness, and felt sure that their days of training slaves were probably over. They had no need to do that any more. What a magnificent submissive Lynne would make, if she did indeed choose that particular path, which now seemed quite likely. However, she would always retain her independence; Francis would never be able to humiliate her and he would always have to be aware that there was a line drawn beyond which he should not cross, and perhaps sometimes she would feel the need to resort to being dominant, albeit only occasionally.

Liam thought of Caroline and realised he was eager to get back to her. He spent an enjoyable afternoon at Beech House and extended an invitation for them both to come and visit him very soon. Taking a fond leave of his hosts, Liam left soon after dinner, anxious to return and tell Caroline of what had transpired. He hoped she would understand why he hadn't told her where he was going and hoped that, like Francis and Lynne, he and Caroline could reach a mutual understanding and perhaps, in time, come to love each other.

Liam drove home in the gathering dusk, feeling a stirring of sexual excitement as he thought of the coming night with Caroline.

He did not know that someone else, someone he had always thought of as good friend, had also decided to spend some more time with Caroline.

Mrs Davies' mood had altered substantially and she had been unusually kind to Caroline when they returned to the house. She had removed the nappy, plastic pants and the harness and had allowed Caroline to use the bathroom, albeit while she watched. This was no longer such an embarrassment for Caroline, as she was used to performing heretofore private functions very publicly now. Indeed, she was not allowed to do anything in private any more. Mrs Davies watched approvingly as she urinated, and used her mouth to dry Caroline off afterwards.

Caroline felt very sore and bruised from her afternoon and was grateful when Mrs Davies allowed her to lie on her side so that she did not lie on any part of her that had been whipped and spanked – areas which were extremely sore. Mrs Davies contented herself with strapping Caroline to the bed. When she had finished, she stood back and picked up the things she had removed from Caroline.

'I won't be gone long so, as a special treat, I'm going to trust you. I won't gag you. You can scream as loud as you like in any event. There's only Mr Clive and a few servants in the house and none of them will help you, if you're thinking of escape.'

Caroline could have told Mrs Davies that escape was the last thing on her mind. She couldn't wait for Liam to return. She realised, however, that this was all part of the game, so she said nothing, listening patiently while Mrs Davies continued.

'As you've clearly seen today, there's no one for miles around who would hear your screams, so I would advise you not to waste your breath, but save it until I come back. The Master won't be back for some hours yet. When he and Mr Francis get together –'

'Francis?'

Mrs Davies looked outraged and Caroline quickly realised her mistake.

'I'm sorry, Mistress, Master Francis.'

'Yes, that's where he's gone. Didn't he tell you? It was arranged a few days ago. Anyway, he'll be away until quite late, so you and I can have some fun when I return.'

Caroline nodded and Mrs Davies went out, locking the door behind her. She left the key in the lock after she had turned it, in case Caroline needed to be seen to by one of the other servants in the unlikely event that someone called at the house. Leaving instructions to that effect, Mrs Davies went out.

In her room, Caroline's thoughts were in a turmoil. Liam had gone to see Francis. Why? Why hadn't he told her? Would he tell her when he returned? Was she going to be sent back to Beech House and, if so, how did she feel about that? There was no question of how she felt. She did not want to go back! She cared too much for Liam, she knew that now. She would not let thoughts of Clive intrude. She wouldn't think about that.

Lying with her back to the door and lost in her own thoughts, Caroline was not aware of the door silently opening. Like the shadow he seemed to emulate, Clive entered the room and closed the door noiselessly behind him, turning the key silently in the lock. Daring it to rustle, Clive placed the bag he carried on to the floor beside him. With his back to the door, he leant against it, contemplating Caroline's inert body. He was grateful to her for what she had allowed him to learn about himself, the surety she had given him which was allowing him to map out his future path. He replayed in his mind scenes from his encounters with Caroline. She had indeed served her purpose, albeit unknowingly. Now it was time for him to move on. He had at one point even considered taking Caroline with him. He felt a strong enough assurance in his hold over her to believe that he could have successfully won her over to the idea of leaving Liam and going with him. He realised now that this was not what he wanted. Clive had always travelled better alone. He wanted freedom to experiment with his newly discovered powers of control. Yes, he had always revelled in his previous success with partners and, after discovering Liam's penchant for owning and training slaves, had even toyed with the idea of trying it himself. Now he had experimented with power control and mind-games and realised he not only enjoyed it, he was very good at it. Yes, he reflected, it was indeed time to move on. His business ties with Liam had, broadly speaking, run their course. They could now be severed with no great financial loss to either man. Clive felt his cock harden as he thought about the submissive partners he would have, the pleasure that could be enjoyed in teaching them to obey and service their Master. Power was certainly an aphrodisiac, he thought as he stroked his stiffening cock through the material of his neatly tailored and carefully ironed trousers. He thought about Caroline and the immediate future. He wanted to demonstrate his control over her again. He wanted sexual satisfaction and he wanted to leave Caroline and Liam with a memento that they would remember him by. He smiled almost pityingly as he looked down at the bag resting on the floor beside him. He had no wish to hurt Caroline, wanted in fact to give her pleasure, but he owed Liam a small amount of revenge for the rejection he had suffered at his hands. What he had in mind, with the aid of one of the contents of the bag, would satisfy him in more ways than one. It would avenge him and would refine and perfect his control over Caroline and, in the future, many others like her.

Caroline sighed and moved restlessly, prompting Clive to move towards the bed on silent feet. Caroline was not aware of the presence of another person in the room until she felt a strong hand over her mouth.

'Easy, sweetheart. Time for another lesson.'

Caroline lay still, watching Clive as if he were indeed the teacher and she his eager-to-learn pupil. He had gently removed the straps imprisoning her to the bed without saying anything. She wasn't sure what she wanted to do. She could cry out, but that would surely only result in the replacement of his hand over her mouth, silencing her. Besides, what was there to cry out for? As she studied Clive, she knew that she wanted him there with her. She had really wanted Liam, but he wasn't there. Clive was, and he fascinated her. When she looked into those black eyes, she only knew that she wanted to please him. She would do anything for him. It wasn't love she felt for Clive, but a desire to obey him, to see pleasure in those eyes which could sometimes be so cold. It was almost like a challenge. She wanted to please him in a way that was palpable; something tangible to which she could point and feel pride in her achievement.

'You want to obey me, Caroline, don't you?'

She wasn't gagged but she might as well have been because she couldn't find her voice. She just nodded.

'Good.'

Clive crouched down by the bed, stroking her hair with a mesmeric touch.

'I want to cane you, my darling. Will you let me?'

Again the affirmative nod. Clive felt his growing excitement at her acquiescence. He gently helped her to sit up and guided her hands behind her back. Efficient in everything he did, Clive crossed her wrists and tied them together with rope he had concealed in his pocket. Sitting beside her on the bed, he resumed his caressing of her hair.

'I'm not going to gag you. I want your promise that you will not cry out when I strike you. I want you to show me that I can trust you. Will you do that?'

He watched the uncertainty in her face, watched the resolution firming in her eyes. Then the whispered 'Yes.'

With mounting passion, Clive pressed his lips against her forehead before assisting her to stand and leading her over to a hook in the ceiling. Caroline had noticed this before but she had not dared to let herself wonder too much about it.

'Bend over, my darling.'

Like an automaton, she obeyed, bending at the waist. Clive slipped a length of rope through the bonds at her wrists, looping and tying one end to the hook. He pulled on the rope so that Caroline's bound wrists were pulled upwards. She felt the strain in her arm sockets and made a soft, whispered protest.

'Remember your promise, my darling. I am counting on you.'

Annoyed with herself, she immediately closed her lips, pressing them into a firm line, resolved not to utter another sound until the punishment had finished. When he was satisfied with the position of her arms, Clive tied the rope off, knotting it tightly around the hook. He stood back to admire the picture that Caroline now presented, her hair brushing the floor, her buttocks pleasingly presented. Clive bent down and took her left nipple between thumb and forefinger, squeezing it tightly, making her silently struggle. Mentally he applauded her courage.

'You are beautiful, my dear. I'm hurting your nipple, am I not?'

Mutely she nodded.

'You know I'm doing this because I enjoy it, because it gives me pleasure, don't you?'

Again the helpless nod.

'You like giving me pleasure, don't you?'

The hair swayed against the floor as she nodded again. Clive moved his other hand to her clitoris, revelling in the way she was so open to him. Now it was harder for Caroline to keep quiet. He rewarded each of her little moans of pleasure with a sharp, stinging slap across her bottom. She was very wet and he brought his fingers up to her mouth and, by insistent pressure on her lips, encouraged her to lick his fingers, tasting her own juices on him. Clive could feel liquid escaping from the tip of his cock and moved away to facilitate the removal of his clothing, dropping them unceremoniously to the floor. He retrieved the bag he had brought with him and extracted a thin cane, which he bent along its pliant length as he returned to Caroline. He probed her again, this time letting his fingers slip into her, enjoying the ease with which he gained entry. He slapped her buttocks again as she moaned softly, but he knew she was enjoying this as well. Almost reluctantly, Clive moved away, measuring the distance to ensure that the cane would strike her on the sensitive crease between buttock cheeks and thighs. He noted with approval the marks left on her bottom by this afternoon's encounter with Mrs Davies and felt a momentary reluctance that Mrs Davies was not accompanying him in his own foray into slave training. She would indeed have been invaluable. Pushing such thoughts to one side, Clive brought the cane down with precision, laying a pleasing red line across Caroline's white skin. She did not cry out.

Caroline felt tears stinging her eyes as the pain reverberated through her, but also a pride in the fact that she had not cried out. She wanted to please Clive. She wanted Clive to return his fingers to her swollen clit, give her the release for which she craved. She would stand any amount of pain for that. The strokes were laid almost lovingly on the unmarked skin on the insides of her thighs. She held her breath at the pause between the strokes, the excitement of the beating exacerbated by the close proximity of each blow to her slit. Clive was an expert, knowing just how far to take her, knowing where the delineating line between pleasure and pain stood and never crossing over it.

Clive's own need was growing stronger. Eventually, he threw the cane down and pulled Caroline back towards him, using her own juices to lubricate the entry to her anal passage. The heat and stinging sensations in Caroline's bottom had dulled a little, but her desire had not. She felt Clive's penis pushing at her anus, demanding entry. She relaxed and bore down, easing that entry. She felt her reward as Clive slipped into her and used one hand to massage her clitoris. The other hand was placed firmly over her mouth. It was this pressure, reminding her of her submissiveness that she gave as a willing gift to Clive, that triggered her orgasm, making her push back against him, answering his thrusts with her own pleasure. The hand was removed from her mouth, both breasts squeezed painfully tight in his eagerly grasping hands, as Clive shuddered with his own climax, more powerful than any he could remember. Caroline was exhausted, was not even conscious as she had been of the rope pulling her arms upwards. She was replete but, more than that, she was ecstatic that her teacher was undoubtedly happy with his pupil.

* * *

Clive had released her and was now lying beside her on the bed, massaging her shoulders, easing the strain that had been put on them. He gently ran his fingers over the rope marks on her wrists.

'I can't tell you how pleased I am with you, my darling. You have given me so much pleasure,' he said.

Clive didn't pause to question who had had the real power during their encounter. It didn't seem to matter. In any event, it was Clive who had ensured Caroline's silence beneath the beating he had administered to her. His control had determined that. That had been enough to elicit from him enormous satisfaction for which he was grateful to her.

'I didn't make any sound while you were beating me. Did that please you?' she asked in a small voice.

'Oh, my dear, you have no idea how much.'

Clive resumed his massaging of her nipples.

'There is one other thing that you can do for me . . . if you want to.'

She looked at him, meaning what she said. 'You know that you can ask anything of me. I want to please you.'

Clive felt the stirring in his cock that such evidence of his control brought.

'I see that Liam has had you marked.'

She didn't answer the rhetorical question, merely closing her eyes to fully enjoy the exquisite sensations he was eliciting.

'That means a lot to Liam, I know, and it would also mean a lot to me.'

Her eyes flew open and she stared at him, her eyes full of questions. With unerring accuracy at guessing her needs, Clive pressed his mouth over hers, finding her tongue with his own, kissing her deeply, dulling her questions. When he pulled back and looked at her, he saw the desire to please him evident in her eyes.

'I want to mark you too. Will you let me?'

'How? How do . . .?'

Clive got off the bed, returning with the whip he had extracted from his bag. He saw fear in her eyes as she looked at the bull-whip, looked at its thick leather length, the plaited fronds promising pain.

'If I use this on you – just one stroke, I promise – you will always carry my mark. It will be more permanent than Liam's. Then, wherever I go . . .'

'Where are you going?' she asked, alarmed more at the prospect of his departure than at the possibility of the pain she was facing.

Clive sat down beside her and cradled her in his arms.

'Darling, I have to go away on business sometimes. I thought you knew that.'

'I did, but not so soon . . .'

'I'll be back soon, my darling, and while I'm away, I can think of my mark on you. It would give me so much pleasure. It would show me how much you want to give me that pleasure.'

'What about Liam? What will I tell him?'

'You can say that it was Mrs Davies who did it. I know you don't like her, don't want her around. He'll get rid of her if he thinks she did that to you.'

Clive didn't tell Caroline about his empty room or the packed bags awaiting his collection, denoting his lack of intention to return. He didn't tell her about the copies of the tapes that Mrs Davies had made, ensuring that her revelations would soon convince Liam that it was Clive and not she who had marked Caroline. There was probably a tape running somewhere even now, recording the events taking place in this room.

Caroline looked at him, her eyes limpid with trust and desire . . . desire to please him no matter what the consequences to herself might be.

'Will it hurt very much?'

He clasped her tighter, gratefully accepting the gift that he knew she was bestowing on him.

'I'll try to make it as easy for you as possible, my sweet. Thank you. You have given me so much pleasure.'

Clive meant it. He would indeed do his utmost to make the experience as bearable as possible for Caroline. He felt the doubts at the back of his mind but drove them away with thoughts of Liam's constant refusals of his advances, even though he regarded Liam and himself as kindred spirits. It didn't matter now. He had other battles to fight and the prize would be the total submission of his willing slaves. It was a pity about Caroline but he could not back down now. He would leave this house with his bridges totally burnt!

As Clive moved to get something else from his bag, Caroline could not suppress her rising excitement. She was scared, yes, but she wanted so much to give this man what he most desired. She felt her arousal at her very submission. This was where she belonged, submitting to the desires of her Masters.

Clive returned to her carrying a black shiny garment.

'Would you put this on for me, please?' he asked.

It was a request, almost humbly put. Caroline got off the bed and slipped her arms into the sleeves of the black rubber garment. It was only as she did so that she realised that the sleeves ended in straps. She felt Clive doing up the back of the jacket with what felt like more straps. Before she could give much thought to this, Clive caught hold of the ones on the sleeves and, crossing her arms in front of her, pulled the ends of the sleeves behind her, strapping them tightly into place. She now realised that she was wearing a strait-jacket. She tried to move her hands and arms, finding that they had been totally immobilised within the confines of the smoothly sensual rubber. There was no escape, but she knew that she didn't want one. She had made her decision and she was not going to back out of it. Clive returned to stand in front of her, taking her helpless body in his arms and kissing her passionately, his tongue probing her willing mouth. When the kiss ended, Caroline was straining against him as her body demanded further satisfaction. Clive kissed her softly.

'Later,' he promised. 'I won't ask you to keep quiet this time. I'll give you something to scream into. It will help.'

So saying, Clive pushed a black, rubber ball into her mouth and strapped it firmly behind her head. Caroline tested it with her lips and tongue. Although it filled her mouth, it was soft enough for her to bite into if she needed to.

'You look wonderful,' Clive said with undisguised admiration. He knew that he was going to need to push his cock into that secret place of hers again. He took the hardness of his penis into his hands and stroked it, remembering with pleasure how her tight little anus felt around him. Business first, he reminded himself, gently helping Caroline to lie face down on the bed. He positioned himself so that he was standing beside the middle of the bed as he unfurled the whip to its full length. Clive imagined how the weal would look, how Liam would feel every time he thrust his cock into his slave, seeing the unmistakable imprint that Clive had made, always reminding him of what Clive had done, of what Caroline had allowed him to do. He raised his arm, almost regretting the action he was about to take, but reminding himself of the pleasure to come afterwards as he comforted Caroline, showed her his gratitude.

Clive had carefully chosen the spot he intended to mark. He thought about telling Caroline to ready herself, but knew it would be kinder just to do it with no warning, so he remained silent, measuring his aim. With an indrawn breath, tensing his arm muscles to increase the strength of the blow, he started the downward stroke ... the stroke that would indelibly mark Caroline as his property.

Suddenly he felt the whip being forcefully wrenched from his grip and heard a voice that quivered with rage.

'What the fucking hell do you think you're doing?'

Chapter Twelve

Liam looked up from some business papers he was studying, frowning with annoyance at the interruption, as the gentle knocking on the door of his study was repeated.

'Come in!'

The door opened and Liam caught his breath as he looked at the beautiful girl who stood there. Her long blonde hair was loose and had been brushed until it shone. Her slim, shapely body was shown off to best advantage by the tight-fitting rubber corset she wore, which pushed up her breasts but left them bare. The matching black rubber suspender belt held in place black latex stockings that clung to her legs like a second skin. Her shoes were black patent with four-inch heels. Around her neck she wore a wide, black leather collar, the chain attached to the ring set in the collar hung loosely, the leash awaiting an owner.

Liam stood up and went over to the girl. He ran his hands approvingly over her rubber-clad body. Taking the leash in his hand he twisted the chain until her face was forced close to his.

'You are beautiful,' he whispered before plunging his tongue into her willing mouth. They clung together, experiencing waves of sexual excitement until Liam held her away from him.

'I still can't believe you're really mine,' he said, embarrassing her with the open frankness of his admiration and desire.

'I'm sorry to interrupt you, but I wondered how long you were going to be.'

'Because?'

'Because I'd like to go to bed and I thought that, before I did, I would see if my Lord and Master wanted anything.'

Liam frowned, pretending to consider the question seriously.

'There is something actually,' he said.

She looked at him expectantly and Liam smiled.

'Have you been beaten today?'

They both laughed and she looked demurely at him.

'I haven't, Master. Did you want to see to that before I retire?'

'I believe so. I suggest we go to the bedroom where we can be comfortable and you can tell me how many strokes you think you deserve.'

'Yes, Master,' she said, and preceded him up the stairs to the bedroom.

Liam followed his delicious-looking slave upstairs, again marvelling at his ownership of her. He frowned as he noticed the remnants of some bruising on her thighs, the only surviving visible sign that Clive had left for them. That was three weeks ago, he reflected, and it had taken that long for the marks left by the cane to fade, longer still for the memories. Even now, he trembled with rage as he recalled walking into the room just in time to stop Clive from permanently marking Caroline.

Caroline had frozen at the sound of Liam's voice. It was so unexpected. She had believed herself to be falling in love with Clive, had desperately wanted to please him. She had even considered asking Clive to take her with him, believing that she wanted nothing more than to live with him, serving and loving him.

After Liam had wrenched the whip from Clive's hand, there had been a strained silence. Eventually, Liam had moved to the bed and unstrapped the strait-jacket from Caroline's limp body. As he removed the gag from her mouth and helped her to sit up, she realised that she felt as if she had battled through a great storm and now felt too weak to do anything. She couldn't meet Liam's eyes and kept her own lowered. She shivered convulsively and Liam immediately and almost automatically wrapped a blanket around her bare shoulders. She stole a glance at him as he did so and realised that Liam was moving as if in a state of shock. She felt tears stinging her eyes until a solitary drop of liquid forced itself from her left eye and rolled miserably towards her chin. Liam sat on the bed beside her. She hoped he would put his arm around her but knew that she didn't deserve that kindness. That was for other people, those who didn't practise deceit. And she had been deceitful, she told herself, remembering how she had welcomed the prospect of Clive marking her, how she had planned to plead with him to take her with him.

Clive himself was standing motionless by the bed, his arms slack at his sides. His thoughts, though, were far from confused. He had to extricate himself from this as quickly and as easily as possible. Looking at Liam's stricken face, he knew that Liam had overheard enough of what had taken place to realise that Caroline was no unwilling victim. In one corner of Clive's mind, the part that wasn't desperately formulating his escape route, he felt satisfaction. He felt he had been avenged. He wasn't concerned about Caroline. She would have to fend for herself. As always, Clive put his own interests first.

'Liam . . .' Clive made his voice sound tentative.

Liam raised his head and looked at Clive with undisguised contempt.

245

'You have five minutes of my time. After that you can get out!'

'I understand how you feel, Liam. I never intended to hurt you. That's why I refused to take Caroline with me . . .'

Clive had known this was a gamble. He was counting on the fact that Liam would only have been listening outside the door for a few minutes before deciding to stop things from going any further. Clive used all of the instincts that had made his business acumen highly respected and himself fairly well-off.

Caroline looked at him mutely. How had he known?

'Caroline and I were attracted to each other from the first. We neither of us wanted to hurt you, Liam, please believe that. We talked about this a lot. Even though Caroline begged me to take her with me, I couldn't do that to you, so I –'

'Liar!'

With a speed that surprised everyone, Caroline leapt off the bed and slapped Clive, swinging her arm with a force fuelled by her anger. She had listened with growing disbelief to Clive's words, seeing him properly for the first time. She felt anger at what he was saying, an anger that washed away the fact that she had indeed wanted to leave with Clive. She now saw him clearly for what he was: clever, manipulative and totally selfish. The fascination she had had with him disappeared. She felt anger at herself, too, for being such an easy prey, for turning away from Liam, the man she truly loved. She had slapped Clive with all the impotent fury she felt at herself, at the whole situation. How could she convince Liam of the truth? How could she tell him everything and make him believe her?

She felt gentle hands on her arms, stopping her from continuing her assault.

'It's OK, Caroline. There's no point.'

Wordlessly, she turned to Liam, who saw the fear in her eyes.

'He's not worth it,' Liam said, smiling at her, knowing that there was a lot to be sorted out between them, but that it *could* be sorted out. He looked at Clive.

'I don't really want to hear any more from you,' Liam said, his voice dangerous in its quietness. 'I want you out of here now. Any business matters that need to be sorted out between us can be dealt with by our lawyers. I never want to see you again.'

Not able to believe his luck at the ease with which he was able to walk away from this, Clive simply nodded. He did not risk even a glance at Caroline as he walked from the room, carrying the imprint of her hand on his cheek.

Liam had put Caroline to bed in his own room and left her to sleep a long and exhausted sleep. He had not allowed her to attempt any explanations, insisting that there was plenty of time for that later, that now she needed rest. She slept as a free woman. He had told her this before he put her to bed. He gave the servants instructions that Caroline was to be treated in future as a guest, that she was free to come and go as she pleased and that she was to be left to sleep until she awoke naturally. During the night, Liam kept watch over her, sleeping in a chair in the bedroom in case she needed anything. He slept badly, going over in his mind what he had heard before he stopped Clive from marking Caroline. He knew that he did not have the whole story as yet but, in his wakefulness, he knew that he would listen with sympathy to what Caroline eventually told him. He wanted to believe her . . . needed to.

After a restless night, Liam showered and dressed before going over to the bed to check on Caroline. She was awake and, when she saw him, smiled tremulously, uncertain of her reception. He sat on the bed beside her.

'I'm giving you your freedom, my dear. You can leave whenever you want. Tell me where you want to go and I will take you there. I'd just like you to know, before you go, that I love you.'

Almost embarrassed by his declaration, Liam stood up.

'I'll go and get you some breakfast and, afterwards, you can let me know when you want to leave.'

Liam prepared her breakfast himself, spilling things in the process because, as he later admitted to himself, he was nervous of facing her again, of hearing her say she wanted to leave, perhaps that day. He took a deep breath and picked up the tray. She was sitting up in bed and she smiled at him. He sat down beside her and watched her eat.

Caroline ate with an enthusiasm that surprised her in view of all that had happened. Was it because she knew herself to be a free woman or perhaps because she didn't want that at all? There were things that needed to be said and she felt the need for strength and a clear head before she began. There was also a burning question in her mind that needed answering before anything else. She finished eating, pushing her plate away with gratitude before looking seriously at Liam.

'What happened with Francis?' At his look of surprise she said, 'Mrs Davies told me.'

Liam told her what had happened and then, as he removed the tray, looked at her with pleading in his eyes.

'I have no right to ask, Caroline, but I can't stand not knowing when it is I am to lose you.'

They looked at each other for several moments, neither of them speaking, then Caroline said three simple words.

'I'm not going.'

They had talked for hours, honestly and openly. Haltingly at first, Caroline related her experiences with Clive. Holding nothing back, she told Liam how she seemed to have fallen under Clive's spell.

'I don't know what it was about him. I knew by then that I loved you, wanted only you.'

Liam pressed her to him. There was a pause while he kissed her deeply, their tongues intermingling, both feeling the stirrings of arousal. Reluctantly, Caroline pulled away slightly. She wanted to get everything clear between them.

'Clive seemed to have some kind of hold over me. He demanded my submission and eventually . . .' She paused, looking at Liam almost questioningly, begging his understanding, '. . . I gave it to him. He didn't force me, Liam. I was willing to do what he wanted. I even –' she dropped her eyes, wanting Liam to know the truth yet unwilling to meet his eyes while she told him – 'I even found the idea of him marking me with that whip exciting. I wanted him to do it.'

'My darling, I think Clive was forcing you in ways you didn't realise. I am aware of the power of Clive's personality. He created that power, nurtured it. I think that you were the final test. He wants to control people, the way he controlled you. He's become very good at it. It's one of the reasons that he's a successful businessman and will continue to be so. He manipulates people in a way that they cannot see. They come to think, as you did, that they are making their own free decisions, but they're not. Neither were you. There is no reason to be ashamed, my darling.

249

I'm the one who needs to ask himself questions. Why didn't I see what was going on right under my nose?'

Caroline felt a huge wave of relief at Liam's words. She had feared that her disclosures would alienate him but, far from it, they seemed to be bringing them closer together. Because she didn't want them to have any more secrets from each other, she then told Liam about Mrs Davies and the various incidents that had taken place.

'My poor darling, I had no idea. I'll dismiss her immediately.'

Liam got off the bed, determined to deal with this, but Caroline put a hand on his arm.

'No, Liam. Where would she go?' Caroline told Liam the parts of Mrs Davies' history she had learned. 'I feel sorry for her and, while we're being honest with each other, I have to confess that I did enjoy a lot of what she did to me.'

Again, the downcast expression. What must Liam think of her now? She felt a finger under her chin, tilting her face up to meet his eyes. She saw love, warmth and, yes, there was a definite gleam of amusement there.

'I'm very glad that you enjoy being tied up and punished, my dear,' Liam's voice had taken on the unmistakable tone of the Master, 'because I intend that you will spend a considerable part of each day in bondage and, of course, I shall have to punish you most severely for your confessed wanton behaviour!'

Caroline looked at him wide-eyed. Seeing her look, he smiled.

'And I promise you, you'll enjoy every minute of it!'

Now, they entered their bedroom as willing slave and very proud Master.

'Bring me the cane,' Liam ordered her, dropping the leash attached to her collar.

'Yes, Master,' Caroline responded and went to get the cane.

She returned with it and knelt before him offering the implement.

'How many strokes?'

'Twelve, please, Master.'

'Bring me the rope.'

She hastened to obey, returning with the white silken cords which could be tied tightly, but did not damage the skin. She offered them to him and was then ordered to turn around and put her hands behind her back. She did so and Liam tied the longest piece tightly around her breasts, looping the cord around each breast, framing their perfect shapes and gently flicking the cord against her sensitive nipples as he did so. He tied further lengths of cord around her elbows and then around her wrists, immobilising her while she struggled helplessly, something which they both enjoyed.

'Go and kneel on the bed with your back to me and present your bottom for punishment.'

Caroline got up with some difficulty and then knelt on the bed in the prescribed manner, bending forward so that her head was resting on the pillows. Liam went over to her, admiring her lovely bottom and running his hands over it. She felt the cane being stroked over her buttocks lovingly. She knew he would not tell her when he was going to strike, but she tensed in expectation of the first stroke. When it came, it was a stinging blow, but lovingly delivered. Liam took a pride in his handiwork and took care that the red stripes were laid in a pleasingly symmetrical pattern. In between strokes, he pushed his probing fingers into Caroline's already wet cunt, alternating his fingers with the cane, pulling playfully at the initials dangling from the ring. Just as she was moaning with pleasure, he delivered some further stinging strokes with the cane. There was an element of punishment in these harder strokes.

'You didn't ask my permission to come, slave!'

'Please, Master, please may I come?'

'You may, but you'll have another six strokes for extra punishment first!'

Before he delivered the extra strokes, he pushed a piece of black rubber between her lips.

'Just to ensure your silence under the punishment, slave!'

Caroline felt the rubber growing in her mouth as Liam inflated the gag, making protests impossible. Liam resumed the caning, enjoying marking her bottom with dual parallel red lines, his penis growing hard with excitement at the sight of his beautiful slave, tied up, gagged and at his mercy. Caroline gasped into her gag in the throes of orgasm, arching her body spasmodically. Liam threw down the cane, probing the entry to her anus, first with his tongue and then his cock, which was engorged with his passion and lust. Caroline whimpered and moaned into her gag, her excitement rising again to match his. She strained against her bonds, feeling the thrill that now always stirred her sexually as she felt the pull of the restraints. Liam grabbed a handful of her hair, pulling her head up as he came, his cries of 'Dirty little slut' and 'Bitch' fuelling their simultaneous orgasms.

A long time afterwards, Liam cradled her in his arms. He had untied her and removed her gag. He gently massaged her stinging buttocks, both of them revelling in their shared sexuality. Liam gently turned her over, running his hands lovingly over her rubber-clad body. Caroline responded by arching her back sensuously. She was grateful for the way things had turned out, grateful that Liam had helped her to see her fascination for Clive in its true light. Part of her mind wondered what would happen to Clive but this was not considered with any concern. The Clives of the world would always be all right. They knew how to turn events to their advantage and, with a lift of their superior eyebrows, were well able to cope when things didn't go their way. She opened her eyes and looked at Liam who appeared to be totally absorbed in the massaging of her body. She loved him so much and, now fully aware of their shared sexual enjoyment, she was a willing participant in their 'games'.

'You know, I've been thinking.' Liam's voice interrupted her thoughts and she looked enquiringly at him.

'Perhaps Clive had the right idea when he attempted to control you.'

She looked at him with some surprise.

'Oh, he went too far, but the idea of totally controlling you is not such a bad one. Do you think I have total control over you?'

'Of course, Master,' she responded, the perfect slave.

'Well, I'm not so sure. Are you prepared to try a little experiment with me?'

Caroline looked at her Master, excitement building.

'Yes, Master. What did you have in mind?'

Liam got off the bed and gestured that Caroline should follow his example. Liam's bed was a king-size four-poster, to which Caroline had been tied in many differing ways. Now, she found herself positioned with her back to one of the posts at the bottom of the bed. She could feel a wetness between her legs as she

253

watched Liam select several pieces of rope and return to her. His stiffening cock showed her that her excitement was shared. She felt her arms drawn behind her, felt rope binding her wrists tightly. Liam was very thorough as he bound Caroline securely to the post, tying her arms, breasts and ankles, checking each knot before he was satisfied. He positioned her head against the post before tying a scarf around her mouth and knotting it behind the post. He stood back, surveyed his work and smiled at her. Caroline realised that the gag not only effectively silenced her, but also kept her head still.

'I don't want you to be able to struggle too much,' Liam explained. 'I don't want you to obtain any relief until I allow it.'

His words made her attempt to struggle, to test the limits. She found she had been tied very securely and could move only fractionally. Liam moved behind the post again and she was suddenly plunged into darkness as a thick scarf was tied over her eyes and secured behind the post.

'I want you to feel everything, my darling.' Liam's words dripped into her ear like thick treacle, promising much. 'I want you to feel without any distractions to your senses, because I am going to do everything I can to you to make you come ... But, of course, you are not allowed to orgasm until I tell you.'

She made small ineffectual whimpering noises into her gag. She knew Liam's skills, knew her own inability to obey him rather than her body's urgings.

'If you disobey me,' Liam continued, as if reading her thoughts, 'you will be punished most severely.' His voice moved seductively closer to her ear. 'I have a new whip that I am longing to try out on you.'

Liam knew the effect his words would be having on Caroline and smiled as he let her hear the buzz of the vibrator in his hands, tormenting her with all the possible uses he could make of that little toy. Caroline had never been able to withstand the insistence of the vibrator. If Liam was to apply this to her clitoris she knew she was lost. Liam, however, wanted to take his time and switched off the vibrator, tantalisingly leaving the memory of its buzzing in Caroline's mind. Liam knelt in front of Caroline, gently pushing at the hood and revealing the swollen clitoris. He flicked it gently with his fingers and then leant forward and took the pulsating bud into his mouth, pushing the hood further back with his fingers, leaving the clitoris fully exposed. Liam was not inclined to show any mercy as he gently licked and sucked, but not enough to trigger the orgasm he knew she wanted to have. Liam moved his tongue inside her, again doing just enough to send her into paroxysms of desire ... but not release. When he felt she could not take any more, Liam stood up and, with his lips and tongue, caressed her nipples, which were exquisitely framed by the rope. He delighted in Caroline's helpless squirming, knew that the ropes must be digging into her flesh, fuelling her excitement ... as if any further encouragement were needed. With a mischievous smile, Liam switched on the vibrator, knowing that if Caroline were able to speak she would be begging him to stop or give her permission for her release, neither of which he had any intention of doing. He was enjoying himself too much and knew that, in spite of her discomfort, or maybe because of it, so also was Caroline.

Caroline, helpless in her darkened world, the victim of continuous orgasmic sensations, did her best to obey her Master. She tried frantically to think of other things, to concentrate on something and help her body in its futile battle. Ironically, she remembered being at the mercy of the equally intractabe Mrs Davies as she struggled not to wet her nappy. She had lost that fight too, just as she knew she was going to lose this one. She tried desperately to think of Mrs Davies. Liam had let her stay, her powers within the household much curtailed. She thought of Mrs Davies being in this room now, watching and silently encouraging Liam, holding the whip in readiness.

Liam had spent several minutes stroking the vibrator over her body, letting it move closer to its objective. Deciding that his cock was in need of some attention, he chose to bring this particular game to a close. He moved the vibrator until it was nudging Caroline's clitoris and that was enough. She relinquished her efforts to hold out and felt the sweet aching that presaged her orgasm giving way to the flood of feeling that swept through her. She pulled at her bindings as her body bucked as much as it was able with the force of her orgasm, confused pictures swirling in her mind of Francis, Clive, Mrs Davies, settling, as if someone had fine-tuned the picture, into one single image, that of her Master, the man she loved.

Liam did not allow her orgasm to subside before he replaced the vibrator with his cock, pushing its way into her slit, gaining easy access with the lubrication of her juices. Caroline felt the pressure, felt the heat as Liam's semen invaded her, shuddered with the force of her second orgasm as Liam held her tightly, murmuring his love for her.

After a while, when they had both recovered a little, Liam untied her, smiling as he removed her gag and blindfold. He guided her gently towards the bed and they lay together, sated and at perfect peace.

* * *

Caroline realised that she must have slept and awoke to find Liam looking at her meditatively.

'You are a lovely slave,' he said, kissing her gently and then, with renewed passion, pushing his tongue into her mouth and feeling her excitement. He pushed his fingers into her slit and felt her juices, using them to lubricate his fingers before massaging her clitoris in a slow sensual manner, his tongue in her mouth imitating his fingers until, gasping, they moved slightly apart.

'And you are a wonderful Master,' she told him.

'There is of course the matter of your disobedience,' Liam said with mock severity. 'I think I mentioned a new whip I was keen to try.'

As she felt his cock harden against her, Caroline held up the ropes with which she had been tied, acknowledging that punishment was certainly due. Smiling with almost cat-like satisfaction she watched as the man, to whom she was such a willing slave, again slipped the ropes around her wrists.

NEW BOOKS

Coming up from Nexus and Black Lace

Nexus

The Test by Nadine Somers
January 1998   Price £5.99   ISBN: 0352 33320 0
When Rachel starts working for Michael, a high-ranking Government minister, she doesn't realise exactly what kind of job training he has in store for her. She is to be initiated into a mysterious and perverse group of female devotees of discipline; total obedience is expected of new recruits, and bizarre and lewd demands are made of them. Will Rachel pass the test?

Exposing Louisa by Jean Aveline
January 1998   Price £5.99   ISBN: 0352 33321 9
Anton and Magdalena are brother and sister, separated at birth but reunited as teenagers. The forbidden nature of their love for each other only serves to intensify their passion for experimentation – for the darkest of sexual games. Working as dancers, they fall under the spell of the manipulative Sophie and the masterful Dieter, both of whom have secret and perverse plans for the couple. By the author of *Sisters of Severcy*.

There are three Nexus titles published in February

The Submission of Stella by Yolanda Celbridge
February 1999   Price £5.99   ISBN: 0 352 33334 0
Stella Shawn, dominant Headmistress of Kernece College, craves to rediscover the joys of submission. Her friend Morag suggests an instructive leave of absence, and enrols her at High Towers, a finishing school in Devon, whose regime is total submission of women to women. The strict rules and stern discipline at High Towers ensure that even Stella can learn once more how to submit to the lash. By the outher of *The Schooling of Stella*.

Bad Penny by Penny Birch

February 1999   Price £5.99   ISBN: 0 352 33335 9

Penny Birch is a very naughty girl. Not only has she shamelessly revealed her love of the bizarre world of pony-girl carting in *Penny in Harness*, but she has also let us know dark secrets about her best friend in *A Taste of Amber*, and has now, in *Bad Penny*, told us everything we ever wanted to know about her cheeky activities. Fans of Penny's writing will know what to expect from this collection of stories – the uninitiated are in for a treat.

The Image – A Nexus Classic by Jean de Berg

February 1999   Price £5.99   ISBN: 0 352 33350 2

The Image was first published in Paris in 1956, and was suppressed almost immediately. In this piece of classic erotica, the story is simple yet subtle, intriguing and very erotic. The narrator, Jean de Berg, is drawn to the delectable and apparently innocent Anne. But Anne is the sex slave of Claire, an icy beauty whom Jean knew years previously. He becomes involved in the women's games of ritual punishment – but who is seducing whom? This is the first in a series of Nexus Classics – a unique collection devoted to bringing the finest works of erotic fiction to a new audience.

A Feast for the Senses by Martine Marquand
January 1998   Price £5.99   ISBN: 0 352 33310 3
Claira Fairfax leaves her innocent life in Georgian England to
embark on the Grand Tour of Europe. She travels through the deca-
dent cities – from icebound Amsterdam to sultry Constantinople –
undergoing lessons in perverse pleasure from the mysterious and
eccentric Count Anton di Maliban.

The Transformation by Natasha Rostova
January 1998   Price £5.99   ISBN: 0 352 33311 1
Three friends, one location – San Francisco. This book contains three
interlinked and very modern stories which have their links in fairy
tales. There's nothing innocent about Lydia, Molly and Cassie, however, as one summer provides them with revelatory sexual experiences
which transform their lives.

Mixed Doubles by Zoe le Verdier
February 1999   Price £5.99   ISBN: 0 352 33312 X
Natalie takes over the running of an exclusive tennis club in the
wealthy suburbs of Surrey, England. When she poaches tennis coach,
Chris, from a rival sports club, women come flocking to Natalie's
new business. Chris is skilled in more kinds of adult sport than tennis,
though, and the female clients are soon booking up of extra tuition.

Shadowplay by Portia da Costa
February 1999   Price £5.99   ISBN: 0 352 33313 8
Daniel Woodforde-Ranelagh lives a reclusive but privileged existence,
obsessed with mysticism and the paranormal. When the wayward and
sensual Christabel Sutherland walks into his life, they find they have
a lot in common. Despite their numerous responsibilities, they
immerse themselves in a fantasy world where sexual experimentation
takes pride of place.

NEXUS BACKLIST

All books are priced £4.99 unless another price is given. If a date is supplied, the book in question will not be available until that month in 1998.

CONTEMPORARY EROTICA

THE ACADEMY	Arabella Knight		
AGONY AUNT	G. C. Scott		
ALLISON'S AWAKENING	Lauren King		
AMAZON SLAVE	Lisette Ashton	£5.99	
THE BLACK GARTER	Lisette Ashton	£5.99	Sept
THE BLACK ROOM	Lisette Ashton		
BOUND TO OBEY	Amanda Ware	£5.99	Dec
BOUND TO SUBMIT	Amanda Ware		
CANDIDA IN PARIS	Virginia Lasalle		
CHAINS OF SHAME	Brigitte Markham	£5.99	July
A CHAMBER OF DELIGHTS	Katrina Young		
DARK DELIGHTS	Maria del Rey	£5.99	Aug
DARLINE DOMINANT	Tania d'Alanis	£5.99	Oct
A DEGREE OF DISCIPLINE	Zoe Templeton		
THE DISCIPLINE OF NURSE RIDING	Yolanda Celbridge	£5.99	Nov
THE DOMINO TATTOO	Cyrian Amberlake		
THE DOMINO QUEEN	Cyrian Amberlake		
EDEN UNVEILED	Maria del Rey		
EDUCATING ELLA	Stephen Ferris		
EMMA'S SECRET DOMINATION	Hilary James		
FAIRGROUND ATTRACTIONS	Lisette Ashton	£5.99	Dec
THE TRAINING OF FALLEN ANGELS	Kendal Grahame		
HEART OF DESIRE	Maria del Rey		

ANCIENT & FANTASY SETTINGS

THE CLOAK OF APHRODITE	Kendal Grahame		
DEMONIA	Kendal Grahame		
THE DUNGEONS OF LIDIR	Aran Ashe		
THE FOREST OF BONDAGE	Aran Ashe		
NYMPHS OF DIONYSUS	Susan Tinoff		
THE WARRIOR QUEEN	Kendal Grahame	£5.99	Dec

EDWARDIAN, VICTORIAN & OLDER EROTICA

ANNIE	Evelyn Culber	£5.99	
ANNIE AND THE COUNTESS	Evelyn Culber	£5.99	
BEATRICE	Anonymous		
THE CORRECTION OF AN ESSEX MAID	Yolanda Celbridge	£5.99	
DEAR FANNY	Michelle Clare		
LYDIA IN THE HAREM	Philippa Masters		
LURE OF THE MANOR	Barbra Baron		
MAN WITH A MAID 3	Anonymous		
MEMOIRS OF A CORNISH GOVERNESS	Yolanda Celbridge		
THE GOVERNESS AT ST AGATHA'S	Yolanda Celbridge		
MISS RATTAN'S LESSON	Yolanda Celbridge	£5.99	Aug
PRIVATE MEMOIRS OF A KENTISH HEADMISTRESS	Yolanda Celbridge		
SISTERS OF SEVERCY	Jean Aveline		

SAMPLERS & COLLECTIONS

EROTICON 3	Various		
EROTICON 4	Various	£5.99	July
THE FIESTA LETTERS	ed. Chris Lloyd		
NEW EROTICA 2	ed. Esme Ombreux		
NEW EROTICA 3	ed. Esme Ombreux		
NEW EROTICA 4	ed. Esme Ombreux	£5.99	Sept

NON-FICTION

Please send me the books I have ticked above.

Name ....

Address ....

....

....

.... Post code.........................

Send to: **Cash Sales, Nexus Books, Thames Wharf Studios, Rainville Road, London W6 9HT**

Please enclose a cheque or postal order, made payable to **Nexus Books**, to the value of the books you have ordered plus postage and packing costs as follows:

UK and BFPO – £1.00 for the first book, 50p for the second book and 30p for each subsequent book to a maximum of £3.00;

Overseas (including Republic of Ireland) – £2.00 for the first book, £1.00 for the second book and 50p for each subsequent book.

If you would prefer to pay by VISA or ACCESS/MASTER-CARD, please write your card number and expiry date here:

....

Please allow up to 28 days for delivery.

Signature ....